B.C. CROW

THE NEPHILIM DEVICE

**BLUE HOUSE
PUBLISHING**

an imprint of

Light Minded art 

11 N. 500 W.
Springville, UT 84663

Picture of Earth: Courtesy of Nasa

For information regarding bulk purchases, send a request to Blue House Publishing, or email us at BCCrow@BlueHPublishing.com

First print run April 2015 by Blue House Publishing

ISBN-10: 1943239002

ISBN-13: 978-1-943239-00-9

Library of Congress Control Number: 2015905442

Special thanks to my wonderful wife, and the patience she had for listening to me obsess about this book series, and for the patience she continues to have for me while I continue to pursue future novels.

Thanks to my editor, Carolyn Haley, for helping me advance my storytelling abilities. May my future novels benefit even more than this one did because of your advice.

And an especially sincere thanks to
YOU, THE READER,
for giving me a chance. You are what makes
this all possible!

Chapter 1

3026 B.C.

My name is Ramuk, and I transcribe my journal onto these golden plates. Though I now look back on these entries with a different perspective, I copy them here in their original wording. This I do to present you with a clearer understanding of who we are, where we came from, and most importantly, how we killed everyone.

T-1 Day

The clouds drifted by on this monumental day before we launched. I carried my freckle-faced daughter on my shoulders through the towering green gate that surrounded the World Science Achievement compound. She pointed up into the sky as a massive airship cut through a low-hanging pillow of cloud. Natine loved everything about flight, making this one of the most enjoyable times in her life. The blimp dipped out of sight, into the WSA stadium, as a prelude to the event that was about to ensue. It was the first time in years that a scientific breakthrough of this magnitude had been discovered.

From outside the gates I heard cheers, laughter, and crying coming from the stadium. The security woman at the entrance checked my ID badge shortly before flashing a smile and a wink at my little Natine. She told her that she would give anything to be where my daughter was going. Her playful comments made my daughter giggle as we bounced along into the stadium. I've often commented to my wife how precious our girl's little laughter is, something the security guard was all too happy to confirm.

My wife stood waiting for us as we passed through a tunnel below the bleachers in a hallway cordoned off for the VIPs. Most people would consider her a strict-looking woman, but I knew better. She had a strong will and attacked everything in life with focused intensity. Her force of character was often accented by her short fire-red hair. Today was no different, but when Natine called out to her, her face lit up and she reached out to sweep Natine off my shoulders.

"Ooof, you're almost too big for me to lift now, and aren't you looking adorable!"

She often said things like this of late, being so consumed by her work, that we had little time together to just be a family.

The girl then let herself to the ground and complained, "Mommy, Daddy made me wear the purple dress."

"Ramuk, how could you," my wife accused playfully, knowing full well that she was the one who'd picked the outfit the night before. She'd wanted to return to the lab after dinner to work through the night, fine-tuning her equipment. Obviously, she wouldn't be available to get Natine ready in the morning.

We hurried through the maze of corridors, technicians, and journalists. We found our seats behind the podium just moments before the band finished the WSA anthem. The audience was standing when the president of the foundation walked up to the microphone. The podium was amplified on a giant video screen with speakers that were hanging from the blimp about seventy-five cubits from the ground. The top of the blimp crested the top row of seats, allowing all of the twenty-five thousand spectators to see the screen. President Juhodo was a round, soggy-looking man. He was dressed elegantly in a green-and-white button up suit, the formal WSA uniform. The crowd went silent as he smiled and waved them down to their seats. His flapping cheeks seemed to wave them down at the same time.

"Today is a very proud day for all the people of Mars," he began in a voice unexpectedly crisp and smooth, proving that he had been a public speaker his whole life. "Today we announce to the world that we are no longer bound to this terrestrial sphere!"

Cheers and applause followed each sentence as he pushed through his oration. "A new age is upon us, one where only our imagination is the limit. Yesterday our ancestors were pioneering the possibilities of steam engines. Today we dominate our skies and oceans with airships and nuclear-powered watercraft. But tomorrow we will launch the first spacecraft capable of interstellar and faster-than-light travel!"

He continued like this for a good fifteen minutes or more, adding the usual pomp and spit that any politician could manage. The speech was broadcast simultaneously in several languages throughout Mars. When he finished the crowd erupted with shouts, cheers, and whistles.

The past hundred years had seen new technologies, and innovations that had made the world a better place. Three and a half years ago, the team my wife and I had been working with finally made the breakthrough discovery that would permit us to travel faster than the speed of light. This prompted the government to give the WSA a grant to build a spacecraft that would carry a team of pioneers, explorers, and scientists to the far corners of our galaxy. The passengers of the recently completed spaceship included my small family, three other scientists who'd been working on the ship's new wave drive, small teams of astronomers, geologists, physicians, and, of course, a crew of twenty men and women to operate and maintain the ship.

There were only two families allowed to go. Mine was one of them. Granted, most of the others didn't have families. The few that did, thought it reckless to bring kids on this journey. The WSA was of a similar mind, since originally, families were prohibited. For me, there was no way I'd leave my little girl behind for the two-month voyage. So I persuaded the program manager, a lifelong friend, to make an exception. The other full family that came, did so by riding the success of my exemption. The program manager passed it off as an opportunity to study the feasibility of families living in a spacecraft environment for an extended period.

My wife was going because she'd been involved in developing the new technology. I earned my ticket not only because I was a scientist, but also because I had a substantial background in journalism. This combination gave me the unique ability to translate the complicated technical jargon into words that the average person could understand.

After the president's speech, a few members of the scientific teams made their remarks to the crowd. I was one of the last to stand and offer my perspective on the mission. Before doing so, I kissed my daughter's forehead and asked her to wish me luck. Then I stepped up to the podium and recited the oration I'd been practicing for the past week.

"I just asked my daughter for luck, but what I should have asked for was a towel to dry my sweaty palms on."

A courtesy laugh rippled through the stadium, which was more than that joke deserved. I may be a journalist, just not the speaking kind.

"It has been my pleasure to be chosen, along with my family, to accompany this brave crew of men and women to explore our galaxy. I intend to record and broadcast home everything about our adventure. Although we are among the first to go, I feel confident that the age of space travel will bring opportunities for everyone to see new worlds and establish new colonies across this amazing universe. I see an age of giant spacecraft exploring many different galaxies, and with luck they will find even more planets that can support life. One of the most exciting things I'm looking forward to is visiting Earth. We know it has life, and from our distant observations it appears even to be sentient. Beyond that, we know very little about them. This will be an excellent chance to visit and learn about the inhabitants there.

"As our teams have been unraveling the mysteries of physics, I can say that we never imagined the full scope of what we might be able to accomplish. Only now as I prepare to embark on this voyage do I see all the possibilities that lie before our people. As elected spokesman for the team, I have been asked by them to convey how our technology can propel such a large craft out of our atmosphere and through space. I will attempt to explain this.

"As you know, propulsion is the means by which all our airships have moved for decades. Some use rotary engines with propellers attached, and some use rockets. Our new technology is totally different. What we do is create a space bubble with our ship inside, then bend space around the bubble. This creates the equivalent of a wave. The bubble is then pushed through space as though it were a bottle being carried by a wave on the ocean. By controlling the harmonics of the bubble, we can control the space wave carrying us. Our calculations show that this will allow us to travel much faster than the speed of light. Because we will be enclosed in a special pocket of space, we should not even be aware of the inertia caused by our accelerations and decelerations. This is because we will not actually be moving, but space will be bending around us.

"Our first task will be to leave the Martian atmosphere. Once in high orbit, we'll have a brief pause, mostly to wave hello to everyone back home. Our first destination will be Earth, followed by the asteroid belt. Then we'll explore the gas giant Jupiter, with all its moons. For our final destination before returning home, we'll attempt to visit our next-closest neighboring star. We'll push the wave drive into full power and see how fast we can really go.

"This is an exciting time, and our team thanks you, the people, for supporting us in this endeavor. We look forward to not only this trip, but also the day when our people will travel the universe as easily as we travel through our cities. Thank you again, and may God bless us all!"

Several deafening whistles pierced the roaring

crowd as I finished my speech. My presentation must have been better than I thought it would turn out. There was one other speaker, then the conference was opened up for questions. Every journalist asked their bits. The part I found most perplexing was when one of the reporters turned out to be part of the small group of protesters. They expressed irrational concerns that we were messing with technology, the likes of which could have devastating consequences. We'd heard it all before: Just because we have the ability to do something doesn't mean we should. I don't know if they're religious radicals, fearful of science, or if they're just plain paranoid. In either case I was glad when the president of the WSA stood again and announced that there'd be no more questions.

The brass band filled the stadium with a triumphant marching tune. Reporters were still screaming to get their questions answered, but nobody paid them any attention as the airship hovered higher and started dropping a dazzling display of fireworks. The speeches and questions had lasted a good hour, and the WSA was committed to giving everyone a good show in addition to our dissertations. While this was going on, we were ushered away from the stage.

On the way home, we stopped at my brother's quiet restaurant near our house. Our whole family was waiting for us. We joked around and told stories. We had a big day ahead of us, and since we'd be gone for two months, we thought the best way to spend our last day with family.

Day 1: Doomsday

Yesterday my words could not fully express my excitement for our mission. Tonight, however, my soul grieves more than I thought was possible. I write this down now, only because I need an outlet. I don't know if anyone will ever read it, but I know of nothing else to do at this time. I, along with all those on board this damnable ship, am in a state of total despair.

This morning started out as expected. I think the only person to get any sleep last night was my daughter, bless her soul. Had she been left behind, I would have nothing left to live for.

Anyhow, upon arriving at the launch site, we all took our places in the spacecraft. It goes without saying that we were brimming with anticipation. The cameras, the people, even the manic protesters added to our euphoria. We were really going to visit the far reaches of our solar system!

As the countdown began, we looked out our window. Three, two, one . . . then it happened. At first we didn't know what to think. We didn't even know if we were moving. All we saw was a blinding fire raging outside the windows. In the fraction of a second that it took to reach space, the bubble around our ship disengaged. The fireball that had engulfed our ship was immediately sucked out into the great vacuum of space. Warning lights and sirens went off as rooms were sealed to prevent the damaged areas from compromising the entire ship.

Everyone scrambled to different stations to check equipment and radio down for help. It was then that my daughter pointed out the window and asked, "What is that?"

I glanced out the window and saw our planet. It took me a second to understand what I was seeing. I could hardly speak. I think I tried to shout; however, it came out a feeble squawk. In no time, we were all striving to peer through the melted and marbled glass window. Once everyone finally found a section of burned window to clearly see out, a stunned silence ensued. A few of us vomited. The putrid smell of our bile, floating in the zero-gravity environment, mirrored the rancid feelings in our consciences.

A hellish conflagration was consuming our world. We watched the giant fire cloud as it blazed across the circumference of our planet, and we knew it had to be a result of our launch. When the inferno died down, it left behind a scorched and barren planet. The crew of our ship tried desperately for the rest of the day to contact anyone on the surface. But most of us knew that it was futile.

Some blaming went around, then some crying. None of us knew how to deal with it. The captain gathered all the scientists and asked what we could make of the situation. After brainstorming, which was in itself difficult and entirely awkward, we came up with the only likely explanation.

When we'd tested the wave drive, we did it on a scaled-down model. Each time we performed the test, we did so within a vacuum in order to simulate traveling through space. The difference this time was that we'd launched our spacecraft from the planet's surface. When the space bubble was initiated around our ship, it did exactly what it was supposed to do—it split space. That process is the only way to protect the ship as it slides along the spatial wave. Only this time it didn't just split space, it must have also split any atom that was between our bubble of space and the outside space. Since our atmosphere was full of nitrogen and oxygen, when it split the nitrogen, it would have released all that energy, creating a nuclear plasma cloud. This caused a chain reaction to occur, resulting in our atmosphere burning up, disintegrating all life on Mars. Nothing could have survived. Even our great oceans had become a charred wasteland. Nothing would ever be able to live there again. We alone survived.

Day 2: Coping with the Nightmare

Nobody slept last night. Even my daughter, who is still too young to know what has happened, could sense the tension in the air. She asked me this morning when we could go home.

I don't think she'd ever seen me cry before. It scared her, yet I couldn't stop the gasping sobs. It would have been better if none of us on this flying boat had ever been born. Our captain is just barely managing to hold us together. Our only option is to land on the third planet from our star. It is similar enough to our own and the only other place we know of in the galaxy that can support life. We don't have any choice. Though many of us feel responsible, some of the crew had no part in the development of this ship and are simply survivors. The rest of us are mass murderers. We will live for the survivors, and they will keep our race alive. I feel—

I just had to leave for a small while; it seems that we have less time than we thought. When the atmosphere inside our space bubble ignited, it seriously damaged the hull of the ship. Had we not disengaged our wave drive as quickly as we did, we would have been destroyed also. As it stands, our ship is falling apart. Two of the scientists who were taking inventory of some equipment in one room were sucked into space when the room lost hull integrity. The hatchway to their compartment automatically closed, but we have been hearing the stress and groaning of the ship more frequently.

While we have food to last for many days, we fear that if we don't make it to the planet soon, we won't survive more than a day or two. The bigger trick will be landing our ship on the planet's surface. We now have only a couple windows offering any visibility, and all external scopes and sensors were destroyed. I have faith in our crew to land us, even if a part of me hopes that I don't survive. Our wave drive is still operable, and as long as we engage it out here in space, where the creation of our space bubble can't split any more atoms, we should be able to safely fly to the planet and disengage it without harming that world. The captain has told us to get some rest. Tomorrow we'll give it a try. Until then he's working with the pilots to find a way to land safely.

I am exhausted, and may very well fall asleep tonight. My guilt is the only thing that might prevent me from getting any rest, as my heart and stomach feel as though they are being strangled from within. I greatly fear that if sleep does come, dreams will haunt me tonight, and for the rest of my life. The funny thing is, I hope they terrify me. I hope I suffer every sleeping minute I can find. I will never forgive myself.

Day 3: A New World
We've landed safely. The crew managed to pull it off. When we disengaged the space bubble for the final time, we landed between the largest continent and a smaller one next to it. We had no landing gear, and the combination of landing and the seizure of the planet's increased gravity caused our ship to buckle and crack. It'll never fly again. This world may be similar to our own, but it'll never feel like home.

Day 11: Adapting
The work has completely drained my energy. Building a sufficient shelter has proven very difficult. The location where we landed is not the most

hospitable environment that we'd have hoped for. Most of us have little experience in tilling land and surviving in the wilderness. There'll be little relief for us here if we don't learn to adapt. We are, however, receiving some help from the natives.

The indigenous people of this world, primitive as they seem, are more similar to us than we'd imagined. Our physician believes that their DNA is likely close enough to ours that we might even be a compatible species. The only exception is that they are, in most cases, much shorter than us, standing only to about the middle of our torsos.

Our physician has theorized why they would be so similar yet so different in size. This planet is larger than ours, and the gravity here is over two and a half times stronger. This suggests that despite a similar evolution, the people's growth here has evolved to accommodate the pressure. They seem surprisingly strong for their size. As for us, we all tire much faster. Our bodies weren't meant to handle this type of pressure. I'm sure we'll adapt. We'll have to. Nevertheless, it's highly frustrating.

One surprising effect brought on by our difference in height is evidenced by how the natives have started treating us. When we first landed, the residents of a small settlement near our crash site came out to see what had happened. At first we weren't sure if they were friendly. We assumed that our size would intimidate them, so we offered them food from our ship's provisions. This helped us develop friendly relations but also added a quirk. I can't be sure, but they seem to regard us as some sort of deities. It'll be nice to eventually understand their language, then perhaps we can better clarify our intentions. But for now, having them worship us is far better than having them skewer and roast us over an open flame. They don't have much, so they cannot offer much by way of assistance. Despite this, we've been able to observe. This has helped us learn what we must do to survive here.

Day 62: Naturalizing

This will be my final entry. Over the course of the last several days, we have labored long and endured more than we ever would have expected. We are finally getting more comfortable here. Some of us have even begun to understand small pieces of the language. My daughter has made some friends among the native children. Our way of life is much different now than it ever was back home, and we lack the ability to create the society to which we had become accustomed to on our planet. But this is our home now, and we will adapt.

Using an iron pen with a diamond tip that I was able to procure, I have taken some thin metal sheets from inside our spacecraft, and I will soon engrave these choice selections from my journal onto them. I do this because I believe that my ancestors will live on. Already I see some from our crew forming bonds with the natives. One native woman already carries the unborn child of one of our younger crew members.

Since there will obviously now be descendants of our population, I wish them to know where they came from and how they got here. I cannot include our entire history, as I lack the material and time to engrave a lasting transcript memorializing our entire planet. But I can provide certain things that I hope will be beneficial.

I will include my journal entries, and also those items that might eventually benefit our descendants and those who called this planet home long before we showed up. I also engrave these things so our language may be preserved to some degree. Most important, these engravings must serve to let our descendants learn from our mistakes.

I don't know when the people of this world will achieve our level of technology. But someday when they do, they must know the fate of our world. We were once a proud people. We considered ourselves smart, and then we destroyed everything.

Be smart, and be wise, but most of all take care. Some things can never be replaced.

Chapter 2

Two years ago

Flint Krieger placed a hand on his wife's bulging belly. A tiny foot stretched out to meet him. Flint smiled. A half-laugh betrayed a sense of excitement and a tinge of eeriness. Flint exaggerated a shiver.

"It's not that weird, Lydia, his wife of three years, scolded.

"Easy for you to say," Flint joked. "You live with it every day. I only get to see it occasionally after I get home each night. To me it looks like some alien trying to break through your stomach."

"Won't be long, and that's exactly what it might try doing," Lydia replied.

After a year and a half of trying, plus nine months of incubation, their miracle boy was about to be born. Flint had been married to his wife for three years, and they both felt that it was time for a child in their lives. For the last eight months, they stewed over a name. Once they'd picked one, they started calling the bump on her belly by it, only to find the title unfitting after a few weeks. Then it was back yo brainstorming.

As the time for delivery neared, Lydia became more certain that she wanted to name the child after her father. Flint secretly protested, thinking that his own father's name should be the one handed down to their firstborn. Ultimately it was destined to remain undecided until his birth.

At last the anticipated month arrived, but a complication arose. Lydia just finished a late lunch when her water broke. She was seized by what could only be labor pains. The baby was coming, and Flint was still at work. Lydia inhaled deeply to calm her breathing. Their planned induction wasn't for another few days.

"It's ok," she told herself. "My mom had long deliveries, I've got time."

She placed a call to Flint. His phone went straight to voicemail. She bit her lip, today would be full of meetings for Flint. Even if he could break away, his commute back might be a good hour and a half. That was time Lydia didn't dare gamble on.

Mentally, she scrolled through the list of people she could call to give her a ride to the hospital, an ambulance not even once crossing her mind. She didn't feel comfortable asking any of her neighbors.

As she slid the keys into the ignition of her small Toyota Corolla, she got the impression that she shouldn't be driving. The hospital wasn't far, so she ignored the prompting. When she felt the Ford diesel slam into the back of her car, she immediately regretted everything. There was no avoiding the secondary accidents as her car skid into the busy intersection. In the few minutes that past after the accident, Lydia and Flint lost their soon-to-be child.

The driver of the Ford was reported by witnesses to be a woman. After trying to help for a few minutes, she ran from the scene, never to be found again. They described her as being athletically fit with dark, even hair. She seemed savvy enough as she tried to help Lydia with a calm and calculated demeanor. To the onlookers' surprise, she never spoke a word, or even hinted at any emotion for the tragedy she'd helped create. The police found the truck she was driving to have been stolen, and there remained no evidence as to her identity.

August 1

Present Day

Sweat filtered down the clean-cut brown hair. Gravity tugged on the salty droplets, pulling the beads into Flint's deep blue eyes. The wall his back was pressed against was about thirty degrees cooler than the air from which he'd just come. Still, the perspiration continued flowing across the whole of his narrow, finely sculpted face. At first he'd welcomed the cooler temperature, but now, being suspended in the hollow shaft, with the dark gaping hole below, a hint of worry crept to the front of his mind. The daylight above was all but vanished, leaving him surrounded by darkness. All that remained to be seen from the world above was a pinhead of white, a star that dimly reminded him that he was nearly 250 feet below the sandy surface.

At first Flint didn't have any reservation about climbing unaided down the ancient well. The limestone pavers that lined these old Egyptian wells held firmly in place, a credit to their builders some thousands of years ago. If they lasted this long, maybe they would continue to keep back the thousands of tons of Earth that threatened to crush him now.

The further he descended down the narrow shaft, the more the dark claustrophobic space worked on him. His tired body shook uncontrollably. Flint considered himself to be in great physical condition for the task when he started. Maybe he shouldn't have gaged his ability by comparing himself to other people.

True, some of the jocks from his high school years spent their free time in the gym, keeping in shape. But the majority of the people he'd grown up with sported the soggy waists of office induced atrophy. Friends that were more athletic in those early years were now easily paled by Flint's current state of physical ability.

A life of being active had kept him from following the degenerative path of so many others. Flint knew himself to be mildly handsome, but nothing much to view with his clothing on. Take his shirt off though, and the nonthreatening form would reveal a clearly defined structure with medium built muscles, toned more for strength and endurance than for size. Nobody would argue against his state of fitness.

A lot of good that would do him now. The shakes were nearly enough to cause a fall, perhaps to his death. Preferably to his death. He imagined being stuck at the bottom of a forgotten well with a broken leg.

Having no ropes to assist him, only the friction of his five foot, ten inch body against the old limestone walls, he found it more difficult than he expected. The sides of the abandoned well had a few surprises in store for the young thrill seeker. More than once it let him slide a few feet before he regained sufficient pressure to halt his descent. His eyes now stung from the sand that permeated the air. He didn't dare take his palms away from the walls to rub them clean.

Another fifty feet down, and he found the bottom. It was dry. Flint's throat burned with thirst, each breath drew in another exhausted reminder of his urgent need for water. Although there had been a large stone covering the ancient well, Flint shouldn't have expected the stone cap to protect such a scarce commodity.

The disappointment of not finding water waxed stronger as the tension from the climb down disappeared. Even if there was water, he wouldn't have been able to get to it from above. "Only one thing left to do," he sighed. Taking only a minute to rest, he clawed his fingers into the dry floor. He first dug a hole, then piling the sand and crusted mud up against one side of the pit, he held it back with his feet, then his calves. His fingernails felt soft, and with each blistering fist full of dirt, he wondered why he was even here in the first place.

Two Years ago

Lydia had stayed in the intensive care unit for a couple days, then remained under observation for a couple more. She was an emotional jigsaw puzzle, with several pieces missing. Any worse, and she might have been put on suicide watch. Flint wished now that would have happened. But her stay hadn't been long when the doctors said that she'd be able to go home. Lydia had spoken very little since the crash. Flint feared that she blamed him, and somewhere inside he blamed himself, also.

While he rarely left her side during that time, on

the day he was to bring her home from the hospital, he left for a couple hours to make sure she would come home to a clean and warm feeling home. When he returned to pick her up, she was gone.

The nurses claimed that she'd checked herself out. But she never made it home. Even her own mother didn't hear from her. It was as if she'd blamed the whole world, and decided to disappear from the face of it.

For two weeks, Flint searched desperately for her, every clue led to a dead end. Then that letter came in the mail. It was missing a return address, but its message was clear. Even if Flint did try to track her down, it would be too late. He'd since read it a thousand times. He knew it by heart. It was still hard to believe.

Dear Flint,

I know you don't blame me for what happened to our boy, but I can't shake the feeling that I should have taken more care to get to the hospital. I am to blame, and even if you forgive me, I cannot forgive myself. By the time you read this, I will be dead. Don't bother looking for my body, I've made sure that nobody will ever find me.

I'm so sorry for the pain I've caused you, and am likely causing you now. But I cannot live with this regret. Know that I love you, but that I want you to move on with your life. There are many other women out there who deserve a man like you, far more than I ever did. Tell my mother that I love her too, and that I never meant to hurt anyone. But after this, I'll never hurt anyone ever again.

With love and regret,

Lydia Krieger

Months went by. Eventually everyone came to the sad conclusion that she really must have taken her life in some remote place. After a year the family held a funeral in her honor. Flint hoped she was alive somewhere, but deep in the pit of his stomach, he believed he'd never see her again.

As soon as the funeral was over, Flint bought a plane ticket to Alaska. After hiring a bush pilot for a day, he parachuted into a dense forest in the southern part of the state. There he spent the next month alone, with nothing more than a Ruger .357 Magnum pistol, a knife, and a lighter. After finally emerging from the soul-searching survival trip, he began to lose himself in his work.

A heap of dry silt against his calf and two years of mourning now placed him here. The memory still burned deep. He had little desire to find another love to fill the void. He knew he shouldn't feel responsible, but it was easier to blame himself. Had he been there to drive her to the hospital, he could now be bouncing a little toddler on his knee right now. Lydia would be at his side. Flint felt that any attempt to find that type of happiness again would blaspheme her memory and his conscience.

As despair crept deeper into his life, Flint fought back in the only two ways he knew how. First, he fully immersed himself in work. With his mind occupied, he had little time to dwell on the past. The second way came in the form of his vacations. Flint didn't consider himself a normal relaxing vacationer. It was too simple and ordinary. Besides, he rarely found idleness to be relaxing. Rather, he chose to simply run away and lose himself in a more formidable setting. The time alone on these adventures gave him opportunity to clear his mind.

On this sorrowful anniversary, Flint was again losing himself. This time it was no Alaskan forest, but the Egyptian desert.

One week ago in the small town of Ras Shukheir, he paid a man to ferry him across the Gulf of Suez. There he set out on his hike across the desert terrain that would eventually lead him into Israel. If he found the time, he wasn't against stopping by Jordan. After all, the ancient ruins built into those desert cliffs held some intrigue. But for the most part, he didn't have a firm plan on where to travel; just a general direction and a time frame.

Also, since he didn't know how long it would take, or where his little adventure might lead, he made sure to take a full month off from work. In the financial world where Flint was employed, month-long vacations were highly discouraged. When dealing with other people's money in the stock market, clients tended to be very unforgiving when their accounts got neglected.

Flint still put in 72 to 80 hours each week. The only reason he could get away with the excessive vacation was because he'd only just started managing real funds, so his clientele list was still small enough to temporarily pawn off on a co-worker.

In his backpack he carried very little food, and water, appropriate for a survival trip. He had his binoculars, knife, a folding AK-47, a burlap sack, a satellite telephone, and enough cash in various currencies to get him by. When his friend, Philip Noon, discovered the details of Flint's vacation, he immediately picked up his cell and ordered a satellite phone. Flint tried talking him down, but Philip ignored him. Flint's whole idea was to lose himself; to shut out the world and be alone with his thoughts.

Flint's rejection proved useless; Noon had slipped the phone into Flint's bags before he left. Flint doubted that he'd even touch it, as it now lay in the bottom of his pack. He knew that having a phone wasn't a bad idea, in case of emergency. But the thought of it defeated his goal of completely cutting off ties to his normal world. To his eventual surprise, this phone would soon help launch him into a situation further from his normal world than he could have imagined.

The AK-47 was Flint's idea, though. In a Middle Eastern country, the nice Ruger .357 Magnum that he had preferred in Alaska was a dead giveaway that he was American. The rustic AK-47, however, would fit in better. Not wanting to attract attention, Flint considered every detail that would allow himself to blend in.

Aside from the gun, his clothing was meant to blend. He even had a burlap sack to cover his framed hiking backpack for when he came to populated areas. While Egypt and Israel were generally friendly to Americans, he would be traveling close to Saudi Arabia. Most towns he'd pass would not be on the general tourist routes.

With a worn-out kaffiyeh wrapped around his head, his plain ragged clothes, and a nice tan, the only way to know that Flint was American was if he spoke. Maybe up close, Flint could be distinguished as American, but he tried to keep a safe distance. Under the Kaffiyeh was a thick set of sandy brown hair, hinting at an early blond childhood. His whole physic had that sort of trim fullness that shows a balance of good diet and an active lifestyle. While not large, he wasn't gauntly either. Flint's softly chiseled features gave him an appearance that was almost akin to a dedicated runner or cycler, though neither of these activities interested him in the least. Since leaving the boat at the beginning of his hike, he had only encountered one group of people. They, however, had paid little attention to him.

Now that he was at the bottom of this dark abyss, with dry ground at his feet, Flint questioned his judgment for his trip down the ancient abandoned well. Had he just wasted a lot of time and precious energy? He dug his fingernails as deep into the earth as possible. His breath quickened, and he furiously attacked the well bottom. A muddy layer of silt now appeared on the sandy floor, and Flint knew it wouldn't take much before he could access water. His first attempt to scrape it away was met by a static discharge. Flint found that odd at first, but then finished scraping away the mud.

Soon the muddy cavity was filled with muddy water. It was slow, but it was water. He waited a few minutes for most of the silt in the water to settle. When he guessed that the water was somewhat clear, he filled, then drank the first two bottles.

The water had a gritty earthy taste. If he'd seen the water in daylight, he might never have touched it to his lips. It's surprising how much a little darkness can filter a bottle of water. The third bottle was emptied directly over his head. After refilling the bottles one more time, he braced his hands and feet against the sides of the well.

His arms were all too eager to remind him of his exhaustion as he climbed back up. Going up was easier than coming down. The weight of extra water and fatigue didn't help much, but Flint didn't notice until he was a third of the way up. Every few minutes he stopped to rest.

Held above certain death with only friction keeping him aloft. The pauses, though necessary, were the most frightening moments in the climb. During these breaks his limbs were more likely to convulse. Terror of falling ebbed him on faster, forgoing any prolonged breathers. Trembling his way out, he collapsed to the desert floor.

It had been a risk going into the well, but Flint had exhausted his water supply more quickly than planned. The last two nights, he had survived by collecting desert insects when they appeared under the moonlight. He then squished the bugs into a wet pulp. This kept him going, but if forced to do that for two more nights, he might just cave in and pull out his satellite phone.

After replacing the stone over the top of the well, he sank to a sitting position next to it. A wave of satisfaction swept over him. "And Philip thought I couldn't handle the desert on my own!" he reminisced.

The sun was sinking below the horizon. Between pursed lips, he released a few long sighs. It was time to pack up his primitive camp. The air was still warm, but would soon cool down. He quickly learned after the first day of hiking that he preferred to travel at night.

This was much more to his advantage. Not only could he save water and escape the desert sun's wrath, but also he could forage for food. This simple revelation had saved his life. Despite the fact that the sun was Flint's first reason for attempting to travel at night, he realized that the barren desert came alive after the sun had vanished. He correctly assumed that this was because years of evolution had taught the inhabitants of the dry wilderness climate to be nocturnal. Having no fear of insects, except the occasional spider, he discovered that they were a decent enough meal. As he had brought very little in the way of food, this made surviving much easier.

He didn't see any people around, and didn't expect to run into any. So with little effort to keep up his disguise, Flint swung the aluminum-framed backpack over his shoulders. He didn't even bother to camouflage it with his ragged gunnysack. His legs were still a little shaky as he began to walk in a northeasterly direction, but he believed that walking would do him much better than sitting.

In the second hour of the hike, his eyes found a few unlucky insects. The beetles were easily pluck up and placed in a little cotton bag. The scorpions were a little more tricky. He used a stick to pin them down while he cut off their stingers before adding them to his stock pile. In the third hour, he stopped for a small break. Opening up the pouch, he withdrew a few of the bugs that would constitute his first meal of the evening. The taste was still foreign to him, but not detestable. The texture of the creature's soft abdomens took a little more getting used to. But every night it got easier. He was almost to the point where it was no harder to eat an insect than an egg.

Flints chest rose and fell with each heavy breath. His throat was dry, but he feared to break into his new meager supply of water just yet. After a fifteen-minute breather, he raised his first bottle of well water to his lips. With lips pursed tightly, Flint took a slow but small drink of water. He'd purposely waited until he was ready to start hiking again. If he drank immediately after deciding to rest, he knew his impulse would be to guzzle the live-sustaining liquid. If he waited for his body to cool down on its own, then he wouldn't feel as thirsty and could survive on much less.

He put his gear back together and continued his

trek. Occasionally he glanced at his compass, but even that felt a little like cheating. Usually he relied on the stars. Sure, he didn't know enough about them to really navigate, but wasn't that the whole point of his journey, to get lost and risk it all for a little fun?

Flint pondered how bright the nighttime lit up once away from the city. Though he carried a flashlight, he chose not to use it most nights. Once his eyes adjusted to the darkness, the sky provided enough light. Even when the moon was not visible, the stars were so glorious that the landscape seemed to illuminate and worship the heavens. It caused Flint to think about his wife. Could she be alive, or was she up there in the skies, dancing between the stars, and peering down at him? Sure she'd been an emotional wreck, but suicide? He would never have guessed.

Sometimes he'd pick a star and talk to it as if it were Lydia. "If you are up there, my sweet, I hope you are taking good care of our boy."

Sometimes he would even carry on a conversation for hours at a time, only to end it by falling to his knees and crying. Tears would not come, though. Maybe because of a lack of water. Maybe because he'd worn out his tears. Still, sometimes he wished the heavens would pluck him up and take him away. But he would never take his own life. Put himself in the Alaskan wilderness or the Egyptian desert with very little provisions, yes. But to give up was not his way. He was a fighter. His father was a fighter, and so was his father before that. Perhaps that was why he went on these survival expeditions. If he could survive, then he could prove that he was stronger than he felt.

After another hour of hiking, he came to a rocky

outcrop. Scaling the rocks for a better view, he gazed upon a moonlit series of stubby plateaus with deep canyons. A brief glance at his compass made him scratch his head. The needle was pointing north, but for nearly ten seconds it spun. Then it immediately returned to pointing north.

Knowing only a little about geology, he figured if there had been iron deposits in the rocks, then his compass would still not have been acting this way. Iron would either completely throw his compass off, or it wouldn't. *This has to be something different*, he thought. *But what could do this in the middle of a desert? Maybe there's some hidden military or terrorist base nearby that's experimenting with different weapons. If that's the case, though, wouldn't there be additional signs of activity?*

It was a far-fetched idea, but just then a helicopter flew right over him. He hadn't heard it coming. This chopper had obviously been rigged for silent flight operations. He got down on the ground, hoping the pilot hadn't already seen him. But if the chopper was outfitted with silencing technology, then Flint could safely assume that it was also outfitted with night vision.

As he expected, the chopper began to circle. A cold sweat clung to his back, drawing his attention to the pack resting on it, as if it were a huge mountain standing atop his shoulders, waving at the possibly unfriendly visitor. Swinging it off his back, he unstrapped the AK-47, Flint injected one of the copper-coated rounds into the assault rifle's chamber. Quickly adjusting the range on the open sights for five hundred meters, he thumbed the safety off.

Crouching behind a rock for additional protection, Flint felt relieved that he'd brought the AK-47 instead of his Ruger, a minor consolation. The pistol would have offered no protection against a militant hostile in a helicopter. Even the assault rifle was a long shot, but it was better than nothing. Back home he had often shot the AK-47 with his friends. The solid bullet he used was made to have little if any expansion on impact. This made it good at piercing dense material. He had often lined up several logs to see how many the bullet could pass through before it came to rest. As long as the helicopter wasn't armor plated, the copper coated projectile would offer some defense.

Surprisingly, the chopper didn't swing all the way around. Before completing its turn, it slowly descended into one of the larger canyons to the south. Exhaling with relief, Flint's first instinct was to get moving as fast as he could in the other direction. But he was in unfamiliar territory, and his curiosity got the better of him.

"After all," he said to himself, "it would be rude to just ignore my new neighbors."

He slowly crept across the rocky terrain with his gun at the ready. Only as he approached the rim of the small valley where the chopper had landed did he finally relax his rifle a degree. Stepping cautiously to avoid kicking any rocks or to stumble across any perimeter defense mechanisms, he approached the rocky outcrop at the edge of the canyon. Peeking over the edge, he didn't see a large base camp. But something didn't seem right about the whole situation.

In the basin, about two hundred yards away from the helicopter was a single military-style tent. Bars were being pulled down as the tent was being deconstructed. Flint pulled out his binoculars to study the small camp. With only the natural illumination from the night sky and a few dim lights around the chopper, Flint had to really struggle to see through the binoculars. What he could see, though not very clearly, were two men with rifles and one man with no visible weapon. He wore a button-up shirt with slacks and a full-brimmed hat. Flint's neck hair prickled. The man carried himself as if he was important. *What could they be up to in the middle of the night out here?*

They were miles away from anybody else. They just had a single tent, guarded by armed men. Nothing was coming out of the tent that was being taken down. This bizarre encounter was suspicious. Whatever their purpose for being here, they seemed to be finishing it up. Flint's first thought was that it was a mobile terrorist training camp. But even that didn't quite mesh with the scene he was spying on.

Flint followed the leader's movements, until he suddenly disappeared.

No person could just disappear.

Fixing his gaze on the point where the man had vanished, Flint realized that there must be an opening in the hill at the bottom of the valley; a cave of some sort. Perhaps they were mining something of great value. Only why, then, would there be no miners, but rifle toting bodyguards instead?

After a few minutes, the tent was fully packed into the chopper. The man then emerged from the hidden opening. This time he came out with two more guards and a woman.

When he focused on the woman, a rush of adrenaline spiked in Flint. He had to take the binoculars down and squint for a second. Shaking his head, he thought his mind must have deceived him. After a deep breath, he again lifted the magnifying lenses to his eyes for a better look. His hands had started shaking. He was forced to reposition himself to get a more steady and clear image. Even still, the woman he saw looked too familiar . . . but could it be? Focusing in on her, he tried to tell himself it was impossible. They were still pretty far away, and it was too difficult to know, but she looked remarkably like his own wife of two years ago, minus a pregnant belly of course.

It's just the dark. It can't possibly be her. How could it be? But curiosity and confusion gnawed at him. As he watched her, he could only imagine Lydia, with her mid-length, smooth blonde hair. From this distance the woman appeared to stand about the same five foot nine as his wife.

He remembered the way she would shift her stance in public. It was almost a nervous tic but it came with the grace reminiscent of shampoo commercials. Only his Lydia had a way of involuntarily doing it with her whole body, not just her hair. It was one way she always stood out in a crowd. The fact that she had no awareness of this simple act only added to her mystique. When combined with her smile and quick laugh, her motion made all other women appear stale. Flint thought he saw that characteristic movement in the woman just moments ago.

Refocusing on the scene below, he could see that the man was carrying two large briefcases. What they contained, he could only guess. As he shifted his focus back to the woman, he realized that she was resisting. The two guards were holding on to her, and she appeared to be straining against them, as if she wanted to return to the hole in the earth. This protest forced them to drag her toward the chopper. Flint's temper went from a warm nervousness to hot anger.

Wife or not, Flint disapproved. His assumption

of a terrorist or mining camp was abolished by the only scenario left for him to conjure. He'd heard of the sex trafficking that took place around the world, but never thought he'd see it for himself. Even if he was mistaken, she was still in distress, and he knew that he was the only person around who might be able to help her.

His biggest and most obvious obstacle was the four armed guards. Sneaking around the edge of the canyon, Flint looked for a way down. If the chopper stayed in place for a little longer, he might find an opportunity to get to the woman.

Thanks to a full moon and clear sky, he found a path in under a minute that skirted the canyon walls, leading down to the people below. It offered sufficient concealment for most of his descent, as long as he could keep from kicking any rocks down as he passed through the more open portions of the natural staircase.

Never taking his eyes off the guards, he inched his way closer to the chopper. When his foot suddenly snagged something, he silently cursed.

Time slowed to a crawl, as the peril of his situation dawned on him. He'd been hiking in this climate for the last week, and had run across every form of plant life indigenous to the region. The new tug on his foot was no plant, but a trip wire. Flint knew in the pit of his stomach that he was going to die.

The sky lit up, and Flint shut his eyes. It didn't hurt, but it was blinding. After waiting a few seconds he reopened his eyes. He wasn't dead. The string he'd tripped was only connected to an aerial flare. He was relieved that he hadn't been killed by a bomb, but with the arching red flame of the flare pointing its tail down on him from the sky, there was no doubt he would be discovered.

Chancing a look over a large boulder, he was stung in the face by chips of the metamorphic rock as rifles down below targeted his location. Two more bullets hit nearby. One of them passed so close that he felt the disturbance in the air as it whizzed by his forehead.

The thick chunk of rock that stood between him and the deadly aim of his attackers was sufficiently protecting him for now. But to retreat would expose him too much. He was effectively pinned down. All they had to do was flank him from the side, or gun him down if he tried to run. His heart was thumping, but he forced down the panic. The terror was still real, but he knew that if he let his fear get to him, then it would become his greatest enemy.

As he calmed, he tried to think from the perspective of the men below. They knew where he was but didn't know that he was alone. This gave him some advantage. They would doubtlessly approach him with caution, which would slow them down.

Since the trail he was on, was the only way to scale the canyon wall, he knew where they would approach him from. They would also be stupid to leave their boss man and their chopper unguarded. With this understanding, Flint guessed that two of them would stay by the chopper, ready to snipe at anyone that moved. While they stood guard, the other two men would make their way up the steep path and attempt to flank him.

Flint realized he had a few minutes to prepare before they intercepted him. The one thing that he hoped they would not expect would be for him to continue down the trail toward the camp. It would be his only chance.

He unslung his backpack from his shoulders and pulled out the old gunnysack. He then placed it in front of his backpack, being careful to lay it on the rocks in a particular shape to resemble a hiding person. Then, leaving his pack behind, he held himself as close to the ground as possible.

The next twenty yards of path that hugged the canyon wall were relatively flat. As long as he shimmied along on his belly, the men below wouldn't see him from their angle.

Scooting down, he barely registered the discomfort of the ground as it scratched across his chest. His concentration was fixed on an outcropping of rocks just ahead. The formation created a roofless tunnel, with the canyon wall ascending a good fifty feet up on one side, and the wall of the valley side providing at least six feet of vertical height. It would be plenty tall for Flint to stand, hidden from those below.

Inside this protected area, he found that some old fallen rocks were lodged in a portion of the trail. A one-foot gap presented itself beneath these boulders, creating an opportune place to hide. The gap didn't extend very far back, but Flint managed to shimmy into the crevice.

Feeling reasonably concealed, he reached for his AK-47 that he'd set down seconds ago. He just managed to pull the rifle in with him as two guards crept up the trail. The squawk on their radios was in English, but indiscernible enough to sound foreign to him; still, he instinctively knew that the men below must be telling them where he was supposed to be hiding.

Their feet crunched over the rocks within a foot of Flint's rifle as they passed. Flint wiggled out enough to see their backs more clearly. They were dressed in dark uniforms with assault rifles butted against their arms. They walked as though they had done this many times before. Flint observed that their uniforms were composed of body armor. But he also knew that the average Kevlar suit would be no match for the fully copper-jacketed bullets from his AK-47, especially at close range. Flint tensed, not wanting to pull his trigger.

As soon as the men came around the corner to see Flint's abandoned pack, they fired several quick bursts into the decoy. Fear of being killed temporarily replaced most of his fear of killing, and Flint took this opportunity to empty three rounds into the back of each man. The bullets tore through the first side of their vests. The Kevlar only managed to slow the momentum, leaving the projectiles sandwiched inside their chests. They were dead before they hit the ground.

Never before had Flint killed a man, and now in a split second he had dispatched two complete strangers. Vomit rose in his throat. He hadn't believed it in himself to kill another human being.

Now two real men were real dead. He dropped the gun and buried his face in his bicep, attempting to wipe the sweat from his face in the process. Doubt burned into his mind. *Maybe I shouldn't have stuck my nose into this hornets' nest*, he thought. *What if they were good men, and I just created a large misunderstanding?* Choking back bile, he forced himself to take a few deep breaths. *No. Honest men wouldn't attack so quickly.*

Flint shimmied out of the crevice, determined to move on. The two assassins had failed, and their comrades below would have seen them go down. They would also know by now that he was armed. An AK-47 was all too common for the region. Sound recognition alone would ensure that they knew of their comrade's failure, especially since his shots were the last ones fired. Crouching to collect his thoughts, he tried again to guess their next move. Only two armed men were left below. But there was also the man in charge, who might be armed and dangerous. And what of the woman? Was she with them, or was she being held against her will?

Not sure what he was up against, Flint decided the best course of action would be to crawl back to his pack and strip the dead guards of their vests. If he could double up the vests, he would have some measure of protection against the remaining men.

As soon as he was lying down next to one of the dead assailants, he unstrapped their body armor. The Velcro was easy enough to undo, but rolling over the lifeless mass of flesh to pull out the back side of the blood-soaked vest was more difficult. Flint guessed that the man weighed close to two hundred pounds, but his dead weight seemed to add an extra hundred. Just as the vest came loose, he heard an unfamiliar *phzz*, lasting no more than half a second.

The sheltered outcropping where he had just come from suddenly thundered with an explosion that shook the whole mountainside. The flash of light and the concussion of the rocket-propelled grenade threw him over the dead man's body. He landed on the narrow trail between the two corpses. He just had time to pull one of them over his own body before the canyon wall above him erupted in another explosion.

Stunned, he lay there long enough to question his own ability to move. His ears were numb, and he didn't dare budge. The landscape around him would be deformed, and any sign of movement might trigger another barrage of rocket fire from below. Only after several minutes did he dare test his muscles.

His body was not only pinned by the weight of the

man he'd pulled onto himself, but also by the other corpse that had rolled over during the explosion. Their combined bulk, along with the weight of some debris from the canyon wall, was enough to almost suffocate him. Had the dead men not been covering him, the fallen shards of stone would have lacerated him, or worse. The boulders he'd previously hid behind were dislodged and had fallen down below.

Craning his head around, he could see the chopper speeding up its propellers. The man in the button-up shirt shoved the distressed woman into the backseat, with the remaining guards following close behind. Within a minute the machine had lifted off, and was disappearing over the canyon.

Never before had Flint felt so miserable. The numbing of his ears was turning into a throbbing pain. Even worse was the ringing that he was beginning to notice. But at least there was the ringing; that meant he hadn't lost his hearing. His whole body ached, and it took every bit of strength to pull himself out from under the men and debris. To his surprise, he had no broken bones, though the bruises would take weeks to heal.

Limping over to the edge of the trail, he sat down on some rubble next to his half-buried hiking pack. Looking down into the canyon, he could see a faint light. It came from the place where he suspected an underground opening to be. He wondered if the light had always been there, or if it was new. He couldn't remember it before, but that didn't mean it wasn't there.

He found his gun to still be in good shape, if a little dirtied. Then with pained effort, he limped down the trail. Having come this far, he might as well know why he'd just killed two men and nearly died himself. Reaching the bottom, he realized that a cave did indeed exist in a gap between two small hills.

As he cautiously approached the entrance, shouting voices caused him to stumble with surprise. *"Mangyarin, ipaalam sa amin, kami ay gawin!"* They weren't cries of alarm, but sounded more like cries for help.

Flint raised his rifle at the thin face behind a chain-link fence.

"Hindi! Hindi! No!" the man cried and put his arms up and fell to his knees.

Lowering his rifle, Flint realized that these men were not violent. Taking a brief look around, he saw the lock that held the chain-link fence shut. The men appeared to be of some Asian descent, but he couldn't place them. All he knew was that they were being held inside the cave against their will. Risking being found for an American, Flint asked, "Do you speak English?"

"Ingles," the closest man shouted back as others ran up to the gate.

"Ingles, Americano, you G.I. Joe!" they proclaimed.

"Hey Joe, you help, you help," they continued in their broken English.

"Hold on, get back," Flint ordered, motioning for them to step away from the gate.

Raising his gun again, he aimed at the lock. The men ran to the other side of the gate and put their hands over their ears. The sound of the rifle hurt Flint's ears. He winced, even though he felt half deaf anyway. Luckily he had only to discharge a single round. The lock shredded off, and the gate swung wide open.

The four captives ran out of the cave. Some were crying, and some were saying things he couldn't understand. Cautiously Flint entered the cave. After about twenty feet of an angled descent, he came into a room that was clearly not a natural formation. It looked ancient, and he felt as though he'd stepped inside a submarine. But how could a submarine this old and this far out in the desert even exist? The bulkheads and compartments were nearly rusted into nothing. The wall flaked into pieces at the slightest touch. This room had to predate any modern submarine he had ever heard about. The thing was truly ancient.

As he inched his way around, he began to question his assumption. The scale of the passageways was larger than any submarine he had previously imagined, giving more than enough headroom. There were also corridors that went perpendicular to the room he'd first entered, suggesting a very large vessel.

With his mouth open and lip twisted in awe, Flint wanted to venture in farther. He wanted to find some explanation for what he was seeing. For the moment, the only hypothesis that he could conjure, he immediately knew to be false. After all, the famed *Nautilus* of Captain Nemo was just a work of fiction.

A hand grabbed his arm. Spinning around with gun at the ready, he saw one of the men he'd freed moments ago.

"No here, no here," the man said urgently. Then he grabbed Flint's arm and tugged him toward the entrance.

Flint wanted to explore further, or at least to ask what this place was, but the stress in the young man's face worried him. "American Joe, trust me," the man said. "We Filipino, not lie to you."

The cool fresh air of night contrasted brilliantly from the stale thing he'd come out of. As if waking from a dream, the urgency of the moment dawned on him. Flint noticed the three others running toward the canyon wall, soon to be followed by the man who'd just pulled him from the underground lair.

Then he remembered the chopper. What if it circled back around? They couldn't hide underground; they'd be trapped, but they had no place to hide in the valley. Trusting in his new friends, Flint was about to follow, but recalled that he'd left his backpack up on the other trail.

Changing course to go back up the trail, the Filipinos only shouted a meager protest. They didn't seem interested in following him up. He guessed they knew of a different way out of the valley, but Flint needed to get his pack. Upon reaching the spot where he'd left the dead guards, he dug his belongings out of the rubble.

Then, reaching down to the bottom of the bag, he conceded, "Okay, Philip, you win," as he pulled out the satellite phone.

He pressed the red button and held it until the phone's screen glowed in bright indigo. After a minute it was ready to use. There was only one number saved in the phone and Flint knew it would connect him to a voice that would proclaim, "I told you so."

He hesitated, then pressed Send, the screen lit up with a message: "Searching . . . Searching . . ."

After repeating this for a minute or two, it said, "No reception."

"What good are you," Flint scolded the phone.

He'd never used a satellite phone before, but he thought it should be simple enough. The only option he had was to get out of the canyon completely and hope for a better signal.

The walk back to the canyon rim was uneventful. He tried not to look at the phone, since the glowing screen adversely affected his night vision. After having survived the night's encounters, he didn't want to end his luck by tripping on a small stone and falling down the canyon to his death. He only wished that he could have gotten to his backpack without looking again upon the two corpses who died at his hand. He wondered if everyone who killed felt as guilty as he did, even if the act was prompted by self-defense.

As soon as he was on the rim of the canyon, he tried the phone again. It took five minutes of redialing before the phone began to ring.

After a full minute of ringing, the phone clicked, and a laugh came through the receiver as Philip Noon answered on the other end.

"Don't you dare say a thing until you hear what I have to tell you," Flint began, remembering his last conversation with Philip.

"You'll never make it alone out there," his old mentor had warned, just before forcing the phone into Flint's pack. "When you end up stranded in the middle of the desert, don't expect any sympathy from me, I just want to hear your last dying breath so that I can tell you I told you so."

Flint knew he could count on Philip. They joked like this occasionally. Philip had hired him when he was eighteen, six years before he married Lydia. With Flint's dad having died that year, Philip had not been just another employer, but had become a good friend and almost like a second father to Flint.

"I think I've gotten myself into something pretty big here. I'm not sure what I've found, but it nearly cost me my life. Two other men weren't so lucky," Flint started.

He then recited the evening's events to Philip. When he got to the part where the Filipino had pulled him out of the cave, the whole canyon flashed bright. Flint instinctively reached for his ears, but before he could prepare himself, the concussion of the explosion below knocked him to the ground.

"Aaaaghhhh!" he shouted as he pressed his palms against his throbbing ears. "Enough with the explosions already!"

If permanent hearing damage hadn't already occurred, he wouldn't be surprised if this one did him in. Then he reached over and picked up the phone. The main screen was cracked slightly but still glowing. "Are you still there?"

Flint was relieved when he could hear Philip's voice from the phone before he fully brought it back to his ear.

"What just happened?" Philip asked.

"A change of plans, Noon," Flint replied as he strained to stand up. "I need a chopper here ASAP. I've stumbled onto something, and I don't think I'm finished yet."

Flint listened as Philip tried to reason with him.

"Look, I just killed two men, saved a few more innocent men," Flint argued back. "And I'm pretty sure there's one woman who's still in serious danger. I came looking for an adventure, and maybe I didn't expect this turn, but I've still got three weeks till I need to be back—I'm going after her."

Pausing for a moment, Flint began to piece things together. The men from the chopper had a bomb placed at the bottom of the canyon, most likely to cover up whatever it was they were doing. The Filipinos were meant to be killed in the explosion. This didn't surprise him much, as Filipinos were often taken advantage of. They were very poor, and were willing to do just about anything if it meant they could support their families. In Japan most of the prostitutes were brought in from the Philippines. The house laborers in Saudi Arabia were often Filipinos who were treated like house slaves. They always seemed to get the bum deals.

Then there were the men and that woman who'd flown away in the chopper. It had been too dark to get a good look at them. However, the two he had killed didn't look as though they were from the Middle East. This would suggest that they were not a local outfit.

St. Catherine and Sharm El Sheikh were the two closest international airports in the direction that the helicopter had come from. Knowing they likely would go back that way to refuel, he lifted the phone back to his ear.

"Get me a chopper out here now, and let them know that I need to go directly to Sharm El Sheikh," Flint said.

That airport seemed a more likely destination than St. Catherine. While they were both international airports, the one at Sharm El Sheikh was larger, and would be more accommodating for a long-haul trip. A militarized helicopter flying into the touristy St. Catherine airport would raise more suspicion. With any luck he might even be able to get there and find the helicopter before it left again for its final destination. It was a long shot, but he knew if there was any hope for the woman on board, it would be up to him.

"A helicopter isn't cheap you know," Philip stated lightly. "This is going to come out of your Christmas bonus."

"You find a good reason to skip my bonus each year anyway," Flint reminded. "At least this time I get to choose where it goes."

Philip laughed, "I may be cheap with you, but

just wait till you take over and are making the big bucks."

"Careful," Flint joked, "When that time comes, I might find a good excuse to cut your pension down."

"You know I won't have a pension from the company," Philip stated.

"That was easy," Flint chided. Both chuckled slightly, acutely aware of the seriousness of the situation.

After hanging up the satellite phone, Flint played with it until he found out how to use the e-mail function. Then he typed a short message to one other person who he hoped might be able to help.

Chapter 3

August 2

Philip Noon hung up the phone. The Middle East peoples had been fighting one another for generations, and he knew that wouldn't change in the near future. Now Flint was pushing him right into the middle of somebody else's war. But he also knew that once Flint set his mind to something, you would have to knock his head clean off his shoulders in order to change it. This was the reason why Philip was in Egypt to start with.

A few years back, a good buddy by the name of Jim Krieger came to Philip with a request. Jim had been diagnosed with cancer when his son, Flint, was seventeen years old. With less than a year to live, and few relatives to lean on, Jim wanted to make sure that his boy would be well taken care of. Even though Flint was just about to turn eighteen and would be free to pursue his own life, Jim still wanted somebody there to mentor and help guide the boy along. Since Philip was one of Jim's lifelong and closest friends, the dying man entrusted him with the care of his son.

Because Jim had worked the factories in Michigan for much of his life before moving to Wyoming to chase after oil, all he knew was manual labor. Though he regarded the lifestyle as a respectable one, he always wanted something better for his son. Philip, on the other hand, had started a few businesses and later gotten involved in the financial markets as a hedge fund manager. To many people Philip had been known as a jovial but shrewd businessman. He'd done very well for himself, and could have retired early. But his love for that next big deal always propelled him forward. This mentality appealed to Jim, but even more, their close friendship had made him like a brother. So when Jim asked Philip to watch over Flint, he accepted the responsibility without hesitation.

With two girls and no sons of his own, Philip took Flint under his wing, and treated him as the son he never had. Their friendship grew, and when Flint finished college, Philip offered to let Flint take over the business he'd been developing. Granted, Flint still had much to learn, but for the last eleven years, Philip had been moving Flint around the company. He hoped that by giving the young man experience doing everything from cleaning toilets to holding investor conferences that Flint might get a better appreciation for all that went into running a successful business. After all, in Philip's opinion, school could only teach you so much. It helped expand your ability to think, even if it didn't always give much in the way of practical working knowledge.

The first time that Flint had ventured out after his wife's disappearance, he gave Philip little notice. Philip didn't like the way Flint was coping with the loss of his child and disappearance of his wife. But he tried not to read much into it. It wasn't until a month later, when Flint finally returned to work, that Philip found out just how dangerous the young man's little Alaskan trip had been. So when Flint insisted on taking another month off for an adventure, Philip judged that Flint had become addicted to danger.

Whether Flint was hoping he wouldn't make it home, or he just liked the thrill of the adventure, Philip didn't know. He wasn't sure if Flint even knew himself, but he felt responsible for his friend's son. So when Flint had wanted to trek across the Egyptian desert, Philip was more than a little concerned. He didn't let Flint leave without first sticking a satellite phone in his backpack. Philip had no doubt that it would get used along the way. Then he took a flight a day later to Egypt to be close at hand if Flint actually did get into trouble.

For the past week, Philip had enjoyed a nice vacation. He spent a little time seeing the sights in Egypt and planned to visit Jordan. Eventually he'd end up in Israel. But today he was relaxing in the desert mountains of St. Catherine. Each morning at the hotels, he checked up on his business for an hour or two via the Internet, keeping his phone free in case Flint called. This morning he was just waking up and getting ready to start this routine. The sky was still dark but hinting at dawn when the half anticipated call came in.

Not wanting to sound too concerned, Philip had forced a laugh when he answered the phone, but what Flint had to say was far from what he would've expected.

"Are you nuts?" Philip had asked. "You just about died, and now you want to go chase some girl and a few terrorists across the Middle East?"

Had he not known Flint for so long, he would've guessed the young man was playing a joke on him. But the tone in Flint's voice was as serious as a heart attack.

"I can get you a helicopter and bring you over here to St. Catherine airport," Philip began. But Flint told him that the terrorists' chopper was more likely to head down south to the next airport.

Philip could see that Flint was determined to help this lady and he knew that once Flint had made up his mind, he would unrelentingly see it through. The best thing he could do now, would be to help get this over with as quickly as possible. With any luck he could just turn the terrorists over to the airport police.

"I'll use the GPS app on your satellite phone to send a chopper your way. But if this is that important to you, I'll head down to that airport and keep an eye out for them."

If Philip's being in Egypt surprised Flint, he didn't let on. But Philip knew he'd have to get involved. He didn't want Flint chasing down a terrorist group by himself, and he doubted the ability of the authorities to apprehend the militant group.

Philip's suggestion sounded good enough to Flint and they hung up their phones. Philip soon realized there was only one helicopter available at this airport. Even if he sent the chopper to Flint, it would never catch up to the terrorists in time. However, if he first flew down to Sharm El Sheikh Airport, then he could at least do a little digging while his rented chopper went to pick up Flint. Philip didn't like getting into this mess to begin with, but Flint always had a way with persuading people to do anything. It was something Philip admired about him. But now this ability was turning into a curse for Philip.

The St. Catherine airport was only ten minutes away from his hotel. In the darkness of the early morning, Philip was relieved to find not only a helicopter, but it's pilot there with it. The chopper itself seemed in good condition, which was more than Philip could say about the pilot. Even Philip, with his fully white Beatles hair style and hardened red face, looked younger at sixty-four than the dark-haired pilot who could only be pushing fifty. The pilot's face was worn by too many days in the sun, and by too many vices. This made his body appear ragged and tired. Philip couldn't tell who was taller, since the pilot had a permanent slouch, making him stand about an inch shorter than Philip's five foot eight. As for the chopper, it appeared to be about twenty to thirty years old and well maintained.

"Does it have GPS navigation on board?" Philip asked the thin pilot.

"Nope, I don't need GPS," the pilot replied with a British accent. "I know all the best places to visit, been showin' folks around these parts for years. I know every ruin and hot spot for a thousand kilometers in each direction. You'll get your money's worth."

"I'm not interested in sights, I'm interested in getting my friend and myself to Sharm El Sheikh," Philip said quietly, as he realized the pilot had probably fallen asleep drunk inside the cockpit and was now fighting off a hangover.

The edges of the pilot's left eye lowered to meet the rising corner of his lip. Puzzled, he said, "Don't get me wrong, I do like the business, but there's a couple of flights each day that go down that way, and you can bet they're cheaper than booking a flight on my chopper."

"I need to get there quickly, then I need you to pick up my friend who is out in the mountains and bring him over. We're in a rush."

The pilot had to force a pained expression on his face. "Oh, I didn't realize your friend was in the mountains. You need me for the rest of the day, then. I don't usually do private charters like this. They have a tendency to come with more baggage than I bargained for."

"We'll be no trouble at all, trust me," Philip replied.

"Oh, I've heard that before—it got me locked up for a full month once. Egyptian prisons are very uncomfortable. I want five thousand American dollars up front."

"That's outrageous!" Philip claimed. "What makes you even think I would carry that much money?"

The pilot's face remained passive as he replied, "If you like, you can look around for another helicopter, which you won't find. Or you can just wait for a plane to take you, and hope you find a pilot there with a better deal to pick up your friend."

Philip's face reddened with mounting frustration. "You know what, I don't even want to go. You just gave me a good excuse to extend my vacation here for a little longer."

Turning to leave, Philip took a few steps in the other direction. The pilot was obviously startled. Only a moment ago, he must have felt sure that Philip urgently needed transport. Now Philip guessed that the pilot was beginning to think he'd overestimated Philip's need.

"All right, you convinced me. Four thousand and

not a penny less," the pilot said.

Philip hadn't been aware that he was holding his breath until he sighed with relief. Realizing that he now had the upper hand, Philip casually replied, "I'll give you one thousand now, and two more when you deliver my friend."

"I've never been hired for a full day's work for so little," the pilot lied.

Philip continued to walk away. "I didn't say you had to accept it."

After years of running a business, Philip had learned that the best place to be when negotiating was to not actually need the other person's contribution. Still the bluff was no less difficult.

"Come back, I'll take you," the pilot exclaimed as he mumbled a few words in some Arabic tongue that Philip guessed were curses.

Philip knew the pilot would consider three thousand dollars to be fair or better, even if he was a little disappointed. Business around here was likely slow, owing to the region's unrest. Tourism had gone down, and there weren't nearly as many visitors to charter a sightseeing helicopter.

The little chopper was small but adequate, at least for a little group of sightseers. After ten minutes of preflight inspections and preparations, and a couple private minutes where Philip guessed the pilot was trying to do something about a hangover, they were ready to take off. Philip placed a call to his hotel asking them to hold his bags until he returned or sent for them. He didn't like leaving his luggage, but he didn't have enough time to retrieve it.

The helicopter sped along, and conversation between Philip and the pilot was sparse. He couldn't tell the man anything about what Flint had found, because he didn't know if the tour guide could be trusted. Often in that line of work, guides were paid for their entertainment value, which led many of them to be great storytellers. The last thing Philip needed was his story being told. More to the point, Philip wasn't sure himself what he'd gotten involved with. Occasionally the pilot tried to inject some comment about a particular landscape feature or a bit of historical trivia. Philip, however, was focused on figuring out what he would do when he got to the airport.

At Sharm El Sheik, the chopper hovered for a few seconds before its wheels touched down. The rotor slowed to a windy idle, then the pilot shut the engine off all together. Philip thought helicopter pilots always left their rotors moving, but he tried disregarded this for now.

He checked his phone one last time and gave Flint's coordinates to the pilot. Since there wasn't a GPS computer in his chopper, the pilot had to rely on cumbersome aviation charts.

"This is in the middle of nowhere," the pilot said. "How did your friend end up there in the first place?"

"He likes to get himself lost every now and then," Philip replied. "But don't ask me why he does it."

The fuel truck arrived and the pilot had the workers top off the tank.

"Good luck," Philip said as the pilot stepped into his chopper.

"Why, am I going to need it?" he asked seriously.

"Just find him quickly and get him back here," Philip said. "I'll be waiting for you."

Wind from the rotors washed across his squinting face and Philip was left alone on the tarmac. Unsure of what to do, he walked to a small building, which he had been informed was the FBO, or fixed-base operator. Most private flights would have to go through this office for fuel and other services. As soon as he stepped up to the door, he took one last look around and noticed that another helicopter was on approach for landing. But it was heading toward a hangar, not this FBO.

Philip walked halfway around the building, careful not to draw attention to himself. He wanted a closer look at the chopper that was about to land. Since neither of the two other choppers on the ground matched Flint's description, the one coming in was most likely the one Flint had seen earlier. This chopper was incredibly quiet and looked more military than pleasure. Stepping back around the building, Philip walked into the FBO office, which along with the fence, stood as a main barrier between the tarmac and the outside of this portion of the airport.

"How may I help you?" the man at the front desk asked.

Philip was surprised by the man's British accent. "Does everybody here speak English?"

"Of course, it's the language of aviation," the man replied. "All pilots are required to know it if they are to fly and communicate legally, or at least in most countries."

"Well, I'm no pilot," Philip began. "But I am interested in a helicopter—in particular, the one landing at the hangar a few buildings down."

The man had been monitoring the radio behind his desk. He knew the chopper, but a puzzled look came across his face.

"I'm afraid I can't help you with that. We have a couple choppers for rent here, and we can sell you one. But the one you are referring to is privately owned."

"Oh, who owns it?" Philip asked casually.

"I wouldn't know. They fly in and out of here all the time, but they are based somewhere international."

"International," Philip said. "You mean, like Saudi Arabia or Jordan?"

"No, they have a jet also, and it is made for longer flights than that. But I don't know where they go. They keep to themselves."

Philip realized that if they only used the chopper for the short flight to where Flint was, then they would soon be departing on their jet for their final destination. If this happened, and they really were holding someone captive, then he had to find a way to track the jet before they switched aircraft. Back in the states, Philip knew that he might be able to track a plane's flight plan, but here he wasn't too sure. Even if a flight plan was required to be filed, if these people wanted to keep a secret, they would likely file a false plan. In any case, Philip was sure that they had some way of eluding a tail.

"I just realized something," Philip told the man, as he tried to think of a good excuse to leave. With nothing coming to mind, he just ended with, "I'll be back in a few minutes."

Philip stepped back outside and began to walk casually toward the hangar that would undoubtedly hold the jet. On his way he sent a quick text message, letting Flint know he was enabling the GPS on his phone. This would allow Flint to track the jet once he placed the phone inside the airplane.

When he reached the sandy colored hangar, he slowed his pace. Casual, but discreet, he circled the building, taking notice of any person or surveillance cameras. A couple of people were milling about their own business in this early hour, giving Philip less than a moment of their attention.

For an international airport, this one was small. On the south side were a few commercial jets, the northern end where Philip was now, had recently been converted into what resembled a smaller municipal airport. Security, though present, was more lax in this area. There was almost a dangerous sense of disregard compared to the airports he was used to. Philip guessed they were simply turning a blind eye with a gold patch.

He only found one camera, and it was positioned above the entrance to an office area. Even this seemed more for the occupants of the hanger than for the airport security. His only other entry into the hangar would be through the open bay door. Sneaking around to the bay door area, he moved his head just enough to look inside at a man in blue coveralls. His back faced Philip. Sensing little danger at being found, he risked coming a little more into the open. The man was talking on a small radio. Four other men dressed in mechanic's coveralls were scattered around the interior.

On the inside of the hangar, Philip observed a large private jet and the military-styled chopper, which had just been taxied under the protective roof. On the right side of the cavernous building were extra doors. He guessed that they led to the offices and supply rooms he'd noticed a few minutes ago. That might also be where passengers would stay until the jet was ready to leave.

The jet was a Cessna Citation X, one of the fastest private jets available on the market. With a top speed of Mach 0.92, the airplane could make an international trip very convenient. The main hatch on the port side of the craft was open, and a few attached stairs protruded outward.

Philip looked at the mechanics again. One was

standing with his back to him; two were refueling the chopper; the last one had just finished stowing some bags in the jet, and was heading back to the office for more. Satisfied that they were sufficiently distracted, he sprinted as fast as tip-toes would allow, until he climbed into the jet.

Short excited breaths tried to keep pace with his beating heart. Adrenaline was pumping through his body, fueling the adventurous emotions that he hadn't felt since he was much younger. He wondered if the pace was a little too much for his aging health.

The interior was not the business look he had expected. It shouted classic Asian style. There were vibrant reds mixed with expensive gold and jade artifacts and decorations from China.

Calculating eyes stared in amazement at the expensive decor. A deep fear began to replace the earlier adrenaline. Whoever owned this was, from Flint's description, heavily armed. Now Philip could see that they were also well financed. Resisting the urge to follow his senses and run back out of the plane, he took out his phone. Sliding his daypack from his shoulders, he also pulled out a charger. If these guys were going far, his satellite phone wouldn't last much more than a day, especially since it would constantly be transmitting a GPS signal.

Next to one of the plush red seats at the back of the plane, he found an outlet that was almost hidden by the side of a luxury recliner. Philip plugged in the charger, and then hid the phone under the seat. The design of the bulky chair prevented anyone from casually noticing the phone. The outlet would not likely be discovered unless somebody needed to charge something as well. It wasn't the only outlet and he gambled that the other outlets in the attached tablet consoles would prove easier, should that necessity arise. Confident in his job, Philip eased his way back to the main hatch on the jet.

Chancing a quick glance outside, he couldn't see anybody. Even the mechanics from earlier had vanished. Philip quietly stepped out of the plane and turned to look under the jet, making sure there were no people on the other side of the plane before he continued.

The sudden lack of people made him nervous, and he was extra cautious as he ran back to the hangar door. Once outside, he relaxed a little. He'd done it. Now it was up to Flint to continue the pursuit. If Flint wanted to play knight in shining armor, that was his business and Philip wanted nothing more to do with it. Mostly though, he hoped Flint would eventually come to his better judgment, once he saw what he was getting into. Philip, on the other hand, was ready to pack up and head somewhere more tropical.

As he was about to round the corner of the building, a pang of guilt seized him, and he realized that he couldn't encourage Flint. He was just turning around to take the phone back from the jet, but he barely had enough time to gasp. One of the men in a blue mechanic's suit came around from the outside corner where he must have been waiting. Before Philip could react, the man rammed the bottom of a heavy red fire extinguisher square into Philip's face.

Chapter 4

Flint's last conversation with Philip had troubled him. Philip was going to place a satellite phone in a jet. He didn't want Philip in that situation, even though he knew it was the only way he would be able to find these people. Checking his phone again, he could see that the dot representing Philip's phone had started moving. The jet was just beginning to take off.

Flint scanned the skies looking for a helicopter. It had been just over an hour since Philip called, and the stars had completely disappeared as the sun began to crest the horizon. Flint had no idea when the chopper would arrive; he just hoped it would be soon. He also looked forward to seeing Philip again.

He was surprised that Philip was even in Egypt, but he knew all too well that Philip had been charged to watch over him. Now he was glad to have his guardian hovering close by.

After the explosion, some Filipinos had come up to join him on the canyon rim. Despite their apparent lack of English, they all knew how to say *Joe*.

"Hey Joe," they declared. "You American hero!"

"My name is Flint, not Joe," he replied.

But they kept saying, "Hey Joe, hey Joe," as they tried to shake his hand even more.

"Do you speak English?" Flint asked.

"Oh-oh, I speak *Ingles*, Joe," one stated, the same man who'd pulled him out of the underground structure.

"Okay, then you can start by calling me Flint, not Joe."

"Very-very good, boss," the man replied. "Gual, my name Gual."

"Okay, Gual. What on earth is going on here?"

Gual looked at him with a strained expression. Flint realized he needed to simplify his language to be understood.

"Okay, Gual, why did that blow up?" Flint pointed down the canyon then made a gesture with his hands to imitate the explosion.

Gual understood and replied, "That is ship from up," as he pointed to the sky.

"Airplane," Flint offered.

But the Filipino shook his head and said, "*Dili-di*, ship like *Star Wars*." Then he hummed part of the theme from the George Lucas movie.

"You mean it was a spaceship?" Flint asked.

"Yes, spaceship!" Gual replied. "Very-very old spaceship."

Flint could tell that it was old. He originally thought it looked like some sort of submarine. This sounded even more ridiculous. It was too old to be a space shuttle, let alone a submarine. The thing had to be over a thousand years old.

After more questioning, Flint discovered that the Filipinos had been hired by a group of Chinese men who were living in the Philippines. They were promised good money to work abroad, but once they signed on, they were shipped out to this site and forced to unbury the ancient ship. One of them had been killed when he complained to the men who were overseeing them.

So far, Flint gathered that the base of operations for this company was in the Philippines. It was a great place to hide a clandestine operation. In that developing country, if you had a lot of money, you could not only hide, but also live in style while keeping the authorities from asking questions. You could also draw from the vast pool of poverty-stricken workers and turn them into slave labor. This was how the Filipinos had ended up here, excavating the site. The Chinese men were clearly after something specific, though not even the Filipinos knew what it was.

Turning his head away from the sky, Flint looked at his new friends. They'd been talking among themselves. Then Gual came back over to him.

"Hey boss, you have fly?" He made a sound of a helicopter.

"I have a helicopter coming for us," Flint replied.

The Filipino smiled and asked, "You take us—America?"

"America?" Flint looked puzzled. "Don't you want to go home?"

"No-no, Philippines very poor. America—land of opportunity."

Flint understood that they had originally wanted to find a better life to support their families. If he returned them to the Philippines, then they would be right back where they started.

"But I need your help," Flint replied. "I need to find these bad men and help the other people they might harm."

Gual looked hurt; he had his mind set on going to America. Then he got an idea. "We help, then go to America?"

Flint knew there was no way he would be able to get them to America, but decided that he could offer them a small consolation. "No, but I need a guide. If you help me find the men who did this to you, I will pay you."

Gual's eyes lit up, and Flint now knew he had a guide around the Philippines. But he wasn't sure if they understood that they would still not be going back with him to the United States. For now, at least, he was just glad to have a little help.

As he pondered the issue, he heard the faint thudding of a helicopter. After all that had just happened, his first impulse was to find cover. But he doubted the enemy would be returning in another chopper. They'd buried their mess and coming back to clean up any further might be overkill. Besides, if they were coming back, why would they return in a different chopper? Still, he maintained a little caution.

Once he saw the helicopter, he could tell it was for tourism. The flashy paint job advertised "The Best Sightseeing Above Mount Sinai." For good measure, until Flint was sure the chopper was truly friendly, he kept a finger around the trigger of his AK-47. Since the gun was concealed in the backpack, which he casually held in the other hand, the pilot might only see Flint as a man digging through his pack, feeling for some object of little importance.

The Egyptian who'd been flying, stepped out and shouted with a jolly English accent, "Would you be Flint?"

Only now did Flint relax his grip on his firearm. "I am, and I have a few others with me."

"Now wait a minute," the pilot began slyly. "I was told to pick you up, not to taxi a bunch of dirty desert rats."

"These men are stranded here and I've promised them a ticket back home," Flint stated. "Besides, you seem to have enough room on your chopper if we all squeeze together."

The pilot waved his hands. "You don't understand. It's not the amount of people that I'm worried about, it's the weight."

Flint immediately saw through this excuse. Before his father died, they had taken flying lessons together. He'd only reached the level of private pilot. Single-engine airplanes were the scope of his knowledge when it came to aircraft. But he knew many of the basics that governed all aircraft. This gave him just enough of an edge to know how to talk to the pilot.

"Under normal takeoff circumstances, you would be overweight," Flint replied, "but you have come a long way and have used up quite a bit of fuel. I don't see why you shouldn't be light enough now to handle one or two extra passengers. Besides, they're Filipinos. It takes two or three to weigh as much as one of us."

The pilot mumbled to himself. Flint guessed that Philip had already been nickel-and-diming the man. He didn't seem too pleased about the arrangements, but Flint could care less.

"Fine," the pilot grunted. "Since I'm already here, I might as well. But this isn't a free service—I'm still going to charge you for the extra passengers."

"Sounds like extortion to me," Flint replied.

"It's economics, sir. Five hundred American dollars per person," the pilot demanded.

"What difference is one person or five?"

"Do you want a ride or not?"

Flint began to feel frustrated. He half wondered if Philip had found him the most conniving pilot on purpose.

"I don't have that much money," Flint replied.

The pilot headed back to the chopper, "Well, good luck, then."

Now Flint was really steamed. "The best I can do is one hundred per person."

"Two hundred." The pilot paused. "And I want it all in advance."

Flint was half tempted to pull out his rifle to settle the negotiations. Though hidden, his knuckles were turning white as fingers regripped the concealed gun. Suddenly aware of his uncharacteristic lapse of decent judgment, he released the rifle and pulled his hand free of the pack.

He realized how far-fetched this whole adventure was turning. He wasn't even sure if the woman he'd seen was even in any danger. For all he knew, she could be a part of the organization that tried to kill him. But at last he decided that he'd committed and he would see this through.

"Two hundred for them," Flint pointed to the Filipinos. "But you already worked out the price to pick me up with my friend Philip."

The pilot conceded, and Flint pulled out his wallet. He hadn't expected to use up this much money on anything. He paid the pilot four hundred bucks in American dollars, and the other half he had to use Egyptian pounds. He felt he could have gotten the price down further, but he didn't want to deal with it any more.

Flint hefted his heavy backpack into the chopper. Along with its other contents, it now also held four grenades, a pistol with a few extra clips, and a Kevlar vest. At first he felt guilty about stripping these from the fallen mercenaries. But he knew the items might prove useful where he was going, or at the very least, they might be good souvenirs. The next major obstacle facing him would be going international with four undocumented Filipinos and a backpack full of weapons.

The pilot's mood had significantly improved. The extra four passengers were unexpected, but even with the added weight, he would have had no problem flying them all back. He probably would have taken them for no extra charge had Flint negotiated a little harder. But when there were few options, it was easy to gain the upper hand as the pilot so managed. Besides, what did the pilot have to lose by trying? It wasn't like he could get many repeat customers in that line of business, so who cared if you didn't make the customer happy?

"So your friends, they don't speak anything I've heard before. Where'd you say they're from?" the pilot asked after they were airborne.

"I rescued them from some smugglers," Flint said. "Only problem is that I promised these Filipinos that I would get them home to their families."

"Filipinos, ah, well, once we land, you can catch a flight to Cairo," replied the pilot. "From there you should be able to get a flight to the Philippines, or anywhere else you may need."

Flint gaged the pilot for a few minutes. If he was going to get any information, now would be the time. After all, now that the career tour guide had closed the deal, he was slipping back into a tip-generating mood. Flint had no intention of tipping, which the pilot must have known. But after years of taking sightseers around, the optimistic attitude was perhaps more habit than anything.

"So I'm guessing you've been around this area for some time?" Flint asked.

"Oh, I was born here," the pilot boasted. "I've moved around a little, but I've spent the last several years flying tours in this area."

"Well, I shouldn't be asking this, but are there any international charters around here that might occasionally forget to go through customs?"

The pilot looked at Flint through suspicious eyes. "Why would you want to know that?"

"Well," Flint began, choosing each word carefully, "I am a man of my word. While I could easily get through customs, my four new friends have no papers. They've been away from their families for so long already. I'm hoping to avoid all the delays and red tape involved with getting them home."

Only the constant whine of the engine and beating of rotors filled the tense seconds as Flint waited for a response. He wondered if the pilot could sense that there might be more to the story than he was getting. The pilot had seen the site where the explosion had taken place. And though Flint had tried to clean up a little, there was still a hint of blood on his face and clothes. Flint tried to paint a picture of having the best intentions, but he still felt the pilot knew that something bigger was going on.

The faint smell of rum that clung to the pilot didn't soften the scrutiny in the man's eyes. He could see that the pilot was starting to play his cards a little more carefully. The man was becoming nervous, and Flint wondered how much he dared tell him.

"I know a few people at Sharm El Sheikh, but I don't know any of the international players," the pilot replied.

"But there are international charters available from that airport?" Flint asked.

"Oh yes, but you better be careful how you ask people. With terrorism and other upheavals, every pilot lately is on edge."

"Thanks for the tip." Though it didn't really do Flint any good.

A little small talk ensued after that. The pilot slowly seemed to start enjoying Flint's company. He'd never heard of anyone running off to have the type of adventures in the way that Flint did. He told Flint he didn't have the same risk tolerance, but Flint could tell that the thought made him want to get away from things for a while, also.

The pilot even got chummy enough with his new passenger to show Flint how to operate the helicopter. The model they were flying had dual controls, and Flint was able to catch on quickly. After a little while, the pilot turned over the controls to Flint. "We're not far away now," he pointed out. "In twenty minutes we should be ready to land."

Flint was ready to be on the ground. The seats of the helicopter were old and uncomfortable. It felt like he was sitting on hard plywood with just one thin layer of fake leather vinyl.

Suddenly the pilot got a worried expression as he took back the controls. Clicking a button for his radio, he declared on the airport frequency, "This is the helicopter Echo-Charlie-Niner-Hotel, squawking seven-oh-four-two, hailing the Learjet just north of Sharm El Sheikh, do you copy."

There was no answer. "Helicopter Echo-Charlie-Niner-Hotel to Learjet, you are getting very close to my current position."

Flint looked in the direction of the pilot and wondered how he'd missed the plane that was coming straight at them. The pilot nosed the chopper over and did a quick dive, just as the jet blew over them. Flint's seat seemed to flail about wildly as the wind vortex created by the jet's wings buffeted the little helicopter. The Filipinos in back were all shouting their own protests, and the pilot was working on regaining stable flight control.

"In all my years, I've never had a close call like that! Write this down:"

Flint grabbed the pencil and pad the pilot handed him. Then wrote down a few numbers and letters as the pilot spewed them, anger filling his voice. "K-L-2-0-1." Flint was surprised that the pilot had been able to catch the letters on the tail of the plane at all. He seemed determined to find out who was flying that plane and have them cited.

"If I didn't think it absurd, I'd say they meant to take us down," the pilot remarked.

Flint was looking out the window and noticed that the jet seemed to be turning. He then questioned the pilot with a nervous shake in his voice, "Do you know anyone who has a death wish on you?"

"What do you mean?" the pilot asked.

"Well, it looks like that jet is turning around."

The pilot slowed the chopper and let it spin around just enough to see the jet almost fully turned and heading back toward them.

"Oh, this can't be good," he said as he banked the chopper back on course and kicked it into full throttle.

Clicking on the radio button again, he began to hail the Sharm El Sheikh airport.

"I can't get through," he said as he looked at Flint.

"Something is wrong with the radio. What have you gotten me into?"

"Hey, I just wanted a ride to the airport," Flint stated. "I had no idea these guys would be back looking for me."

"Back looking for you?" The pilot's anger shifted from the jet to Flint. "Who are they, and don't pretend that I don't know anything. I saw that big burn spot in the canyon when I flew in to pick you up."

Flint stared hard at the pilot. "I don't know who they are. Everything that I've told you about my hike and looking for an adventure is true. As for those guys, they tried blowing up these Filipinos. All I did was save them from the blast. I'm just trying to get them home to their families."

"Why would they be chasing us now?"

"My guess is that they just wanted to check on any loose ends before they left the site completely," Flint stated. "I swear, though, I didn't think they would be back."

The pilot pointed his finger at Flint and began to say something, but just then there were a couple of heavy thuds and pings throughout the chopper. A siren and flashing lights started going off on the instrument panel.

"They're shooting at us!" the pilot exclaimed. "Those rotten buggers are shooting at us!"

Flint craned his head around, but it was useless, he couldn't see the jet behind them. "What kind of a Learjet is equipped with a gun?"

The jet buzzed over the top of them only about ten feet above the chopper's rotors. The blast of air from the jet caused the chopper to twist and wrench again in the air. To his credit, the pilot was able to regain control and steady it once more.

"They're coming back around," Flint said.

"Our only chance is to get to the airport before they take us down," the pilot replied.

He nosed the chopper over a little more, its airspeed increased as they exchanged altitude for speed. By this time the Learjet had completed its turn and was heading back at them. Flint could see a few small flashes of light coming from the center of the jet's fuselage. Another series of pings and thuds followed almost immediately, attesting to the accuracy of the enemy's aim. The chopper's window cracked like a spider web, but didn't shatter. The jet appeared to have only a single gun mounted on the bottom. But its aim was precise enough that it didn't need any more firepower to cripple the small chopper.

Flint's tour guide began to sway and plunge his craft in an attempt to avoid the onslaught of the gun. Smoke now filled the cockpit, and the pilot began to move the rotary aircraft in such a random pattern that Flint wondered if he had any real control at all. The jet passed over, nearly missing them again. This time the pilot was having a difficult time adjusting back to a stable flight.

"What's wrong?" Flint asked. "Why can't we stabilize?"

The pilot looked over at Flint with a pale face that terrified him. The look reminded him of the last day that his father had been alive. It was the look that came before death, when their eyes look straight at you but don't seem to register your presence. It was a haunting look, one that had greatly unsettled him years ago. Now his pilot was giving him that same death stare.

Flint diverted his eyes from the pilot's face, only to notice that the side of the man's stomach was missing. The pilot tried to say something, but Flint could tell it wouldn't come. Forcing himself to think on the matter at hand, he realized that if any of them were to live it was up to him. His previous fifteen-minute instruction on flying a chopper was all he could rely on now to save them.

Grabbing the controls positioned around his seat, he tested each one for how they would respond. Taking over in stabilized flight proved much easier than recovering from the turbulent shock that they were now in. Something also felt different and Flint knew the controls were most likely damaged in some way. The only option was to take the chopper down.

Flint eased the stick in his right hand lower, and the craft began to sink. He was alarmed at how quickly the chopper wanted to descend. It swayed back and forth as he tumbled through the warming desert air. Despite his best efforts, he knew the landing was going to be brutal. If flying a chopper under normal circumstances required a full measure of concentration, this was taxing his skill beyond the help of experience or intuition.

Flint was so absorbed in handling the chopper that he completely forgot about the jet, which undoubtedly was about to bear down on them again. With the threat finding its way back into his awareness, he risked a quick glance upward to scan the sky for the approaching menace. Unable to see anything, he turned his attention back to the controls. The ground was now only a couple of hundred feet below him. The speed of descent was still too fast, so he pulled up again and tried to hover. This proved impossible for the untrained pilot.

The chopper shot upward at a steep, uncontrolled angle. Dread fluttered from his belly to his head, then back down again. The distress of his overcorrection, and the possibility of crashing and dying, were becoming all too real. Time seemed to slow down for his thoughts, but the chopper still moved in normal time. His only hope was to release control and hope that the machine had some stability built in.

"Here goes nothing," Flint said to himself as he relaxed his grip on the lever. The chopper began again to descend. To his relief the rotors acted like a parachute, slowing their fall enough to keep from squishing them into the sandy earth below.

The landing was still hard. First the front right skate slammed into the ground. Then the chopper bounced ten feet back up. Flint grabbed the controls again but overcompensated, and they came down hard again, this time on the back of the left skate. He tried to keep down by completely cutting all power to the main rotor. The chopper still retained a little desire to bounce before it tilted to one side, digging the blades into the sand, forcing the chopper to whip around and fall completely on its side, smashing the main rotor into pieces.

After the chopper came to a complete stop, Flint unbuckled his safety belt and leaned over to check on the pilot. He was strapped in; however, he had a distinct paleness to his face. His eyes were motionless, staring down past Flint. The windshield had spoiled so completely that Flint couldn't see out. Since his own door was jammed between the wreckage and the sandy floor, he had to either kick his way through the windshield or climb over the dead pilot to get out.

Though the latter would have been easier than risking the shards of windshield, Flint found himself struggling to get in a better position to kick out the main windshield. The thought of climbing over the dead man, who was starting to drip blood on Flint's side, seemed a little too barbaric. After a few attempts, the glass gave way and he was able to throw his backpack out. Flint followed after it.

The Filipinos had no problem climbing out through the rear side door. However, they did have to climb over one of their own dead companions. Gual did his best to relate to Flint that the bullet had come from the pilot's seat. It may have even been the same bullet that ended the pilot's life. The almost lucky Filipino, though injured by the bullet, had only been grazed.

He would have survived had he been buckled into his seat. But since he wasn't, he was thrown too violently in the backseat when they landed. His not-so-fatal injury ripped a little larger and tore a major artery. He bled out in seconds.

"We need to get out of here," Flint said.

Gual pointed back at his lifeless companion and asked, "What to do?"

"We leave him," Flint replied, with more heartless ice in his voice than he meant or felt.

"*No!* No leave—"

Flint cut him off and boldly stated, "If we don't go now, we'll all be dead!" Just in case he didn't fully understand, Flint made a gesture of a plane swooping down and shooting, then pointed to everyone before he ran his flattened palm across his neck in a slitting motion.

Gual looked hard at Flint then back at his dead friend. Then back, peering hard at Flint again, albeit with guilty-looking eyes, he relented. "Okay, we go."

Turning around Gual said something to the other Filipinos. Flint could tell they had a strong respect for Gual, and he felt bad for them, also. He couldn't begin to imagine leaving a friend behind like this. But whatever Gual said to the others, they seemed to accept the next course of action without question. With that, Flint grabbed his pack and started to walk toward the airport. If they hurried, they might be able to get there in an hour.

As soon as they were a few hundred feet away from the crash site, Flint paused. "Wait one minute." He dropped his backpack and ran back to the helicopter. Climbing inside the bloodstained cockpit, he found the pilot just as he'd left him. He grabbed the man's jacket and pulled out a billfold.

"I'm sorry, this doesn't feel right to me, either, but I'm going to need this a lot more than you will," Flint said to the corpse as he pulled out the money. He left the extra money in the billfold that must have been what Philip had paid. "I'm only taking what I need, the rest will be for your family if you have any."

Catching up to the other men, Flint grabbed his pack and retook his position at the front of the line. As they were walking, he had to force himself to keep from vomiting. He was not accustomed to all the death he'd seen so far today. He felt some of it might be his fault. If he hadn't decided to pursue the lady, the pilot would still be alive.

But would he and the Filipinos? Was it better for one or two men to die than four or five?

Then again, the death toll was up to four, if he included the guards he had shot earlier. But they were most likely terrorists, so did they count?

Flint wondered how many people had wrestled with similar thoughts before. Just then, he heard the sound of a jet.

It must have been circling nearby, waiting for the chopper to settle and its passengers to make their move.

"Run, run!" Flint yelled at the Filipinos as they sprinted for some nearby shrubs and rock. Ducking, they watched as the jet came swooping down in their direction.

Chapter 5

Cold water dripping down his neck was the first sensation Philip could feel. His head then slammed back down into the bowl of a cramped lavatory toilet. This time he inhaled some of the water through his nose. Coughing and twisting, he tried to reach for something to hold on to. His consciousness was still fuzzy, but it was coming back fast.

"Stop! Hey—what's going on?" Philip cried as he struggled between gasps.

"Hey boss, he's awake," proclaimed the man who had a viselike grip on the back of Philip's shirt.

A man from farther down the hallway motioned for him to bring Philip over. The brute easily dragged Philip down the hall. This monster of a man reminded him of the cliché Aryan with blond hair and blue eyes, not to mention rock hard muscles accenting an even thicker skull. Philip tried to regain his footing, as well as a recollection of how he'd ended up in this confined hallway, but the man dragging him had so much power that he couldn't find a moment to gain his balance.

The whole area was spinning as he was dropped in the middle of the small hallway. All around him, a dull rumbling sounded as if a large generator was humming with the intention of droning out any sounds from inside this hallway. Blinking a few times, he began to piece together his last memory.

Now looking around he could see that he wasn't in a hallway after all. Small windows lined each side of the corridor. The familiar ornate furnishings proved that he was back inside the airplane where he'd placed his satellite phone. An itchy sweat prickled across his back and chest. Half noticing the tremor in his hands, he realized a new sense of dread, completely foreign until now. The plane was already airborne and the same ruthless people Flint had told him about, were incarcerating him in this flying cage.

"I believe you have a little explaining to do," said the man in a plush recliner.

"What's going on? Where am I?" Philip asked. He decided it was better to play dumb. "Who are you?"

"Don't pretend you don't know who I am," the man stated. "We know you were snooping around this jet right before takeoff."

"I don't have a clue who you are," Philip replied. "I just saw a fancy jet, and wanted a closer look."

The man gave a simple, hardly noticeable nod and a fist crashed into the side of Philip's head. Tasting blood in his mouth, Philip risked a glance in the direction of the blow. The large man who'd dragged him around flashed a small but determined smile.

"Now do we need to rattle your memory any further?" the seated man asked. "Or are you ready to start cooperating?"

Philip, surprised at his own clinging consciousness and clarity of thought, realized that regardless of what they knew or guessed of him, he wouldn't be allowed to live. Whatever they were up to, it had to be serious enough to warrant kidnap and torture. Even if he could convince them that he was just an admirer of airplanes, he figured they would likely kill him. His only chance was to drag out the interrogation and hope that an opportunity arrived to escape. "Well, Suzie, I think that my memory is still a little fuzzy. You're just going to have to help me remember it all."

This response made the brute smile even wider. When his boss gave another slight nod, Philip knew that the grizzly-man next to him would be winding up for another punch. He braced himself for the impact. Still, he was startled at how hard the man's fists were. The punch knocked him flat on the floor of the luxury Citation. Blood trickled into his left eye. His whole head felt like it was swimming in a pool of whining violins.

The boss leaned over in his chair and said, "I'm so glad you're making this interesting. I was afraid I would get bored on our fifteen-hour flight to Cebu."

"Fifteen—" Philip stuttered, right as another punch to the side of his face flattened him back down onto the floor. This was setting up to be the longest flight he'd ever taken. He also wondered where on earth Cebu was.

Philip knew he'd be no match for the approximately 250-pound man who was given the pleasure of beating him and boy did that man take pleasure in it. Philip also knew that his adrenaline would last him for only a few more minutes, then the full pain inflicted by his attacker would set in. Using this time he tried to gain as much understanding of his surroundings as possible before he was further incapacitated.

The first thing he noticed was a beautiful woman struggling to get out of her seat on the other side of the cabin. She clearly protested the way he was being treated. Another man was forced to hold her down. Philip knew she must be the woman Flint was getting all mushy about. Frankly, he couldn't blame him; she was a very attractive girl.

The second thing Philip noticed, when his head was being smashed against the floor, was how hard the carpet felt. He also saw a piece of cord from the charger that was connected to his satellite phone. Though it couldn't do him any good right now, he was relieved that it hadn't been found. As long as he continued to make these dangerous men believe he was of some value to them, he would live. He only hoped that Flint would not decide to stop the chase early.

Though doubt may have ebbed into his mind, consciously he wasn't worried about Flint. Philip knew Flint was a smart young man, and that he would likely find out about his capture. The real trick would be enduring the beating. He'd occasionally wondered how he would stand up under torture. This thought usually came to him after watching some spy movie or reading a suspense novel. He was now beginning to think that he didn't really care to be tested, after all.

"Haven't you heard that torture doesn't produce reliable results?" he asked.

"Please, indulge me," the boss man in the button-up shirt replied. "But remember, this isn't my first rodeo."

Philip groaned under a kick to the stomach. "Listen, Mollie, I've never been a big fan of rodeos." Then, looking up into the man's eyes, he continued, "The clowns seem to say the same old jokes every time."

This earned him a hand around the neck. The guard lifted him up to eye level and said, "You should really learn to respect Mr. Steel. He has no problem killing you."

"You mean," Philip choked, "he has no problem making you kill for him?"

The man dropped Philip, and he collapsed back onto the ground. Propping himself up a little, he looked at the man in the button-up shirt. "So it's Steel, is it? That is starting to sound familiar, now that you mention it," Philip lied.

"Please, now that we're all getting comfortable with one another, why don't you just call me Marshal," the boss replied. "Now it's your turn to tell me your name."

"Sure thing, *Marsha* Steel," Philip said, as he faked a small grin.

This time Marshal let fly his own fist. Philip saw it coming, but was still feeling a little defiant. The blow was not nearly as powerful as the guard's, but his bony fist packed quite a bite.

Managing to look unaffected, Philip smiled at Marshal and teased, "Thanks for giving your brute here a breather. After all, my face was starting to get a little sore."

From across the cabin, the woman laughed. This only infuriated Marshal more, as he massaged his hand. "Sperl, why don't you teach our guest a lesson?"

This time only Marshal had a grin. The brute called Sperl began to wale on Philip with an intensity that even made Marshal turn away. Sperl's eyes had gone cold, and Philip's world got fuzzy again. He could just make out Marshal's words as he said, "Don't kill him yet." He said more, but Philip's waning consciousness had faded out by then.

Blinking as he came back around, he found himself looking up at an angelic face. He was about to talk when she put a finger to her mouth and shook her head. Cocking his head around, he saw that Marshal was busy working on a laptop, and Sperl was in conversation with somebody at the back of the plane. Philip looked back at the woman, and blacked out again.

For the next few hours, Philip drifted in and out of consciousness. With exception of the first time, whenever he woke up, he was met by Sperl. He was never able to stay awake for more than about ten minutes at a time. Sperl purposely tried to avoid hitting his head, so that, in his words, Philip could "savor the pain."

The pain was excruciating. Philip's eyes were filled with dried blood and at least half of his fingers were broken. He knew that he must also have at least one broken rib. During one of the question-and-torment sessions, they grabbed some pliers and pulled out several of his fingernails. But by then they'd stopped asking questions. Either they just wanted to let him know how much pain a body could endure, or they were softening him up for later. In either situation, Philip knew that it must have been working, because he was hurting, and becoming delirious enough to say just about anything.

Every time Philip woke up for his next beating, he'd been at the feet of the woman. He had a hard time seeing her face, but from what he could see, she seemed to be very disturbed by his treatment.

One time he woke up and found her nursing a small gash on the side of her own head. She apparently had tried stopping the abuse of Philip. A backhand from Sperl had sent her crashing into a table. She was no match for the professional mercenaries on board the plane. Instead she was made to suffer as she was forced to watch Philip's torture.

In one of his bouts of forced sleep, Philip dreamed of fighting Sperl. In his dream the mercenary was slapping the woman around. Philip, being a chivalrous man, grabbed Sperl by the shoulder and pinned him against a wall. "It's a weak man who has to hit a woman," he said. "I look forward to giving you a taste of your own medicine."

The man opened his mouth to speak, but Philip couldn't understand the words. Sperl tried to open his mouth again, and only the same dull squeal escaped his lips. The world shook. Philip began to wake up and realized the dull squeal was really the aircraft's wheels bearing down on asphalt. They were landing. He thought they must be stopping to refuel. However, since he'd been unconscious most of the trip, they could very well be at the final destination.

A foot pressed down on his mangled hand. "Rise and shine, sleepyhead." Marshal Steel looked down at the suffering wretch. "I think you'll find the Philippines to be dreadfully uncomfortable. I personally like the humid climate, but sadly for you, I have more friends here who, like Sperl, are going to enjoy your company very much."

With that welcoming, Philip was thrown into the back of a strange truck called a jeepney. These were handmade by the Filipino people, who often took the frames from old World War II trucks and made them look like boxy jeeps. They were a conglomeration of old Toyotas, Mitsubishis, and various other makes.

While the front end looked similar to a shiny chrome jeep or an old Toyota Land Cruiser, the back half stretched on for another fifteen feet. Inside there were two benches reaching up to the front seat, with a partition, similar to that of a stretched limousine, minus the comfort and luxury. The windows were all tinted, and when the doors behind him locked, there was no way for Philip to see where he was being taken.

The jeepney shook as the driver released the clutch. Philip tried unsuccessfully to find a comfortable position on one of the hard benches. Just then a woman's voice cut through the fog in his brain. "How are you feeling?"

Looking up, Philip realized that the woman from the plane was also sitting in the strange truck with him. "Forgive me for not seeing you earlier, I'm still a little new when it comes to captivity."

"I hope you don't mind me saying," the woman started, "but I sure hope you don't feel as terrible as you look."

"Don't worry," Philip replied. "Whatever they did to my face was probably an improvement."

The woman faked a laugh. "So, mind if I inquire as to what your name is?"

"Depends," Philip said. "I'm not even sure I can trust you. For all I know, you're the next attempt to pry information out of me."

"You think I'm with these scumbags?" She sounded insulted.

"Seems classic to me," Philip continued. "First they send in the beast to soften me up, then they send in the beauty to lull me into some carnal security. Before you know it, I'll have spilled my whole life story to these guys."

"My name is Desiree Spring," she said. "But everyone just calls me Dusty." She then reached out a hand to Philip.

"Not that I want to be rude, Dusty, but I'm not in the hand-shaking mood right now." Philip raised his bruised and broken hand for her to see. The crushing weight of boots had caused the hand to swell into a disgusting purple glove of flesh.

"Yeah, I should have known better," Dusty said. "It's just nice to know that somebody is trying to stand up to these guys besides me."

Philip took a hard look at Dusty. It made her stir uncomfortably, as if she felt that he could see into her soul. Then, picking his words carefully so as not to let her know how clueless he really was, he asked, "So if you aren't with them, then what exactly is your role in this whole mess?"

"Well, when I started working with Marshal, he told me we would be excavating something that was so monumental, it would make the discovery of King Tut's tomb look like wilted lettuce. He had already gotten many of the details from some Asian guy named Shen Mao, so it only took us about three years to find it."

Philip listened patiently. Dusty was more forthcoming than he'd anticipated. She continued her story without much hesitation. "At first, Marshal seemed to be just another anthropologist like myself, and we even got a little romantic toward the end of the first year. But then as I started to know him better, I realized he was a greedy crook. I'd occasionally find him illegally selling artifacts on the black market." She paused. "I was so stupid!"

"Don't worry, most girls are a little foolish from time to time," Philip said, hoping to give a little compassion.

Dusty slapped him in the face.

"Not the response I expected," Philip moaned.

Dusty put her hands on his face as if to make it all better. "I'm so sorry. I—well, it's obviously not something I'm very proud to have done."

"That's nice, but please, if you don't mind, my face is already pretty tender. Dusty, was it?" Philip said.

"Yeah, the nickname was given to me as a kid," she explained. "I loved to play in the dirt with the boys. So it kind of fit that I became an anthropologist. My colleagues took my nickname to mean something else. I'd get so engrossed in my work that I rarely found time for a man. So, Dusty Spring became another way of saying, *Guys, don't flirt there, that well is dry.* So, given my solitude, I kind of fell for Marshal a little too easily."

"Well, if you knew what he was like early on, why'd you stick around up until now?" Philip inquired.

"In my line of work," she began, "you don't turn your back on an archaeological dig when it involves a five-thousand-year-old spaceship."

If his swollen face had not mostly covered his eyes, they might have just popped out of his head. Philip couldn't believe what he was hearing. "You mean to tell me that mankind was able to fly to space five thousand years ago?"

"No, of course not," Dusty replied. "I'm saying that a spacecraft from Mars landed here over five thousand years ago." She then paused and looked slyly at Philip. "I'm curious, why do you ask? I thought you already knew about that."

Philip realized his mistake. "I guess it's too late to say that I was just testing you?"

"You're not part of the organization that's been tracking us down, are you?" Dusty pried.

"Us?" Philip fired back. "So you are with these guys after all?"

Dusty turned away in frustration. His question put her back on the defensive. Philip hoped that she was back to wondering if he really did know more than he was letting on. Even if she was good at reading a man's face, he knew that with his being so extensively bruised and swollen, she couldn't have any idea what to believe.

She continued, "Like I said, I want nothing to do with Marshal and his grave robbers. The only reason I stick around is because I want to find a way to stop them and put those artifacts in a museum where they belong."

Philip nodded. "So you're a dedicated one then. Why haven't you gone to the authorities about this?"

"Marshal knows that I don't agree with him on many things, so, I don't think he'd hesitate to have me killed if I went AWOL."

"I'm guessing that Martian artifacts are pretty tempting, too," Philip suggested.

Dusty snorted, obviously offended. For the rest of the drive, she didn't speak or look at him. Once they reached their destination, they threw him into a small cinder-block shack. He was then surprised to find that Dusty was also thrown in and locked up with him. Even she seemed a little shocked that they'd isolate her with the prisoner.

Dusty gave up her silent treatment. "The thing is, there wasn't much left in that ship except for the ship itself. The artifacts that Marshal is taking are pieces of technology."

Philip let a small silence hang for a moment then asked, "So what part of the ship did he take?"

"You really don't know, do you?" Dusty looked inquisitively back at him.

"To be perfectly honest," he said, "I don't know jack. I've only been going along with this up till now, because I think our friend Sperl would have ground me up and fed me to the sharks if they knew I was a nobody."

Philip hadn't wanted to tell her this. He still wasn't sure that she was who she claimed to be. But he was getting tired and decided that if they were going to kill him anyway, he might as well call their hand. Anyways, if she was who she claimed to be, then maybe he had a chance. In either case he wouldn't get anywhere any other way.

Dusty looked puzzled. "I don't get it. If you don't know anything, then who are you, and what were you doing snooping around Marshal's jet?"

"First off, my name is Philip, Philip Noon. Second, I'm not the one Marshal would have any beef with, it's my friend Flint. I'm just the deliveryman."

"I think I'm confused," Dusty said. She sat down in the small room, putting her back against the cinder-block wall.

Philip looked intently at Dusty. "Before we left Egypt, you were at the excavation site, were you not?"

"I was. How did you—"

Philip cut her off and continued. "Right before you left, you ran into a little skirmish with some yahoo. Some of your mercenary friends were killed?"

"That was your friend Flynn?" Dusty guessed.

"Flint," he corrected her.

Still looking confused she asked, "So who does this Flint work for?"

"Why, me, of course." Philip smiled, knowing that he was only confusing her more.

Dusty put her head into her hands and rubbed her temples. "I think I'd learn more by talking to this brick wall."

"Cinder," Philip corrected.

"What?" she mumbled with her head still in her hands.

"It's not a brick wall, it's cinder block. These Filipinos use cinder blocks and bamboo to construct everything that I've seen here so far. I haven't noticed a single brick building yet." Philip was enjoying himself. "You see, a brick is hardened in a kiln, but a cinder block is like a diluted version of concrete that's put out in the sun to dry and harden."

"I'm starting to think that Sperl had the right idea with you," she said.

Philip faked a hurt look, then laughed at himself. He didn't have to fake a hurt look. If anything, he had to fake looking good. "You're welcome to take a swing at me if you like."

Dusty gave a cute snort, and turned away.

"I didn't think you were the type," he continued. "Truth is, Flint was hiking along when he stumbled on you and your companions. He thought you looked distressed, and being the romantic impulsive type, he decided you needed rescuing."

"I don't need rescuing," Dusty said. "Especially from some tourist wannabe hero."

Philip tried to force back another laugh. His face hurt too much to smile. "You know, I kind of think that helping you out is only half the reason Flint is getting involved. He likes a good adventure, and the little ordeal that Marshal and his goons put him through gave him just enough adrenaline to get addicted."

Dusty had a disgusted look on her face. "Sounds pretty stupid to me."

"Any more stupid than spending the last few years helping a murderous grave robber?" Philip shot back.

"That's different," she quickly replied. "I want to preserve those artifacts, and get them where they belong."

"I'm not arguing your motive," Philip countered. "I'm just arguing that you're both equally stupid. Noble, maybe, stupid all the same. You have more in common with Flint than you may want to believe. Frankly I don't care that much, though—I just want to find a way out of this mess. You see, he called me up and had me place a satellite phone in that airplane of yours. He's using it to track us down as we speak. I was never supposed to end up here. Now that I am, I know he'll be that much more motivated to find us."

Dusty thought for a minute. "Sounds like you had your own stumble away from good judgment."

Philip couldn't argue there. He should never have gotten involved.

"He's going to get himself killed, you know," she said. "Marshal would just as soon kill him as look at him. Before we left the excavation site, he set a bomb to blow up the workers he used to dig it out. It didn't even bother him when this Flint guy killed those two mercenaries, and they even seemed to be pretty good friends with each other."

"I'd be lying if I said I wasn't worried about him," Philip began. "But if there's ever someone I'd trust to get me out of a sticky situation like this, Flint would be that guy."

"Well, let's hope you're right," Dusty said quietly. "For both of us."

Philip looked puzzled, "What do you mean, *both of us*? I thought you had the in with these guys."

"I thought I did, too. But now that they have what they want, I can't get to it. They're also aware that I disagree with them. I was able to hide it pretty good, at least until Marshal locked those men in the excavation and set the bomb. Your friend may have been right about me. If he doesn't show up soon, I think we both might be fed to the hogs."

Outside the makeshift prison cell, they heard a couple of pigs squealing, which made Philip shift a little. He was pretty good at acting brave, but inside he was fighting off a cold despair. The heat inside the shack was only about ninety-five, but the humidity made it unbearable. Even with sweat running down his neck, he had to will himself to keep from shivering.

In that little room, after he and Dusty sat silent for a few minutes, a chain jingled outside the door. Once the lock was undone, the door swung open. Sperl stepped in and motioned for Dusty to come out. Dusty hesitated a moment too long. Sperl stepped in and grabbed her by the hair. Dusty squawked in painful protest as Sperl lifted her off the ground and set her on her feet with seemingly little effort.

Philip jumped up as empathetic rage fueled his limp body. Still holding Dusty with one hand, Sperl grabbed Philip by the neck with his other hand. Philip floundered, then clawed at the man's arms with his own battered hands. The mercenary felt as rigid as a car tire.

Sperl smiled, then spit in Philip's face before he threw him into the wall. "I'll be back for you later."

Dusty cried out. She was being dragged off by her hair, but her eyes were locked on Philip.

Philip tried to right himself, if only to look strong for Dusty's sake. His crumpled body ached all over and refused to respond. The door was slammed shut. Philip was left in the dark, again.

Chapter 6

Flint tugged at his weapon, but the gun was stuck on something. He bared his teeth in frustration. He was trying frantically to pull the AK-47 out of his pack when, the jet buzzed him and the other Filipinos. It kicked up dust all around before gaining altitude again. Temporarily abandoning the pack, he ran out of the dust cloud, coughing and spitting sand from his mouth. Gual and the other Filipinos followed close behind, some rubbing their eyes, only to grind the sand deeper under their eyelids.

Gual was the first to speak. "They no shoot."

Flint waited for a moment as he watched the jet, then added, "It's not turning back around, either." In the distance he could see the jet had finished climbing. It turned only ninety degrees before beginning another descent.

"That must be the airport," Flint pointed out. "I bet you anything they're going to come looking for us as soon as they land. We'd better hurry if we're going to find civilization before they catch up to us."

Flint picked his feet up, and moved forward in an easy jog. The Filipinos didn't quite understand what he said, but they could all understand the urgency. They followed as if they were little children, dependent on the better judgment of their father. As they silently trudged behind, Flint couldn't help but worry. Gual quickened his pace, drawing next to Flint. Regardless of the slight language barrier, this man could accurately read Flint's mood.

"Hey Joe—oh, Fa-Flint," Gual stammered. "What think you?"

Flint cocked his head to see the look of compassion mixed with anxiety in his new friend. He could almost sense a deeper wisdom in this man that the others seemed to respect. Even though they'd just met, Flint liked the guy. "Well, it's like this," Flint started, only to remember that Gual's English wasn't that great. "The airport is there," he said, pointing at a small desert mountain. "It will be too hard a climb for your friend." He then gestured toward one of the Filipinos who'd twisted an ankle during the helicopter crash and was struggling to keep up.

"We go round?" Gual suggested.

Flint had already taken the route around the mountain into consideration. The sandy canyon that went perpendicular to the course he wanted to take was not without its risks. "If we go around the mountain," he explained, "we go down the same canyon that the enemy will come up when they start looking for us."

Gual seemed to understand, since he replied casually, "So we go fast."

"If you think your friend can handle it," Flint said.

"No problem. We help him," Gual said before switching to his native tongue, giving directions to the others. Within seconds everyone had doubled their pace. Gual and one Filipino flanked their injured companion. They acted as crutches as he hopped along on his one good foot. The further down the canyon they got, the more relief Flint felt. They were putting some good distance between them and the crash site. With any luck they might make it out without another enemy encounter.

After jogging for at least an hour or more, they came to a small road that looked to have been recently paved. The pitch-black asphalt stood out from the plain desert landscape. It served as a reminder that they weren't far from the borders of the oil-rich neighbors in Saudi Arabia. They followed this road for about two miles, occasionally passing dirt side-roads that joined into it. Most of the side roads looked like they were used by either camels or off-road vehicles. Then one of the Filipinos shouted, *"Kadjut, palihog, kadjut!"*

Gual interpreted, "Wait, can we rest for a minute?" It wasn't as much of a suggestion as a pleading demand.

Flint turned around to see they had stopped. They were good workers, but had been through all they could handle. Flint guessed they hadn't slept for at least thirty-six hours. Now that the midday sun was blazing with all its fury, the men were ready to collapse with fatigue. Flint was also running on fumes, but he fought the lassitude, knowing they needed to keep moving. Their pursuer would soon return by ground to clean up. With little energy left, Flint succumbed to the Filipinos' will.

After resting for about five minutes, he stood up again. He knew from experience that resting too much would cramp their muscles and make walking even worse. The Filipinos, however, were not as enthusiastic.

"No more," Gual said. "Rest longer."

Flint reached for his pack, "We need to keep moving." He could see the defeat in Gual's expression and that of the others. *If only . . .* he thought, and then his spirits lifted as he heard a small rumble. He turned to his companions. "But then again, I never said we had to walk."

The approaching truck was an old diesel tanker. Flint stood on the side of the road and waved at the truck. It continued to barrel down the road at a constant speed, showing no intention of stopping. Right as it was about to pass, Flint reached into his pocket and pulled out the bills he'd taken from the helicopter pilot and waved them in the air. The truck passed him by, but the squeal of old brakes and shifting sand beneath the tires sent a clear signal that cash truly was king. The Filipinos looked as though manna had fallen from heaven. They were on their feet racing toward the truck before Flint could shoulder his pack.

The gnarly old truck looked too old to work. It reminded Flint of the trucks that people let rust into the ground in their backyards, hoping to someday restore. This particular model had a deep hood, with some of its original yellow paint still showing. The rest of the tanker was a mixture of red and rust, with the red almost indistinguishable from the rust. The tank itself was the most well preserved part of the whole truck; while not shiny, it maintained a silver metallic look.

The man driving the truck looked no younger or

kempt than the machine. He eyed Flint with a cold hard stare. Flint guessed that this wasn't the most friendly man he could've met. So he simply said, "Airport."

The driver nodded in understanding then held out his hand. Flint stuck one hundred Egyptian pounds in the man's hand. He took it, then held out his hand again.

Flint stared back at him. The driver didn't even flinch.

Flint stared straight into the man's eyes as he handed him another hundred. As soon as the money was in the driver's hands, he gave Flint a big yellow-toothed grin. The irony of the driver's appearance didn't escape Flint's scrutiny. Even the man's teeth matched the rust-yellow of the truck's hood.

Holding back a chuckle, Flint wondered how he could find humor in a time like this. At least they had a ride now and things were looking a little better. As Flint and the Filipinos hopped onto any portion of the truck that could support them, the rickety diesel ground a gear or two before lurching forward again.

The hot midday breeze felt good. The landscape was full of sand and an occasional group of people with camels. But despite looking like a desert, the humidity was getting more intense. The only other car they passed was a jeep. The jeep was a newer green model, and seemed to be driving much faster. It was, however, going the opposite direction. Flint wondered if it could be the people from the jet, moving to intercept them.

The ride lasted just under twenty minutes, then the driver brought the truck to a stop. He banged on the side of the truck, signaling that this was the end of the line.

Flint and his ragged group stepped off; the driver

dropped the clutch and began to leave them. Flint had barely enough time to drag his pack from the truck before it lumbered away. "How's that for service?" he remarked sarcastically.

The driver had dropped them off about half a mile past a turnoff that led to a series of buildings resembling large white circus tents. It was the Sharm El Sheikh airport. Flint motioned to the Filipinos to follow, and they began to cut across the sand toward the airport.

Instead of heading in the direction of the main buildings, Flint led them to the opposite end. He doubted that he'd run into any trouble, but he figured it would be safe to survey the airport before walking straight into it. While none of his assailants should recognize him, they might recognize his new companions. Besides, he figured it would be silly to walk into an international airport carrying a backpack full of guns and grenades.

At the far end of the airport, away from the commercial airliners, was a section dedicated to private aircraft. The airport security at this point was limited to fences and buildings that blocked entrance to the field. Flint found a small building advertising sightseeing tours. Rather than risk being seen climbing over a fence, he decided to access the field by way of the tour-guide's office. A bell jingled as Flint and the Filipinos entered. Within about a minute, a tall man entered the room. He was thin but had a bulldog chubbiness in his face, the type common among many of British descent. "'Ello," he called out to Flint. "What can I do for you?"

Flint walked up to the counter the man was standing behind. The man tried to hide a look of disapproval as he eyeballed his new guest. Stealing a glance into a reflective glass case, Flint realized how awful he looked. His early-morning adventure had left him looking like he'd just come in from a tornado. Not only were his clothes matted with sweat and dust, giving him the same color as the Egyptian landscape, he also noticed the dark smears and scabs across his face. The Filipinos looked a little better, but he knew they didn't appear to be casual tourists, either. Obviously this Brit was more accustomed to seeing respectable-looking visitors.

"I'm sorry to bother you, but we're looking for a man who might have come in here a little earlier today," Flint began. "He was an American, about sixty-five years old."

"Well, it's been a slow day, but I did have someone in here asking about helicopters," the man replied.

"His name wasn't Philip Noon, by any chance, was it?" Flint asked.

The man at the counter shook his head. "You know, I didn't get his name, but he was mighty curious about the hangar over there." The man pointed in the direction of a private hangar. It was closed, and no aircraft could be seen.

"As I recall, he went over to get a closer look at their chopper. Sure, it was a nicer, newer-looking machine, but I can't understand why he was so interested. Anyhow, I never really saw him after that. If you ask me, I wouldn't have gone over there if I were him in the first place. Those owners never struck me as the friendly sort."

"Well, I was supposed to meet that man," Flint said. "I hope he's still over there; thanks for your help."

Flint opened the side door that would lead him onto the tarmac. The man at the desk was about to object, but then stopped. Flint almost expected the objection, since he would be bypassing security. When the man held his tongue, Flint guessed that he just wanted to avoid the confrontation.

Once he was out on the tarmac, he fully understood how much the man was afraid of confrontation. As he shifted the load that had been on his shoulders, he found about half an inch of black metal was showing through a hole in his backpack. With all of the unrest in the region, Flint knew that this might have scared the man.

Since the metal and the particular bulge might be taken for what they really were, Flint's gun, he tried to smooth over the man's fears. He looked back and gave a friendly wave. The man smiled and waved back, but Flint was still unsure whether or not he would try to warn airport security. Flint's only option was to make haste, assuming that airport security would soon be after him.

With as much speed as he could manage without looking suspicious, Flint and his companions made their way to the hangar. Stealing a glance in the window that was in one of the doors, they could see the helicopter. It was the same one Flint had encountered hours earlier. The hangar door was locked, and nobody was in sight.

Flint knew that Philip had been successful in planting the satellite phone in the jet these guys owned. The jet was nowhere to be found, but neither was Philip. Flint was sure that he'd walked into the only FBO that had helicopter flights for rent, and he knew Philip had been there. Also, since Philip would have expected the helicopter to drop Flint off at that FBO, he should be around. But the man with the British accent hadn't seen him since he left to check out this hangar.

Flint scratched the damp shirt that clung to his

chest. *Where could Philip be?* He feared the worst for his friend and mentor. He hoped there was another FBO that would be used by tourists wanting helicopter rides and began to run along the different hangars, but there only seemed to be private owners remaining. Then he stopped dead in his tracks. On the tarmac before him was parked the same jet that had buzzed him less than an hour ago. A fuel truck was just pulling away from it, and a man who'd been watching over the plane walked over to the FBO, most likely to pay for the fuel.

While the man's back was turned, Flint ran up to the Learjet. The Filipinos started following, but he motioned for them to wait. While this was the jet that attacked them, it wasn't the jet Philip placed his phone in. That jet, last he checked, was moving toward Asia. Flint only hoped that if this was the same group of people, then perhaps he might find Philip being held inside.

Sidling around the nose of the plane, Flint noticed a panel near the bottom. He figured it was meant to hide the large machine gun that had forced his chopper to the ground. The interior was nothing spectacular. It looked very businesslike. Only Flint knew that it was a facade, designed to make the fighter look as if it were simply hauling CEOs around the world. There was relatively little room inside the jet, with the capacity to hold only about eight passengers. The cockpit was also empty, but everything was ready to go at a moment's notice.

If Philip was nowhere around the airport, then he must have taken off, been killed, or been captured. The first option seemed unlikely. Philip wouldn't dash without meeting him. The second option was unthinkable. The only option he entertained was that Philip must have been captured and taken with the other jet.

Outside, the man who'd been paying for fuel started heading back to his plane. Flint knew he wouldn't be able to leave the jet without being spotted. With only a few seconds to react, he decided his best option was to take the jet. It was risky. If security had been alerted, he'd be arrested. No, he needed this jet. He had to get to Philip.

His experience in single-engine propeller airplanes was a far cry from the twin jet engines of the Learjet. Even if he didn't have the recommended experience, he felt more confident in his ability to fly this than the helicopter he'd brought down.

The engines started right up without any problem. Flint looked out the window to see the returning man stop for a moment before sprinting toward him. Behind him, the Filipinos were racing over also. Flint jammed the throttle forward, but the jet engines' response was more sluggish than the propeller-driven aircraft that he was used to. Slowly the jet began to taxi forward. Even though he was gaining speed, he would have to make a sharp turn to taxi towards the runway. This would make him lose precious speed again. The man chasing him was going to catch up.

Keeping the throttle engaged, he slammed his foot hard on the right brake. The jet groaned under the stress, but was quickly turned to face the runway. As Flint feared, he lost too much time. The man jumped into the open hatch with a pistol at hand. Flint quickly pulled the throttle back, so that the jet wouldn't continue to taxi uncontrolled across the runway. He then stood up to face the man.

"You are very bold, but now I have you," the man said in a thick Russian accent. "Maybe if you give me book, you can live."

Flint stood ready, but cocked his head back at

the demand. "What book? I don't even know who you are. And by the way, what are you doing on *my* plane?"

The Russian looked unfazed. "It would be wise for you to not play games. You know what book I speak of, now give me book."

"No, actually, I don't, but if you tell me where my old friend is, I'll be more than happy to help you find this book," Flint replied.

"Enough!" the Russian said. "If you not give me book, you are no good. Good-bye."

The Russian raised his gun. Flint was just about to flinch when he saw a few familiar faces through the window. He smiled.

The Russian paused a moment too long. Before he could shoot, multiple Filipino hands locked around his ankles and yanked him out through the open hatch. The man fell to the asphalt, and a shot rang harmlessly from his pistol.

The Filipinos, already angered at losing their friend in the helicopter crash, didn't hesitate to take their rage out on him. Flint watched their determination as they punished the Russian. The larger man could easily have smashed the Filipinos like ants, but combined, these ants swarmed with pent up fury. They didn't even think of fighting fair. Like the deadly army ants of Central and South America, they overwhelmed the Russian with lethal ambition.

Flint finally had to call them off. When they let up on him, Flint could see the man was disarmed and clearly in no shape to pursue them. He almost felt sorry for the Russian. Flint called for the Filipinos to board the jet with him. Gual was the last one to board. He had to leave one more swift kick to the Russian's jaw.

Flint winced in disapproval, then closed the door

when he saw two security trucks racing in his direction. It seemed to be too quick for security to respond to this incident. The man at the FBO front desk must have tipped them off. Not wanting to see the inside of an Egyptian jail, Flint finished shutting the hatch and ran up to the cockpit. Gual had already taken a seat in the copilot chair. Before seating himself, Flint jammed the double throttle forward. The jet's turbines whined as they wound up to speed.

The tower hailed them as the trucks were closing in. Flint tried to ignore both. There was one last turn before he would be aligned perfectly on the runway, but the Learjet was now going too fast for the tight turn. Flint looked at Gual, who was massaging a rosary around his neck, and said, "If God owes you any favors, you better call on him now to cash those in."

Flint eased his foot into the left brake, arching the aircraft in a slow turn onto the sandy median between a taxi lane and the runway. He had enough speed by now that the plane was able to drive across the sand without slowing down too much. He knew it wouldn't do the landing gear any good, but he didn't plan on keeping the jet forever.

The jet bounced back onto the runway at a forty-five-degree angle. It took all of Flint's luck to swerve onto the runway in the right direction. The trucks were now parallel in an attempt to get in front of the jet. Men in uniform looked eager as they clutched their assault rifles. Flint wondered if this was what airport guards dreamed of doing while they watched tourists from behind X-ray machines.

As he began to lift up on the yoke, a buzz sounded in the cockpit. Gual looked at Flint, the memory of the helicopter ride still fresh in his mind. "We crash again?" he asked.

"Just hold on tight," Flint said. The buzzing continued as the nose began to lift. Flint knew the buzzing was the stall warning. He hadn't quite reached takeoff velocity yet, but the men in the trucks were about to overtake them. Also, his shortcut onto the runway had given him considerably less runway to take off on. All the security guards had to do was get in front of him, slow down, and make the jet coast onto the sands beyond the runway.

Flint was well aware of what was about to happen, but he also knew about ground effect. His mind went back to his training as a private pilot and he hoped his memory was accurate. The principle of ground effect was simple: It often allowed a plane that was either too heavy or too slow to gain additional lift, thereby letting it take off earlier than it should. Usually this temporary force of physics only lasted while the plane was skimming close to the ground. Attempting to gain altitude during it resulted in the plane falling back to the ground in a horrific crash. If Flint could just get the jet off the ground a few feet, then he could work on gaining velocity as he floated just above the flat sandy terrain ahead of him.

With their momentum accelerating, Flint could feel the back half of the jet as it began to struggle into the air. Pointing the nose down just a hair to stabilize the ground effect, he got the jet to hover just a few feet above the sand as the runway disappeared. The security guards had tried to pull in front of him, and they might have succeeded had the jet not gained speed considerably after Flint began his little maneuver. By then the drivers realized that any attempt to pull in front would only cause the jet to collide with them, smashing the wings into their truck. Sure, it would stop the jet, but it would also smear their bodies across their trucks like butter on toast.

The bottom of the jet was within inches of the airport's fence when they cleared the barrier. Their airspeed had finally increased enough so the stall buzzer went quiet. Flint eased the yoke back, and the jet angled into a safe climb to altitude. Flint adjusted his course and leveled off at a thousand feet above sea level. He fumbled around for a minute until he had the autopilot figured out. His rough course would take him in an easterly direction, but now he needed to find some aviation charts.

The owners of this aircraft were undoubtedly world travelers. In an unlocked compartment, Flint found charts that spanned most of the globe. After about five minutes of sorting through them, he settled on two that would show him a suitable route toward the Philippines. Then, talking half to himself and half to Gual, he noted, "I don't know how much fuel this thing sucks, but we'll most likely need to make a few stops before we can get to the Philippines. I just hope that we don't get stopped by their customs."

Flint paused as a thought entered his mind. Quickly he disengaged the autopilot as he remarked, "We have to get below their radar."

He had almost forgotten that the people at the Sharm El Sheikh airport would likely report their incident. The last thing he needed right now was to get shot down by the Egyptian air force. He didn't know how low he needed to fly, but he managed to get within two hundred feet of the sea. He didn't dare fly any closer, as he was afraid of getting hit by a downdraft.

After an hour of tense flying, Flint gained altitude. If they hadn't been spotted by now, then they should be free. After all, they were now beyond the borders of Egypt, flying south over the Red Sea. Feeling a little more relaxed, he turned his focus to the aviation charts.

While studying the charts, he noticed that certain airports were circled with little descriptions alongside them. The descriptions were in English, and the handwriting looked familiar. In fact there was a smell about the whole aircraft that was very familiar. He couldn't quite put his finger on it, but it seemed like a good type of familiar. He figured that a woman had been piloting the jet sometime before he "borrowed" it. Long strands of hair were stuck to the cushions of the pilot's seat, and a familiar perfume wafted out of the upholstery every time he rested against it. Whether or not the smells were the same, everything about this cockpit reminded Flint of Lydia. Even the handwriting on the charts was similar to his wife's writing. Not wanting to dwell too long on the ever-present memory of his beloved, Flint couldn't help but wonder if she was still alive somewhere.

The notes showed a pattern. They marked certain airports that would be small enough to not attract attention, but large enough to supply jet fuel. There were even notations about who to bribe and for how much at certain destinations. Since they'd been flying, Flint had also found the Learjet's manual and calculated their fuel consumption. Using this and the charts, he was able to create a path to the Philippines, and take advantage of the marked airports along the way.

Their first stop would be in Ethiopia, which was about an hour away. They were not out of fuel yet, but the next stretch to India would require a full tank. The only thing that worried Flint now was having enough money to pay for the fuel, but an organization this size wouldn't be flying all over the world without some slush money. He just had to find it.

Since Flint wanted to focus on his flying, he turned to his clueless copilot. "Hey Gual, I think there is money on this plane. We'll need it for fuel. Can you and the others try to find it?"

Gual looked back at Flint with a puzzled look on his face. "Speak slower. You want money?"

"Yes," Flint replied. "Money for fuel."

Gual began to understand, but still didn't know what Flint was asking. "*Pinobre*, we very poor, no money."

"No, no," Flint said. "Here, on the plane, there is money. You find it."

Gual nodded. "Oh, yes-yes, we find, okay, very good." With that he got up and started barking commands to his companions. They all got up and started inching their way all over the plane.

Despite the fact that he was flying a jet, the commotion from his passengers reminded him that the plane was still small. With them moving all around, the plane felt more like a boat rocking on the ocean.

After a few minutes, they located a couple of compartments hidden under the carpeted floor. Here they found a few assault rifles, a sniper rifle, and a small package of plastic explosives. There was even a small mountable turret gun. When Gual came forward to show Flint the weapons, he was holding one of the rifles with his finger on the trigger.

Blood rushed to Flint's head, and before he could be more diplomatic, he yelled, "Get your finger off the damn trigger!" He hadn't meant to scare his new friend, and he rarely found himself swearing, but he had grown up around guns. Only an idiot would carry around or show off a gun with their finger on the trigger, even if it was empty.

Gual was only able to catch the disappointment in Flint's voice, and he dropped the gun to the floor. Picking it up, Flint tried to calm the man down. Struggling to mix hand gestures into his phrasing, he said, "No finger on trigger—very dangerous."

Even with this explanation, Gual looked hurt. "Sorry, sorry," he said guiltily. Flint didn't blame him. Likely, Gual had never used a gun before. He was only doing what he'd seen in the movies.

"It's okay, just be careful," Flint reminded, "and try to find some money."

Their next find was far more disturbing. Inside another hidden compartment, the Filipinos found a large black bag with a zipper. They quickly pulled the zipper down hoping to find money, but instead the whole airplane filled with the distinct smell of decomposing flesh. Inside the bag was the body of a dead man, soaking in a pool of his own half-coagulated blood.

The men quickly zipped the bag back up and replaced the panel over the floor where the compartment was hidden. Now looking around, they found bloodstains smeared on the carpet, which they'd previously dismissed as nothing important. The mood of everyone on board shifted to a more sober realization that they were still in the thick of a tense situation.

A few minutes later, Gual came back and motioned for Flint to take a look at something. Flint reengaged the autopilot and followed him back. They'd found a safe built into the bulkhead of the aircraft. The door was about one foot wide and tall. It looked sturdy enough, but Flint had a hard time believing that it was impenetrable. He gave a satisfied smile and thumbs-up to the Filipinos. "If there is money in this plane, it's in here. Try to find a way to get to it. Tear it out of the wall if you have to."

They seemed to understand and Flint returned to the cockpit. He retook control of the airplane and began his descent to their first refueling stop in Ethiopia. Upon arriving they still hadn't gotten into the safe, but they were determined to do so. Flint was able to use most of his remaining American money to top off the fuel. The whole process at this smaller airport was easy. Nobody asked any questions, just brought the fuel.

Before taking off, Flint took a short walk to stretch his legs. After all the excitement, he realized his last meal had consisted of insect paste the night before. He wasn't sure, but he figured the Filipinos were just as hungry. Sparing a few more minutes, Flint found a small bakeshop near the airport, and picked up a few pastries for the next leg of their trip. Even after considering his nomadic diet, he wondered if he'd ever tasted bread this good before.

The Filipinos had taken a break from busting into the safe while the jet was being fueled, but as soon as they were back in the air, they went at it again with renewed enthusiasm. About an hour into the flight, they were able to tear the safe out of the wall. While the front door of it looked sturdy, the box that had been recessed into the wall consisted of a much flimsier sheet metal.

Once they had it out of the wall, it took them all of ten minutes to pry it open. Inside they found several stacks of nicely bundled American hundred-dollar bills. There were a few other bills of various origins, but the majority was in dollars. For a few guys who might only have ever made a dollar per day if they could even find work, this amounted to way more money than they would have normally seen in their lifetimes combined.

Flint could tell they'd found it by the excited chatter behind him. After a few minutes, Gual came up to him with two bundles of bills. "We find the money!" he said, unable to hold back his excitement.

"How much is there?" Flint asked, knowing they must have counted it.

Gual smiled somewhat mischievously. "Nineteen of this." He waved one of the bundles in front of Flint.

Flint did a quick calculation in his head. Each bundle he knew would contain fifty bills, or five thousand dollars. Nineteen bundles of them added up to ninety-five thousand dollars. Unable to hold back a smile of his own, Flint replied to the overjoyed man, "It looks like we'll make it to the Philippines after all. And I think we might just get to keep a little for ourselves."

Gual's next comment made Flint laugh. In his most dignified voice he said, "Compliments of the villain."

His comment wasn't what made Flint laugh, it was the tone of his voice, and the fact that it was the best sentence of English Gual had constructed since they'd met. "You'll have to remind me to send them a thank-you card later," Flint replied.

Whether he understood or not, Gual smiled and went back to the others to stare at their newfound riches. Flint checked his course, reset the autopilot, and continued studying the aviation charts. They'd hit a small streak of luck getting away from Egypt the way they did. The next biggest challenge lay ahead.

It bothered Flint, since he'd never actually been to the Philippines. He had no idea how to plan his next move for when he got there. He was going to have to improvise the whole thing. He tried shaking off the worry, but he would be in unfamiliar lands, going up against a force whose size he was unsure of. All he knew was that they were extremely danger-ous and had extensive resources backing them up.

Chapter 7

"Sorry for the rough treatment," Marshal Steel began. "I thought it best if that man believed us to be at odds."

Dusty looked at Marshal with disdain. "I would say that you had me pretty convinced, also."

"Please, Dusty, I know we've had some difference of opinions." Marshal took a sip from a bottle of cold beer. "But after all we've been through, I couldn't just throw you out." Then, setting his bottle down, he picked up his brushed-nickel briefcase. After producing a key, he opened the case, pulled out two items, and laid them gently on a bamboo table.

"I'm a little surprised: I thought you would've sold those to the highest bidder already," Dusty said, as she tried to keep a calm demeanor.

Marshal smiled. "You should already know these

have been sold for quite some time. I'm meeting with our buyer and financier tonight." He picked up the small black sphere, which was just under half the size of a bowling ball, and began to examine it.

It had three different indentations where metallic prongs had been plugged in. The dimples not only served as connection points for the metal nodes on the Martian ship, but they also functioned to anchor the device to the ship's mechanicals. Aside from the indentations, there was about a three-inch flat spot on the bottom of the sphere. The whole object looked more like it was made out of a black magnet than anything else.

"It's interesting," he continued, "that something so small could move a ship so large through space at speeds much faster than the speed of light."

Dusty thought it was incredible, but she had become so disgusted with Marshal that she couldn't savor the unprecedented discovery. "Who is our backer, anyhow?" she inquired.

Marshal set the object down next to the golden stack of engraved plates that went along with the treasure. His eyes remained focused on a distant daydream. He replied, "I'm afraid that I can't tell you that." Then he rose and walked over to Dusty. Touching her gentle freckled face with the back of his fingers, he continued, "You see, while I would love to share that with you, I'm afraid he would not approve. He is, after all, a rather paranoid character."

Dusty held back her temper as he caressed her face. She wanted nothing more than to gouge Marshal's eyes out. But the mercenaries in the room would enjoy the opportunity to show her a little pain of their own if she did. She forced a smile and looked up at her partner. "So after all this work, what do we get out of it?"

"You mean the satisfaction of finding the world's most astonishing discovery isn't enough?" Marshal teased.

"Please," she replied. "What good is that discovery if nobody ever knows about it? Unless it goes to a museum, I'll have to keep my mouth shut about it."

He laughed. "And of course that silence comes with a price, doesn't it?"

Dusty simply stared him down. Marshal then circled her with his hand, gracing the small of her back. When he had come around, he grabbed her by the back of the neck and pulled her in for a kiss.

When she resisted his lips, he backed up an inch or two. Then, caressing her face again with the back of his hand, he said, "Dusty, you know I care a great deal for you." His caress ended with an abrupt slap across her face. The blow nearly caused her to lose her balance. "I could have given you everything!"

Though she'd witnessed this sudden change in his demeanor more often in the last few months, it frightened her. He no longer cared to hide the dark canker in his soul that revealed his lack of conscience.

"Imagine what we could do together," Marshal continued. "As soon as our friend finds a way to make this device work, we could visit Mars! Dusty, I'm sorry. I didn't mean to hurt you."

It never failed to amaze Dusty. Marshal could go from nice guy to the offspring of Satan, and back again in seconds. "I have a hard time believing that," she said softly.

"Please," he said, slowly and deliberately, with an almost sincere look of hurt in his eyes. "I on-ly am try-ing to a-chieve the greater good." Sitting back down, he placed two fingers on his long-anticipated treasure. "We are giving this up now so we can visit Mars together and discover so much more."

"But at what expense?" Dusty replied. "And how many people must die?"

Ever so calmly, Marshal just continued, "I don't expect you to approve of all my methods, but I assure you they are necessary. I need you with me, Dusty. I want you with me. If you aren't an asset to me, then you become a liability."

Dusty knew where he was going with this. She also believed that, inside, he really did think he could use charm to win her affection. If this delusion was real, then it might prove to her advantage in the future. For now she was left with the conflict of the moment.

Then he asked the question she knew was coming. It was that conflict which meant either standing for right or caving in. She didn't fear the question so much as she feared her own resolve to answer in a way that wouldn't add shame to her conscience.

He asked, "What did you learn from our new friend in the shed?"

With a sickened expression in her eyes, she looked up at Marshal. "He didn't tell me anything."

He gave her a small frown, but didn't seem disappointed in her answer. "Hey, I know that I've been a jerk, but I want you to know that I won't hurt him. I just want to know who's interfering with our work here. Won't you just help satisfy my curiosity?"

"You won't hurt him, just like you didn't hurt those laborers back in Egypt when you blew up the excavation?" Dusty questioned.

"I had no choice with them," Marshal snapped. "I've already told you that our buyer forced my hand in that case. You must understand that it was as hard for me to do as it was for you to watch it. But he believes that this discovery is far too important to leave loose tongues roaming around. I'm not the killer here. We're just pawns in the most amazing discovery ever. This is a stepping-stone toward Mars. He won't let us in on the discoveries up there if we don't play by his rules down here."

"So what happens if I do tell you about your prisoner? Are you going to let him go, just like that?" Dusty asked.

"Of course I will," Marshal soothed. "Our investor doesn't know anything about him. Once he gets the device and is no longer concerned with our procurement operations, then we can quietly release the man."

Marshal paused as he went into a cooler and produced two more bottles of beer. Opening them both, he presented one to Dusty. "Dusty, we've known each other for several years now. I've done some things that aren't very admirable, but I've always respected you."

Marshal leaned forward and, with a most sincere look on his face, continued, "If you really think this man is a good man, and shouldn't be hurt, I will not hurt him. You have my word."

Dusty shifted uncomfortably, knowing full well the value of his word. Her head was spinning, but she desperately wanted to believe him. She reached for the bottle, but the smell of the beer caused her stomach to twist. Setting it down on the floor, she stared back at the penetrating eyes of her partner. "His name is Philip Noon . . ."

Chapter 8

With the click of a mouse, Shen Mao closed a video conference call on his computer when he noticed his phone ringing. Few people had access to his phone number and there was only one call that he was expecting today. Reaching for the phone with his stubby fingers, he noticed the number was none other than that of Marshal Steel. Shen's paranoia prevented him from saving any number in his phone. He, however, had a way with numbers that enabled him to remember and retain numbers as easily as someone who had a photographic memory. This skill, and an undeterred ambition, had brought the poor, starving Chinese boy out of poverty and into the world of wealth and manipulation.

He brought the phone to his ear. "Marshal Steel, I have been expecting you. I trust that you have had a safe trip?"

Marshal replied humbly, "Yes, sir, we are just tying up a few loose ends now and we'll be stopping by within a few hours."

"What loose ends are you speaking of?" Shen asked with a calm, calculating accent that favored his Chinese upbringing.

Marshal sounded reluctant to make this call, but Mao would have been upset if Marshal hadn't. Nobody knew this better than the stooge on the end of the line. Mao was the type of man who left few things to chance. He wouldn't have hesitated to put Marshal behind the crosshairs of a sniper rifle if he suspected anything foul from the one trusted with his important package.

Marshal explained his delay. "We captured one man, who may or may not be a part of GRIP. We're going to check out his story before we risk leading anyone to you."

"Tell me about this man," Shen proceeded.

Marshal knew he needed to tread carefully. Mao could hear the tension in his voice. "He claims that his name is Philip Noon. He also says that he has a man named Flint who is coming to rescue him. Our lovely interrogator, Dusty, found this out. She, however, doesn't believe they're associated with the organization that's tracking us down. Still, we want to check his story before we kill him."

"I do not know anyone by those names, but very well. If his story checks out, then kill him. If not, then I will send someone over to pick him up in a couple days," Shen said. "In any case, I want my package delivered here before the day is over." Without saying another word, he hung up the phone.

Shen was generally a patient man. He'd trusted Marshal's abilities thus far, but something didn't feel right about the situation. The device he had spent several years and a couple of fortunes to attain was now so close to being his. This recent development, so close to tonight, seemed fishy. As a basic rule, Mao did not believe in coincidences.

He paced between his computer and his dining room table, where a full complement of hors d'oeuvres was constantly replenished by the kitchen staff. He tried to understand this latest situation presented by Marshal. It had to be a trick of GRIP. The organization had been tracking him for some time now. Much of the money that Shen had spent in procuring the device had been spent trying to frustrate GRIP's efforts.

Mao had even been a part of GRIP's organization before he defected. It had been a brief period, several years ago. The experience had taught the shrewd Shen Mao a lesson about finances. It took a whole three weeks after Mao had been invited to join the group before he found that part of his fortune had been diverted by GRIP to finance their operations. By way of consolation, Mao was able to steal some important information before leaving. This information was critical in finding the propulsion device that Marshal now had in his possession. If Marshal was indeed holding one of their operatives captive, it could prove to be a great victory.

Even though Mao had been a temporary member of GRIP, he'd never been allowed to know much. He was just used for his money. Thus far, he knew that GRIP was some form of non-government organization. Similar to Greenpeace, PETA, or any of the countless other organizations out there, GRIP believed themselves to have a superior ethic that necessitated meddling in the affairs of others. Occasionally, some of those organizations had a division that was more focused on forceful actions. Shen wasn't sure if GRIP was that type of NGO or if they were their own organization. All he knew was that they were now well funded, thanks to his contribution. They were also very persistent.

If this man whom Marshal captured, was in fact a part of GRIP, then Marshal was likely being manipulated. It didn't seem reasonable that they'd capture some random person with the resources to stage a real rescue attempt. Marshal was being played. Mao hoped that he had enough time to finish his plans tonight. If GRIP was just now catching up to Marshal, then they shouldn't be able to know about the auction yet, let alone mobilize fast enough to stop it.

Lifting the phone again, Shen dialed a number from memory. It rang twice, then there was a click, but no greeting. Shen was familiar with the protocol and simply stated, "Our friend, Marshal Steel, will be visiting me in a few hours with a delivery. But I also fear that he has lost his edge."

There was no voice to confirm what had been said. The only thing Shen heard was a click, followed by a dial tone. He set the phone down and walked over to his hors d'oeuvres, selecting a fried piece of meat that was delicately wrapped in seaweed and sweet rice. Though harvesting giant stingrays was illegal in the Philippines, it was nonetheless a business that kept his small island-town of Jagna alive. The gristly texture was an acquired taste Shen had come to appreciate.

When the phone rang again, he only bothered to look at the number on the ID screen. It was different than the one he'd called, but he knew it was from the same person he had just spoken to. After two rings, it stopped.

If the assassin understood and was willing to accept the job, he simply called back, using a different phone number. To answer the phone would not only be pointless, but also it would void the arrangement. By doing this, the team on the other end, as well as Mao, were able to add another layer of protection from any unwelcome ears that might be listening in on their activities.

Shen Mao sat down and savored the stingray delicacy. This latest development wouldn't proved to be a large kink in his plans. He was going to dispose of Marshal anyway. True, he'd placed a lot of trust in the man, but even Mao understood Marshal's unstable tendencies. He could not risk keeping the man around for much longer. Marshal was too great a liability. If GRIP really was tracking him, then it was simply a matter of time before Marshal slipped up.

Chapter 9

The screech of the tires was like music to Flint's ears. The trip from Egypt to the Philippines had been exciting and eventful. He'd even bribed a few officials when he refueled in China. Luckily the notes on the aviation charts in the jet offered accurate descriptions of what to expect along the way. The last stop was now a small airport in Lapu-Lapu. Though Flint had enjoyed the adventure, he was growing increasingly concerned for Philip.

From here they would cross a large bridge over to the main island of Cebu, the center hub of the region known as the Visayas in the Philippines. Gual informed Flint that in Cebu, they would find Marshal's base. That was where they would most likely find Philip.

The woman, he learned, was called Dusty. Gual

believed she could be trusted. She'd been working with a man named Marshal, but Gual could tell that she was looking for a way out. This supported Flint's original assumption that she was in distress. It also meant that if they could find Dusty, she might lead them to Philip.

As they stepped out of the airplane, they could see many more jets around the airport. Flint had no idea which one belonged to Philip's captors, but that didn't matter at this time. By way of standard procedure, a few security guards came and escorted them to the main terminal. Gual and the others worked at chumming them up so they didn't feel a need to check the group's pockets or backpack full of weapons and cash. It worked, and within a few minutes they were headed toward the exit of the terminal.

In the corridor leading outside, there was a small band playing for tips and welcoming all the visitors. Feeling generous, Flint tipped them a ten-dollar bill. They were overjoyed at the sight of the American money. Many of them were lucky to make the equivalent of ten dollars in a week.

Flint's group hadn't gotten far when he noticed a small commotion in a parking lot nearby. A white woman with dark brown hair was being pushed into what could only be described as an elongated jeep. Flint had a hard time believing he could be this lucky. Though it had been night when he first saw the woman in Egypt, he believed she was that same woman.

Before he could say anything, Gual spoke up. "That her! That her!" He pointed in the same direction, reaffirming Flint's conviction.

The large man who stuffed the woman into the back of the truck slammed the doors shut and walked to the passenger-side door. The jeepney started up and began rolling toward the road.

With a shout of, "Come on!" to Gual and the others, Flint raced to intercept the vehicle. At that moment a small Mercedes stalled right in front of the road, providing a perfect chance to catch up.

The jeepney stopped, and the driver leaned out the window and shouted at the Mercedes. Then, as he honked his horn, he found his door being swung open.

Flint grabbed the driver and pulled him out of the jeepney. Gual and the others began to beat the driver down. Flint, avoiding the brawl that he'd started, directed his attention to the large soldier getting out of the passenger side. Flint was shocked when he realized the man didn't look surprised. In fact he was smiling as he approached Flint.

Just then two strong men grabbed him from behind, not even giving enough time to reach into his pack to retrieve a weapon. Flint struggled as his gear was stripped away and tossed into the back of the Jeepney. They were too much for him. The only place they could have come from was the Mercedes. Flint realized he'd walked into a setup.

The only way that this foe could have known to trap him was if they'd interrogated Philip and learned that he was coming. Luckily for him, they couldn't have known about the Filipinos he had brought with him. After the abuse these soldiers of fortune had dealt to the Filipinos, the little guys were all too eager to give some payback for their mistreatment.

When they'd finished subduing the driver, they came to assist Flint. One of the men holding Flint left to deal with them. He looked confident that he could handle the small gang. To Flint's dismay, the man's self-confidence proved to be justified. Flint, on the other hand, was unable to pay any more heed to his struggling companions. The big man with the smile had started landing a few good blows to Flint's unprotected belly and face.

"Flint, is it?" the man asked.

Flint spat blood on the ground. "What have you done with my friend?"

"We've been waiting for you. My name is Sperl, and that lovely lady, who you have such a soft spot for, is Dusty. If it wasn't for her, we wouldn't have known you were coming."

Flint didn't even know Dusty, yet he already felt betrayed by her. "Where's Philip?" he demanded.

"Don't worry, you'll be meeting him very soon."

Flint wrestled with this promise as he tried to wrestle himself free. Did Sperl mean that he would see Philip alive, or join him in death?

Sperl opened the back of the jeepney and, assisted by the man holding Flint, roughly ushered him into the back. They slapped him down on the floor of the truck, put a zip tie across his hands, and tightened it. "Just in case." He smiled again.

Turning over, Flint stared up at his captors. Only it was now Flint's turn to show a reddened toothy grin. No sooner had he smiled than Sperl's companion went completely silent and still. Sensing that something had turned away from his advantage, Sperl spun around.

Behind his frozen companion was a thin bald man with the darker skin color. He looked Filipino, but had more resemblance to a man of Hispanic descent rather than Asian. The man was calmly standing about five feet away, with a neutral expression on his face.

Flint noticed Sperl's hesitation. Perhaps it was that the small guy looked Mexican. Still, if Sperl had spent any time here, he'd know that many Filipinos looked more Hispanic than Asian. Flint watched as Sperl came to terms with what had just happened. The conniving brute found the piece of wire sticking into the back of his soldier friend's head, right where his spinal cord connected to his brain. The man who had moments earlier held Flint from behind like a coward, had been killed by this pipsqueak. Though death had been immediate, his body was only now starting to slump to the ground.

Taking advantage of the distraction, Flint jammed his feet hard into the back of Sperl's legs. Sperl groaned as his knees buckled, sending him to the ground on all fours. With a look of fury, the muscular blond bear turned his gaze upward, just in time to see the blur of the bald man's foot as it connected to Sperl's face.

Sperl and the jeepney driver were now temporarily knocked out. With one of the men dead, only a single enemy remained. That man was about to subdue the gang of Filipinos, but he must have known he was now too heavily outnumbered. With the wisdom of a seasoned, albeit selfish soldier, he made the only decision that he could. He abandoned the fight. When he made a run for the Mercedes, the Filipinos chose not to pursue. Bloodied and bruised, they watched as the car fired up and sped away.

By the time Gual made his way back to Flint, the bald man was cutting the zip tie from Flint's wrists. Flint shook his head, forgetting to introduce Gual to his friend. "Well, it sure is nice to see you again, Monk," Flint began. "But couldn't you have shown up before they split my lip?"

Wearing a neutral expression, Monk quoted a passage from the Bible: "But one of the young men told Abigail, Nabal's wife, saying, Behold, David sent messengers out of the wilderness to salute our master; and he railed on them.' 1 Samuel 25:14."

"Oh, you know I'm happy to see you," Flint replied. "I'm sure I would have been in a bad situation if you hadn't shown up when you did." And truly he was grateful to see Monk. When he was still in Egypt, Flint had used his satellite phone to e-mail his old friend. At that time, he didn't know exactly where in the Philippines they would be going. But with Gual's help, he was able to follow up with Monk before they left Ethiopia, giving better directions.

Monk slightly nodded at Flint's greeting. He'd arrived only an hour before Flint. Monk had been visiting Hong Kong, touring the many Buddhist and Confucian temples when Flint first contacted him. Since Manila, the capital of the Philippines, was only a forty-five-minute flight from Hong Kong, he had little trouble getting down. While there was only one flight that day to Lapu-Lapu, it had not been full. Monk had no problem getting a ticket; or at least he didn't have more of a problem than was usual for him.

Flint had known Monk for four and a half years. In that time he'd heard Monk's real name only once, but had since completely forgotten it. All who knew Monk knew him only by the meditative title.

Monk had grown up under the watchful eyes of the Catholic Church. His Mexican parents had deserted him as a toddler while living in California. Many parents would shirk the idea of abandoning their child, but his condition must have proven too much of a burden for them.

As was the case for many autistic children, Monk lacked the ability to interact socially with others. He had a classic detachment of emotions. However, he had one strength, which had manifested while at the Catholic orphanage: an eidetic memory.

Eidetic memories were often confused with photographic memories. However, the eidetic memory not only captured pictures, it also captured smells, sounds, and everything related to an activity. It completely ingrained every experience into someone's life. Instead of memorizing phonebooks or counting toothpicks, though, Monk had memorized the Bible. He rarely spoke, but when he did, he always used a quote from the Scriptures or some other inspirational literature that fit the situation.

While never really subscribing to any single religious denomination, Monk developed his own personal belief about who God was, and wanted desperately to bring his life in harmony with Deity. He believed in the Hebrew God and in Jesus Christ, but he didn't fully discount the other religions either. Allah to him, was just another name for God, and Buddha may as well have been one of God's prophets.

When he became a teenager, he was set up with a job as custodian to a mixed martial arts studio. He never participated, but his excellent memory captured everything that he saw and heard. This all combined to the events that gave Monk his permanent nickname.

While walking to work one day at the age of thirty, he was surrounded by some bullies on the streets of Oakland, California. They had mocked him from a distance before, but on that particular day they advanced to pushing and physically abusing the autistic man. Thirteen years of watching others fight at the gym kicked in. Before anyone had a chance to react, two of the bullies were dead and one was paralyzed.

He spent the next five years behind bars, where the inmates soon learned of his fighting ability and unique way of quoting scripture. They were the ones to give him the name Monk. After those five years, he was moved to an institution more appropriate for his condition. Another five years passed there, and he was released. That was when he met Flint.

Monk had been looking for a place to live, and Flint had recently purchased and renovated a small apartment. After getting to know his tenant, Flint helped Monk find a job in a town where the autistic man was having difficulty adjusting. Over the next four and a half years, Flint often checked in on Monk, and they became good friends. It was not an ordinary friendship, but Flint could see beyond Monk's disability. Despite Monk's lack of outward emotions, Flint sensed that the misunderstood man needed some social interaction aside from his job. Frankly, he enjoyed spending time with the man, anyway.

Occasionally they would go to the gym together, and Flint would spar with him. That was how he learned of Monk's incredible ability to fight. Monk was always considerate of Flint's skill set, and never allowed himself to get carried away. Flint in turn learned a lot about fighting. Not enough to ever beat a professional in a hand-to-hand fight, but enough to hold his own against an average man.

When Flint learned that he would be going to the Philippines and would likely face some danger, he wanted Monk to be there with him. Even though he knew Monk wanted to soak up as much about Chinese religion as he could, he also knew that Monk considered Flint to be his best friend—if not his only friend. If Flint was going into a dangerous situation, Monk wanted to help.

Now, not even fifteen minutes after arriving, Monk had already saved Flint from being captured and possibly killed. Also, they'd succeeded in finding the girl, not to mention another means of transportation. Flint quickly filled Monk in with the details of the situation.

As he wrapped up the briefing, he heard a click. The sound was the familiar cocking of a pistol. He figured that when he'd been on his back and kicked Sperl, he'd bumped into his backpack, causing a pistol to fall out. The girl in the back of the jeepney now had the firearm pointed at Flint.

Monk took a step forward. Flint stretched out his hand to stop him, then said to the girl, "Your mercenary friend said that you tipped him off to our coming. Is that true?"

The gun in her hand was shaking, and her beautiful lips trembled slightly as she replied, "I didn't mean for any of this to happen, I swear, they told me they wouldn't hurt you if I told them about you."

"It's Dusty, right?" Flint began, watching Dusty tremble as she nodded in affirmation. "I don't want these big guys here to wake up while I'm still around, so what do you say we sort this out someplace else? I saw how you reacted when your friend almost blew up those Filipinos, so I doubt you're the type to pull the trigger on that gun now."

Dusty lowered the gun slightly. "What do you mean, *almost*?" Tears filled her eyes. "I thought they—"

Before she could finish her sentence, Flint slammed the back doors to the jeepney, containing her inside the rear passenger section of the vehicle. The door was inoperable from the inside, causing an angry Dusty to pound on the doors.

Flint motioned for the Filipinos to come over. "I don't think we can all fit into the front seats of this thing," he informed them. "And with this girl in the back being a little edgy, we might also need to find a taxi."

"No-no, we okay," Gual said. "We stand." He said something to the others, and they hopped onto the rear bumper of the jeepney.

Flint was a little concerned about the arrangement but didn't want to stick around much longer. He, Monk, and Gual all went up to the front. Finding the keys still in the ignition, Flint started the beast up. He then punched it into gear and they lumbered onto the main road, with Gual giving directions.

After about a mile, Flint began to relax. He noticed that half the other vehicles on the road, which consisted of jeepneys and Multicabs, also had passengers standing on their bumpers. Flint learned as well that the jeepney he was driving had a very interesting horn. Like in many of the other jeepneys, touching two bare wires together honked the automobile's theatrical horn. The catchy tune that blared made it fun for him to use every chance he could. The other jeepney drivers used the horn along with, or in place of turn signals. Frankly, they used it for any number of other reasons. So Flint felt confident in playing it, a lot.

Chapter 10

Marshal sat in the back row of the SuperCat ferry. Aside from the normal curious glances of the natives, he went relatively unnoticed. The trip to Bohol from the island of Cebu would take under an hour. Then there was the two-and-a-half-hour drive to Jagna, where Shen Mao was waiting. Marshal placed a hand across the small of his back to ensure that his shirt was still hiding the Glock automatic tucked into his pants. He'd wanted Sperl to come with him, but Sperl was the most capable of handling the situation back at the airport.

If their prisoner was telling the truth, and the man flying into the airport was just some yahoo looking for adventure, then Sperl would kill him quickly. If he was lying though, and it turned out to be someone from GRIP, then Sperl would need to be there to properly defuse the situation. The black, athletically built mercenary who now sat next to Marshal was Sperl's polar opposite. Sure he was capable, at least for a rugby player or a mixed martial arts contestant, but Marshal knew that Sperl would not have allowed himself to be distracted by the movie playing on the screen in the ferry like this guy was.

Letting out a sigh, Marshal scanned the few passengers who'd chosen a seat in this section of the boat. For the most part, they all seemed normal. There was a small family of Filipinos, and two Mormon missionaries. After cautiously deflecting a little small talk from the missionaries, he was able to avoid any further discussion by simply accepting their Book of Mormon, with the false promise that he would read it someday. Alone again with his bodyguard, Marshal wondered if he could allow himself to relax a little.

The incidents over the last day had not shaken his nerves. But a personal visit to Shen Mao was enough to put him on edge. Though Mao had sounded passive about the latest events, something told Marshal that he needed to approach Mao carefully. He'd only met Mao once in person. That was when he was recruited to find the Martian ship. Since then they'd only spoken through encrypted e-mail messages and telephone. But the one visit with Mao had left a deep impression.

Mao had wanted to ensure that Marshal would know how serious he was. Two other anthropologists had shown up on Mao's yacht the day Marshal was hired. One was a man. The other was a woman. Mao had interviewed them all together before finding the anthropologist he wanted to use. Mao had announced that Marshal would be his man, and had drinks brought in. They all toasted Marshal's success at passing the group interview. But as soon as they sipped their wine, the other man and woman began to choke and convulse.

"I do not tolerate failure." Mao stared directly at Marshal while the other two spasmed. "And I want this to be very clear: You are hired to do a job for me. Do not disappoint me." Two plops to the floor made Mao's point very clear.

Marshal shivered at the memory, and how easily one of those dead anthropologists could have been himself. Then, shifting nervously, he bumped the brushed nickel briefcase that held the piece of technology. Reaching over to steady it, he accidentally knocked over a spare metal briefcase, almost identical in design.

"You okay, boss?" the bodyguard asked as he noticed Marshal fidgeting.

"I'll be fine," Marshal replied. "When we get on shore, keep a good eye out. I've got a bad feeling about this visit."

The mercenary knew the risks, but asked anyway, "What kind of trouble you think we'll see?"

"I don't know yet," Marshal said. Just talking helped ease his tension. "But if I know Shen Mao, we may need a little insurance." Then, looking at the big black man, he patted his other steel briefcase.

The man nodded in understanding. "In that case, maybe it's a good thing I brought little Maggie," he said, referring to the grenade launcher that was packed inside of his own duffel bag.

The mercenary incorrectly believed that the briefcase held a bomb. However, Marshal had something completely different inside, but he let the mercenary believe what he wanted. Inside was a single canister of a black-market nerve agent. If Mao was planning on killing him, he wanted to have a good bargaining chip.

When they arrived at Bohol, Marshal and the mercenary debarked and began walking toward a taxicab. They both looked as casual as could be, but they were deceptively vigilant. They also had one great advantage: They were tall and American. This set them apart from the many Filipinos who were keeping a close eye on them. If Mao wanted to get to them, he would have to do so in front of many witnesses.

After talking to four different taxi drivers, and after being forced to raise the taxi fare considerably, they found one willing to drive them around the island to the small town of Jagna. Along the taxi's windshield were a couple of CDs that had been cut into the symbol of Batman. A rosary, caked in dust, hung idly from the rearview mirror. The driver also had a plastic figurine of a gold-colored Asian cat mounted on the dashboard. The cat's single waving arm seemed to be warning Marshal away from the anticipated meeting.

The driver sped along the beach-front highway, dodging kids, cars, and chickens along the way. The mercenary enjoyed watching the reckless driving that was so common in this part of the world. It never failed to amaze him how close they came to hitting everything along the roadside. Marshal, on the other hand, had spent enough years in third-world countries that he was no longer amused or frightened by the driving habits. Instead, he was lost in thought.

They hadn't seen anyone on their way to the taxi, and nobody seemed to be following. If Mao were to double-cross him, Marshal figured it would be in Jagna. After forty-five minutes of travel, he decided to take a quick nap. He was exhausted. He hadn't fully recovered from the jet lag, and he knew that he'd need his wits about him when he arrived at Mao's mansion.

It seemed he'd just closed his eyes when the mercenary was slapping his leg to wake him up. "We're here, boss."

Marshal sat up quickly, and immediately regretted falling asleep. His neck was kinked from the awkward position, and his mouth was full of dried saliva. He smacked his lips in disgust at his powerful morning breath. Then, pulling out a hand-drawn map, he began to interpret the directions he'd been given. The driver stopped him, though, and said in staccato English, "You wait first, I need gas."

He pulled over to the side of the road. There was no gas pump, but a small roadside shop had gasoline and beer nuts for sale. The driver bought several liters of gas and two small packages of nuts. The mercenary watched with interest and chuckled, "Coke bottles? They sell the gas in coke bottles? I think I'd better be careful about the drinks I buy around here."

Marshal opened the door and spit on the ground, trying to clear the funk in his breath. He took a good stretch before getting back in the car. Then he looked back over to his companion. "It's time to keep your eyes open. Let me know if you notice anything out of place."

"Are you kidding me?" he said. "Everything looks out of place." Then, pointing at the shop wall, he said, "They have a sign there that says, 'No hard liquor for children during school hours.' Man, if Earth had a butt crack, I think we found it."

Marshal glared at the man and simply stated, "Don't let the culture distract you from the task at hand."

"Hey, boss," he replied, "don't worry bout me,

this mission's a breeze. Just don't you worry bout'a thing."

As soon as the driver returned the bottles, he got into the taxi, and Marshal directed him to the house of Shen Mao.

Chapter 11

"The cost is not the issue," came a woman's voice on the other end of the jets passenger phone. "We need those plates."

"I won't fail you again." With that, Lydia hung up. It had taken her considerable effort to bribe several men out of their seats on a plane trip to Cairo. From there Lydia and her team were able to get a flight to Hong Kong with a connection to the Philippines.

"It's a good thing we're able to track our Learjet," Sam, one of Lydia's team, said as he winked at the flight attendant who was replacing the ice on his companion's forehead.

Grisha, who'd been beaten down by the Filipinos at the airport, fumed, "I can't wait to show those men what I think of my new bruises."

"Please, Grisha," Lydia said to the heavily built

Russian, "you're lucky to still be alive."

"I suppose it wasn't bad timing to have airport security show up when they did," Grisha replied. His Russian accent still showed signs of annoyance at the whole incident.

Lydia knew the man's pride had been damaged. He was a good fighter, and a man she trusted with her life. It would have been a sore loss to their organization if he'd been killed.

Picking up the telephone, she swiped a credit card and placed another call. It rang three times before a man named Troy answered.

"Hello, if you want to sell me prescription medications, I already told you that I'm not interested," he answered with his normal muddled accent. Troy was American, but had spent nearly half of his life outside of the country.

"Troy, it's me, Lydia. How are you?"

"Ah, Lydia. How did things go in Egypt?"

"Not good." She sighed. She wanted to voice her annoyance. Continually, she'd been diverted from her original mission of finding a particular miracle plant. Instead, she kept to the most relevant disaster. "I'm afraid they got away with the plates." After all the plates were related to her plant, and if she could find them, she might also discover the secrets behind this moss she was searching for.

There was a brief pause on the other line. Then Troy continued, "I doubt this is the worst of our problems. Our informants have discovered that Shen Mao is holding a private auction tonight for some very big players."

"You mean he's going to auction off the plates?" she asked.

"Even worse, we've learned that he's prepared a demonstration."

Lydia thought for a minute. Then with a bit of understanding, she pried, "That means he must have something other than just the plates. Who's invited to this party?"

"That's what has us worried," Troy said. "He has weapon developers from Iran, North Korea, and a few others. He's also got some names associated with drug cartels in Mexico and China. Your friend Grisha isn't going to like this one, either, but they have a few aeronautical hotshots that are investing billions into the privatization of space travel, among whom are some shady characters from Russia."

Lydia was a little confused. "Why would they invite all those types of people to bid on a plant and some old plates?"

"I doubt they have your plant, and there's more in those plates than just gardening instructions," he replied. "They also contain history and technology designs."

"What kind of technology are we talking about?" Lydia asked.

"Well . . ." Troy hesitated. "The pieces of papyrus we have suggest that they could also contain a schematic for the propulsion drive that brought our ancestors to Earth."

Lydia could see where Troy was going with this, but she let him continue. "If they were able to find not only the plates in the wreck, but also the module that makes the propulsion drive operate, they could build a working replica of the engine."

"But if they're having a demonstration tonight," Lydia said, "how could they assemble something as complex as that in such a short time?"

"I don't know. But one thing is certain: Shen Mao must not be allowed to power up such a machine."

Lydia confirmed with renewed determination, "I'll

be there in nine hours, but you may need to take a group over there in case I get held up."

"We're already there," Troy said, to Lydia's surprise.

"Be careful," she cautioned. "Mao has a bunch of goons and all you have are a few tall men with no combat experience."

Troy gave a half laugh. "I never thought I'd want a gal to come to my rescue, but I'll be happy when you show up."

With that, they ended their call. Lydia had only one call left to make and that was to her contact in Hong Kong. Their connecting flight to the Philippines would be a private charter. Her contact would need to have it stocked with weapons and be ready to go upon her arrival.

Chapter 12

Troy got off the plane at Lapu-Lapu with three other men, all of whom were close to seven feet tall. Troy was the shortest at six foot five. Upon landing he began looking for the men who'd stolen Lydia's jet in Egypt. It had landed here only minutes before his plane touched down.

Troy knew that if he was to stop the demonstration in Bohol from happening, then he must seize the package before it left Cebu. The men who'd stolen the jet, however, were no longer in the airport. All they'd left were a few customs agents they'd either bribed or schmoozed their way around. But when Troy stepped into the parking lot, he received his first stroke of luck.

On the other side of the lot, Troy witnessed all the men who fit the custom agents' description piling into a jeepney. After counting them, he noticed one extra Filipino that the custom agents hadn't mentioned. Troy assumed that the extra Filipino must have been there to meet them with the jeepney. Troy and his men ran to intercept them, but the passenger truck pulled out of the parking lot before they could catch up. Troy looked around where the truck had been. He saw one man who was obviously dead. A couple others were also dead or unconscious. This brutality only confirmed that the men who'd driven away were the ones he was looking for.

He hailed a taxi and they all struggled to fit in. "Follow that jeepney," he directed the driver. The driver didn't see any jeepney, but started off down the road. There was after all, only one way to leave the airport grounds.

"Hurry up!" Troy said to coax the driver faster. Luckily the road leading away from the airport was long and exclusive. By the time it merged into regular traffic, Troy spotted the jeepney that was turning into the main strip that ran along the western end of Lapu-Lapu. This road would eventually lead over the bridge to Cebu. "See them?" He nudged the driver and pointed. "Follow them!

"Okay, boss," the driver said, then asked, "You know how far we go?"

Troy replied, "Nope, but we'll pay you for your time."

Troy guessed the driver had never driven a cab with so many tall men before, but the driver didn't seem too worried "So, you American G.I. Joe?" he asked with a grin that showed several missing teeth. "Or you come for pretty girl?"

"We're just here on business," Troy replied. "In fact, we're scientists."

"Ah, you very-very smart," the driver said. "I don't

go to college, because is poor in the Philippines.”

Troy sighed. “That’s too bad.” He wanted to focus on the mission at hand. But he could already tell that the driver loved the opportunity to practice his English.

The driver then continued, “My daughter, she go to college. Maybe you like, you see her? She very-very pretty.” He then bobbed his eyebrows at Troy in an unmistakable hinting gesture, as if his words failed to bring his obvious intentions to light.

Troy stole a glance in the rearview mirror and noticed his colleagues snickering. He slumped lower in the seat. He hoped they wouldn’t have far to go.

Chapter 13

With Gual as the navigator, Flint maneuvered the sluggish jeepney over the bridge while heading into the crowded streets of Cebu.

"And he looked toward Sodom and Gomorrah, and toward all the land of the plain, and beheld, and, lo, the smoke of the country went up as the smoke of a furnace.' Genesis 19:28," Monk said as he pointed northward at a heaping cloud of black smoke.

"What is that smoke from?" Flint asked.

Gual replied with little care, "That is place of burning the tires."

"It shall not be quenched night nor day; the smoke thereof shall go up for ever: from generation to generation it shall lie waste.' Isaiah 34:10?" Monk asked.

Gual stared at Monk with a quizzical look, then turned to Flint. "He talk hard words?"

Flint interpreted, "He just wants to know if they always burn tires there, or if it's just today."

"They burn all days," Gual said slowly, trying to place all his words carefully.

"Galatians 5:19: 'Now the works of the flesh are manifest, which are these; Adultery, fornication, *uncleanness,* lasciviousness," Monk began, emphasizing uncleanliness. "For this ye know, that no whoremonger, no *unclean* person, nor covetous man, who is an idolater, hath any inheritance in the kingdom of Christ and of God.' Ephesians 5:5."

Flint smiled as he saw Gual's confused face. "Don't worry about it, let's focus on finding Philip." Then he banged his palm on the panel behind the seat and yelled, "Hey, sweetheart, how are you doing back there?"

Dusty's muted reply evidenced her frustration. "Let me out or I'm going to start shooting!"

Flint laughed with only a hint of anxiety, "I almost forgot that I left her back there with all my guns."

Gual gave a nervous groan; to which Monk replied, "It is better to dwell in the wilderness, than with a contentious and an angry woman.' Proverbs 21:19."

"Ha, I wouldn't worry too much about her." Flint smiled. "If you ask me, she's harmless."

Then Flint rapped his knuckles on the panel again and shouted back, "You just sit tight, honey, and we'll be stopping shortly." Then he turned to Gual. "We are close, aren't we?"

"O-yes," he replied. "Maybe three kilometer."

###

In the back of the jeepney, Dusty clenched her

fists in frustration. Looking at the gun, she wondered if she dared to use it. Even if she did, she wasn't sure if she could live with herself if she actually hit someone. But nobody was paying attention to her. She knew from her talks with Philip that Flint was a good guy, but right now she felt like the victim.

The pistol was warm and heavy in her hands. She studied it carefully and could not find a safety switch. Instead of shooting at anyone, she decided to just shoot a hole in the ceiling to show them that she was serious. So pointing the gun upward, she squinted and pulled the trigger.

When she heard a dry click, she jumped and almost fell back. The firearm didn't have a shell in the chamber. The anticipation of the shot had scared her more than anything else. As she tried to calm her breathing, she slowly pulled the gun in closer to examine it.

Growing up, Dusty had only shot guns a few times. Her father had a couple of shotguns and a .22-caliber rifle. She'd shot a pistol once, and that was during one of the few dates she had gone on in college. Despite her lack of experience, she didn't think it would be too hard to operate the weapon. Grabbing the slider, she strained slightly to pull it all the way back. She could almost feel the destructive power of that one bullet now sliding into the chamber. When she was ready to fire, a chill coursed down her spine.

Pointing the gun skyward again, she didn't hesitate. She pulled the trigger and the gun leaped out of her hand. The confined space in the back of the jeepney echoed the report of the shot so strongly that her ears ached with a distinct ringing. The whole world muted and as she pressed her hands tight to the side of her head, she was unable to stop from sobbing.

Outside, two stories up, a woman sitting on the deck of her street-side apartment hand-scrubbing the family's laundry heard a small thud from down in the street, just a moment before a bucket of laundry water above her on the third floor burst, raining dirty suds all over her.

Down below on the jeepney, the Filipinos who were standing on the bumper jumped off, holding on to a grab bar connected to the back of the automobile. They ran and skipped as the jeepney moved along. But it was going too fast, and when it made a sudden swerve, they were forced to let go. Staggering and tumbling, they came to rest with little more than a few scrapes and bruises. Traffic was busy but light compared to a normal day in Cebu City. They were able to avoid getting hit, and found their way off the street.

With shaken nerves one of them said in their Visayan tongue, "What do we do now? Gual and Joe are gone, and we have no money and no way of getting home."

The Filipino who'd taken the first tumble off the jeepney limped up and smiled as he pulled out a small wad of dollar bills that he'd stashed from the airplane. They laughed, and limped away.

Back on the jeepney, less than a minute after Dusty had fired the gun, Gual was acting like a cornered feral cat. Squirming and shouting, he bumped into Flint, causing him to swerve the jeepney.

"Monk, can you give me a hand with this guy?" Flint asked.

Monk reached over and, with a simple pinch of

his finger and twist of his wrist, he applied enough pressure to Gual's hand to make him freeze in his seat. Then Monk said, attempting to reassure the frightened Filipino, "'Always aim at complete harmony of thought and word and deed. Always aim at purifying your thoughts and everything will be well.' Mahatma Gandhi."

Flint just turned to Gual and asked, "If Monk lets you go, will you calm down?"

Gual nodded slightly. Monk released him.

Shaking, Gual asked, "She try kill us?"

"I don't think so," Flint replied. "She didn't shoot into the front where we are and she only fired once. I think we'll be fine. But just in case, we should hurry up and get to where we're going."

Chapter 14

The taxi driver eased on his brakes. Troy watched bewildered as the men who were standing on the back of the jeepney jumped off. The jeepney was still moving and the men ran deliberately, holding to the back. Then the driver swerved and the men lost their grips and tripped on their legs, which were too slow to keep up with their momentum.

The taxi driver turned to Troy and asked, "You want to stop—see if your friends are okay?"

"No, don't worry about them," Troy said. "They'll be fine. Keep following that truck."

The driver shrugged and began talking about the bus system. "You know, if a bus here hit a man, it will back up and hit him again to kill him."

Troy decided to entertain the driver's relentless need to talk; it was easier than explaining why they were following the jeepney. "Why's that?" he asked.

The driver shifted in his seat and began to rant, "You see, my friend, it cost more to take a man to hospital than to pay for funeral. The bus company are very-very big. They get away with many bad thing because of bad politic."

"So there's a little corruption in the government?" Troy asked.

"Some, yes," the driver replied. "But still the Philippines is best place to live on Earth. Very beautiful, and very-very good people. But bus company—no good."

Troy was amused by the driver's story. He had seen much of the world, but had never heard of anything like this. "So why doesn't anyone turn them in?"

The driver replied, "Because they find you. If you talk, they send men and kill you. Filipino are good people, but very-very poor. They not have way of protecting from killer. So if they see the bus kill the person, they keep the mouth shut."

"That's awful," Troy agreed, not missing the irony that this guy couldn't seem to keep his own mouth shut.

"Yes, very-very bad," the driver continued. "But in America, you all very-very rich. You see something, you pay, and everyone know. Bad people get scared to find you."

Troy had listened to him talk about being poor so many times that he found himself defending the wealth of the rest of the world. "It's true, we have more money, but everything we buy also costs a lot more."

This moved the driver from talking about the buses to talking about riches. Troy kicked himself for shifting the conversation to money, but then the jeepney ahead made an abrupt turn into a small street. The street was only big enough for one car to creep into at a time. Troy recognized it for what it was: the end of the line.

"Don't follow them in," Troy said to the driver. "We'll walk from here. What do we owe you?"

The driver didn't have a meter. However, he was familiar with these two parts of the islands, and he said, "Two hundred and forty peso, please."

Troy guessed it was more than what he should have paid. But since that only equated to about five American dollars, he didn't argue.

After the taxi had driven away, they walked down the small alley that the jeepney had gone into. The alley could have concealed a Filipino fairly well, but not a group of seven-foot-tall men. Still, they crouched and snuck along the edges of the walls to hide their movements as much as possible.

At the end, they found the jeepney. It was just coming to a stop. While the narrow alley continued on, there was only one opening on the left wall near the truck. The next opening was a good fifty feet farther down the alley, it was obvious where they were about to go. Troy motioned for one of his men to come forward. Handing him a case, Troy entered a combination into the locks. Once the case was opened, he removed a small Glock for each man in his party. They all cocked their weapons and snuck down a three-foot-wide path.

While not all of the men had received official military combat training, they all knew the stakes. They were prepared to kill or be killed. Troy prided himself on always finding the right people for the job. These men were hard, handy men, and dedicated to their cause.

Chapter 15

Gual had led Flint into a narrow alley to park the jeepney. "We walk now," he said.

Flint killed the engine and stepped out the door. Only he didn't see anybody hanging on to the back of the jeepney.

"Hala!" Gual cried out. *"Asa man sila?"* Then, looking at Flint, he asked, "Where are they?"

Flint's eyes stung with anger. He threw open the back doors and saw Dusty sitting near the rear with the gun at her feet. First Flint snatched the gun and his backpack. There was still that crunchy newspaper feel to the pack, letting him know that Dusty either hadn't discovered or cared about the stash of cash he'd taken from the jet. Then reaching over, he grabbed Dusty by the arm, saying, "Where are my friends? Did you shoot them?"

Dusty allowed herself to be easily pulled from the jeepney. She looked up at Flint. "I shot through the roof." She pointed at the small hole in the ceiling of the truck. "But when I did, they jumped off the back. Last I saw, they were walking away toward the side of the road."

Flint heard only one shot, and he had no reason to doubt Dusty's words. Trusting that the men were okay, he switched topics to the task at hand. "Gual here has helped me get this far, now I need you to help me find Philip."

Dusty looked up at Flint. "I'll help you, and by the way, I really am sorry for all the trouble I've caused you."

"So you're being nice now?" Flint asked.

The corners of Dusty's eyes collected a small pool of tears. "Please, I didn't have a choice. Marshal is a maniac. He would have killed me if I hadn't told him about you."

"Well, now's your chance to redeem yourself. Lucky for you I'm not very good at holding a grudge, especially against a beautiful woman with wet sea-green eyes."

Dusty's face went red and she couldn't help letting a small smile show. Flint was aware that in his present condition he looked like a rather rugged man. Sure, he was dirty and a little smelly, but he thought that might carry certain appeal in her eyes.

She led the way. She stole an occasional look back at him. He'd come to rescue her, and somehow had the feeling that he'd just captured her, in perhaps more ways than one.

Flint grit his teeth. That was a thought for later. He had Philip to worry about.

The narrow path that led between a few buildings opened into a large courtyard after thirty meters.

Dusty turned to Flint and warned, "There's only one guard left behind. It will be the one that got away at the airport, so he'll be expecting you." She then pointed at four buildings. "The one on the right is the guards' quarters; next to it is Marshal's. Behind that is the shed where they keep everything from weapons to artifacts. Philip will be in the back corner shed right by it."

Flint turned to Gual and said, "I want you to hide right here. You've been great so far."

Gual protested, "You save me, I help."

"No," Flint argued. "This is my fight, and you've done enough."

Gual reluctantly tucked himself behind a bush. Flint suspected that secretly Gual was relieved to be out of the line of fire. Monk stepped forward and quoted, "Joshua 6:25: 'And Joshua saved Rahab the harlot alive, and her father's household, and all that she had; and she dwelleth in Israel even unto this day; because she hid the messengers, which Joshua sent to spy out Jericho.'"

"He's right," Flint said to Dusty. "You should hide here with Gual until we get back."

With Flint's quick interpretation, Dusty understood what Monk was trying to say but maintained a confused expression as Gual stepped back out and grabbed her arm.

"He okay, man," Gual said to her. "He just talk in hard words—even for me."

"But, I—" Dusty protested.

Flint chuckled. "It's all right, just wait, we'll be back in no time."

Flint pulled out his AK-47 and skirted the fence. Monk had already split off, snaking his way in the opposite direction. Monk however, preferred not to carry a weapon. Flint carefully examined the buildings where somebody might choose to hide. He snuck completely around one building and near the shed where Philip was supposed to be. To get to Philip, he would have to expose himself to the open property.

Debating his options, he saw movement across from him It was between Marshal's house and the other shed. Flint lifted his rifle, hoping he could resolve the problem without killing anybody else. Flint followed the person's shadow. His heartbeat quickened, causing him to perspire and breathe harder. Trying to steady his gun, he watched and waited with his sweaty finger on the trigger. Just as the head popped up, he quickly lowered the rifle. Flint wondered how Monk could have crossed that distance so quickly. Flint then motioned that he was going to the shed. Monk returned a simple nod.

Hoping that he'd been quiet enough not to alert the guard, Flint made his way into the open. Once he arrived at the shed, he found chains wrapped around two small holes, one in the wall and one in the door. As quietly as he could, he unwrapped the heavy links. The only thing securing them was a metal hook that wedged them into place.

The door creaked slightly as he pulled it open. Cursing the rusty hinges, Flint took a quick scan around. Monk disappeared, but Flint wasn't worried. Nobody seemed to be around. Then pulling the door open a little more, Flint slipped inside.

The shed was poorly constructed, and light shone through all sides. It didn't take long to see there was nobody within. Flint relaxed his grip on the rifle in despair. It seemed his only hope now was that Philip had escaped while the guards were at the airport.

A creak of the door and the shuffle of feet snapped Flint back to attention. In an instant he spun around, and his rifle was up, aimed at the man. The man was clearly unarmed. As he staggered into a ray of light, Flint's eyes could only make out a silhouette. Then he saw it. The haggard man was none other than Philip. His mentor's face was terribly bloodied, bruised, and swollen. A distressed and confused look ran across Flint's own face, but was instantly transformed into near panic when he saw someone hiding behind Philip. The mercenary who'd sped off in the Mercedes at the airport, now had a rifle trained on Philip.

"Don't even think about it," the mercenary said in a stern voice.

Flint let his gun fall to the ground. It made an almost tinkering sound as if he'd let a child's toy hit the compacted dirt. The mercenary then trained his weapon on Flint and said, "You have come a long way just to die. Your friends killed one of mine. When I'm done with you two, they'll die too."

Philip then mumbled, "It's about time."

"So you're ready to die, old man?" The mercenary laughed.

"Just one question," Philip said.

The mercenary conceded, "Go on."

"Why is it that bad guys always talk so much before they kill someone?" Philip tried unsuccessfully to smile.

The mercenary answered, "Don't worry, your wait is over." With that, two loud cracks sounded, followed by the thud of two bodies hitting the floor.

Chapter 16

Marshal handed the cab driver a small wad of bills and said, "I may need a ride back in a little while. Can you stay around?"

The driver looked at Marshal and replied, "Thank you, good-bye."

"Wait, wait!" Marshal exclaimed as the man began to ease off his brakes. "Are you going to be around here in a little while?"

The driver realized that he was being asked a question, but his English wasn't sufficient to comprehend. He looked up at Marshal with a blank expression, raised his hands and he said, "No English good."

Marshal looked to his mercenary companion as if he might know any better way of communicating. The mercenary's solution was to get in the driver's face and shout more loudly and slowly, *"Are you go-ing to be around here in a little while?"*

The driver leaned back to avoid being spit on. Marshal threw up his hands and proclaimed, "This is getting us nowhere." Turning to the mercenary, he instructed, "We need a car in case this thing goes south."

The mercenary reached for the small of his back, a half smile spread over his lips. Marshal interjected, "Let's not make too much noise, or, for that matter, too much of a mess."

The mercenary nodded, reached in the window, and grabbed the driver by the head. The driver had little time to react as he was pulled halfway out of the car. The muffled squeal of the driver's protest was more acceptable than the thunder of a bullet. With one arm locked around the driver's neck, the mercenary tightened his grip. His muscles flexed till both men heard a sickening pop.

The driver went limp.

Marshal and the mercenary moved him into the backseat. They placed a hat over his bloodshot eyes to make him appear to be sleeping. Then Marshal took the keys out of the ignition and stepped away from the car with one of the briefcases he had brought with him. As if nothing had happened, the two men started casually walking up to Shen Mao's mansion.

Unlike Marshal's temporary facility in Cebu, Shen Mao had made a permanent home in this cluster of islands. Bohol was most famous for the geological phenomenon called the Chocolate Hills. A lesser-known fact of the seismically active island was that Bohol was home to some of the most crys-tal-clear waters and white sandy beaches in the world. Jagna was no exception. Though the rivers were stacked high with garbage, the beaches were paradisaical.

Instead of knocking on the door, or ringing a bell, Marshal called out the traditional Filipino greeting, *"Ayo-ayo!"*

Within a minute, a middle-aged Chinese woman opened the door. "Marshal Steel, Shen Mao has been expecting you. Come in."

Marshal entered, and took a look around. While the jet Mao had loaned him was immaculately decorated, it didn't compare to the luxury of his home. There were jade statues that stood almost two meters tall. In the center of the entry hall was a beautifully carved fountain. The red material had a mysterious and ancient appearance. On top of this fountain was a large, shiny metallic-looking pool. Rotating in the center of the fountain's pool was a shiny-pewter, maybe even platinum-looking sphere.

Marshal's curiosity compelled him to touch the eerie liquid, but as soon as he raised a finger to it, the familiar accent of the Chinese businessman stopped him. "Marshal Steel, I am pleased that you have arrived. I see that you have taken interest in my fountain."

Marshal retracted his hand and replied, "I've never seen anything quite like it before."

"And never are you likely to see another like it again," Mao stated. "I had it custom made. In ancient days the Chinese believed it was possible to make special life-altering elixirs from the mysterious liquid metal called mercury. Folklore even talks of elixirs refined from cinnabar that could bestow immortality. You may consider yourself lucky that you did not touch the deadly metal just a moment ago."

Marshal swallowed hard but tried not to show his embarrassment. Mao continued, "The base is carved from cinnabar, the amazing ore from which mercury is refined. The fountain symbolizes the refinement from a coarse state of existence to a pure state of being, in which eternal life is complete in an eternal round. Death is a natural step in the eternal nature of things. Therefore, though ironic, this deadly centerpiece is my own proverbial fountain of immortality."

Before Marshal had a chance to realize it, the Chinese woman who'd answered the door was next to him, reaching for the briefcase. He reacted by pulling away slightly.

"Please, Mr. Steel, do not mind my assistant; she merely wishes to bring the objects to me."

"I'm sorry," Marshal said. "I haven't let this out of my sight since Egypt. I guess I'm just a little skittish about letting it go." Marshal stepped forward to hand the case to Mao.

Mao only looked him in the eye as the woman came up again and snatched the case from Marshal. Mao then turned around and asked, "Mr. Steel, won't you please follow me. I have something you might find very interesting."

As they began walking, Mao paused. Without looking back he stated, "Mr. Steel, you are quite safe here. Please instruct your guard to remain behind."

The woman lifted her arm, pointing to the main lobby and said, "Wait here until they return. You may help yourself to some refreshments on the serving table." Marshal took a short breath as if to protest, but held his tongue. *Is Mao trying to get me alone?* He didn't like the idea, but didn't feel like he had a choice. They all left the lone mercenary and turned down another hallway.

The next room they entered was larger than the lobby. It had several folding tables set up. A kitchen nearby emanated sounds and smells that hinted at a large dinner party. "Any time now, my guests will arrive. Your timing on delivering the device was exceptional."

"I don't think I understand," Marshal said.

"Come, I will show you," Mao replied. Then he walked to the edge of the room, where a beautiful glass staircase seemed to float next to the wall. Mao moved up the staircase with ease. Marshal hugged the side of the wall, since the floating staircase had no railing on the open side. The woman followed quietly behind.

The upper loft was more of an outdoor deck than a room. A roof-like pergola covered most of the platform, allowing for a constant breeze of fresh ocean air. The view all around was spectacular. Marshal almost forgot about his caution. Soaking up the atmosphere, Mao called him over to the center of the platform.

The serenity of the deck was such a welcome distraction, that Marshal nearly missed Mao's centerpiece entirely. Mao directed him over to something about the size of a small to medium steel shipping container. Instead of being a true rectangular shape with graffiti all around, this one was plain and rounded on all sides. The large door on one end had been welded tight, with a round hatch installed on the top. The more he examined the container, the more it resembled a submarine. Even the top hatch had a large wheel lock, just like a submarine door. Two tubes protruded from each side of the object, and ran over the edge of the rooftop patio into the yard, where a few large motors of some sort were resting.

"I give up," Marshal stated. "What is it?"

"Please, Mr. Steel," Mao said with a disappointed

look on his face. "This is what you have been dream-
ing of for the last several years."

Marshal's eyes lit up, and he walked over to examine it. "It can't be, it's too small."

The woman set the briefcase down on a small
glass table, right next to a thick tan folder. A thin
Korean man, who held the air of a gentleman, joined
the woman. He wasn't another server, but one of
Mao's scientific engineers. Promptly he opened the
case that Marshal had previously surrendered to the
woman. Disappointed, Marshal expected more of a
reaction from the three as the heavy sphere was revealed. Seated next to it, in its own foamed-off compartment, was a book made of thin golden plates.

Mao leaned over, but his examination was brief.
Looking back to the Korean scientist, he instructed,
"You may begin your assessment of the device."

The scientist gently removed the sphere. Then,
pulling out a loupe, and with disciplined patience,
he studied every square millimeter of its surface under the ten-power jewelry magnifier.

Five minutes into the inspection, Marshal found
himself increasingly uneasy. Shen Mao had given no
hint of betrayal, so he wondered if he'd simply been
paranoid. His anticipation also began to build, as
well as his impatience. Mao, on the contrary, sat almost motionless on the thickened rail with his legs
crossed, and his arms calmly folded over his knee.

Marshal could stand it no longer and began to
pace. Strolling over to Mao, he asked, "What is taking so long? It is the genuine part."

"Mr. Steel," Mao said with a degree of annoyance.
"I fully trust that the part is genuine. That is not the
purpose of the inspection."

"Well, unless you plan on actually putting it in
that machine you built . . ." Marshal hesitated as he

began to understand.

"I see that you are finally beginning to grasp the situation," Mao said with a slight smirk.

"But how?" Marshal asked. "You didn't even know what to expect until I called you with its description. How can you build a ship without knowing how it works?"

Mao motioned to the woman, who was standing in the background. She stepped over to the table and retrieved the thick tan folder. She took it directly to Marshal instead of Mao. Marshal paced over to the low rail near Mao and rested the folder before opening it. On the first leaf of the folder, Marshal recognized the photocopy of an ancient papyrus. Some of the symbols on it resembled those from the ship he'd excavated. Most, however, were from old Aramaic writings.

"Those are from scrolls dating back to 1000 B.C.," Mao pointed out. "You will find the translations on the next leaf of the folder."

Marshal could hardly believe what he was looking at. Without turning away from the pages, he marveled, "These are blueprints and instructions for their ship. Where did you get these?"

"You see," Mao began. "I have not hired you in vain. I knew all along what I was looking for. I only needed you to help me find it."

Marshal looked up. "But if you have all the plans here, why did you need that part from the ship? Couldn't you just make it?"

"In their wisdom, the ancient Martian descendants separated the plans of the ship from the plans of the engine," Mao explained. "Those scrolls were not the first documents to come from the ship. They, however, made mention of that golden book. In it there is a complete history of their voyage and scientific achievement. There are many more people out there who would kill for that book.

Pieces of it were transferred to scrolls and handed down through many generations. The set of scrolls you see before you are only a small portion of that book."

"So you're telling me that with this golden record, you'll be able to make more ships like this one?"

"I'm afraid that I have too few ambitions toward space travel," Mao replied. "That will be for someone else to do. World peace. Now that is something I don't mind working on. Tonight is one step closer to that dream. I've got money. I'll soon have more. At a certain point, wealth only has utility if one becomes a philanthropist."

World peace? thought Marshal. *How does that fit with Mao?*

"I'm sure you have noticed that I am preparing for guests tonight."

Marshal nodded.

Mao continued, "They are very wealthy and powerful people. After we dine tonight, they will all be brought up here for a demonstration. After the demonstration, we will open the bidding at five billion American dollars. Mr. Steel, I do not wish to fly around in space. I simply want a very comfortable retirement."

"I don't mean to sound selfish," Marshal stated. "But what of our deal? I was told that I'd be able to have passage between here and Mars for archaeological purposes."

"I assure you," Mao said. "You will reap all that you have sown." He then paused and addressed his Korean scientist. "Mr. Jung Ho, what is your analysis?"

Turning around, Marshal noticed the Korean

standing tall. He'd been ready for a few minutes now and was patiently waiting for Mao to finish with Marshal.

"Our theories seem correct," Jung Ho reported. "The device shows minor corrosion, but I believe its integrity has been preserved in good enough condition to work."

"Wait a minute," Marshal interrupted. "How can something that old have survived long enough to still be usable?"

Mao replied, "It is simple. When traveling through space, they might have carried their own air. Since the people of Mars were eventually able to blend in on our planet, we can assume that their anatomy was also similar. Therefore, like us, they would have lived in an oxygen-rich, and possibly humid environment while traveling through space. Most parts of their ship would need to be made out of material that would not corrode easily from the heightened oxygen. Thus they would also logically make their most critical component very durable and resilient."

"You still took a very big risk," Marshal pointed out.

"Oh, how is that?" Mao inquired.

"This." Marshal pointed all around. "You're going to auction off a piece of technology that you aren't even sure works? I never took you for a gambling man."

"Everything in life is a gamble, Mr. Steel. I gambled that I could put my trust in you. I gambled that my breakfast did not contain harmful bacteria. Yes, I even gambled on this device to work for my auction tonight. However, I always hedge my bets. If the device does not perform, then I will sell the golden book and let them find a way to make it work on their own. In any case, I see a very profitable evening tonight."

Mao then instructed Jung Ho to install the device. First he undid the hatch, revealing that the container was not the actual vessel, as Marshal had previously imagined. Inside the hatch was a smaller object that looked like a one-man submersible. It was suspended within the chamber by a series of strong magnets. Jung Ho reached inside and lifted the panel off a compartment.

Inside the compartment, it looked similar to the mechanicals that held the device on the original Martian ship. Jung Ho then placed the orb and closed the ship's compartment. With a cordless drill, four screws were placed on each corner of the compartment, securing the panel. He then closed the larger hatch that held the suspended vessel.

"So why would you put the ship in a container like that?" Marshal asked. "Wouldn't it be easier to show off outside that steel coffin?"

"Mr. Steel," Mao said, sounding slightly irritated. "You are an anthropologist, and I trust your knowledge there completely, but as far as the science of the machine is concerned, I have my own experts in that field. Now if you would excuse me, I have guests arriving, to whom I must attend."

As his unscrupulous host led Marshal back down the stairs to the lobby, a sudden craving for waffles entered Marshal's mind. The thought was almost real enough to smell the peanut butter and raspberry freezer jam on the morning pastry. He could even smell the boysenberry syrup drizzled over his fully loaded comfort food.

Marshal knew this to be a trick of his own mind, but a useful one. In his mind, it was that foreboding voice of warning. It was telling him that he needed to be as far from this place as possible. Marshal wanted to listen to his prompting, but also knew that if he fled the mansion, he'd lose all hope of attaining his goal.

At the bottom of the stairs, his guard was not to be found. This only increased his discomfort. Instead there were six men. Two were obviously of high importance. Each had two men as guards. From their cool, undeviating posture and sharp eyes, the silent guards carried a professional attitude, much like the mercenaries that Marshal had in his employ.

Cursing under his breath, Marshal could see that his opportunity was diminishing. Mao's promise to let him use the technology for a visit to Mars appeared to be a lie. As Mao was greeting the two newcomers, Marshal slipped out the door and headed for the taxi. The "sleeping" driver still lay in the back with the hat covering his face. Opening the door and ignoring the body, he grabbed the other briefcase filled with canisters of nerve gas. *That ship will be mine*, he decided.

Mao was still with the other two guests when Marshal walked back into the mansion. Sneaking a quick glance, he noticed that Mao was busy showing off some Chinese artifacts that decorated his lobby. Seeing the opportunity, he climbed back up to the rooftop.

On the table next to the small ship was the briefcase that originally held the propulsion unit and golden plates. The case was shut and Marshal picked it up. Judging by the weight of the briefcase, Marshal concluded that the plates were still inside. Not wanting to risk being found, he quickly swapped the two briefcases.

He wished that Mao had explained a little more how to operate the device. Now he'd have to wait until after the explanation in front of the guests to make his move.

On the way back to the stairs, he heard a little commotion. Somebody was coming up. Rushing over to the side rails of the deck, he leaned over and placed the briefcase on a small concrete ledge. It was out of sight from the main deck, and the railing was thick enough to conceal the shiny case.

Coming up the stairs was the Chinese lady-butler. She found Marshal leaning up against a pillar looking out over the sea. "Mr. Steel, what brings you back up here?" she asked.

"I just liked the fresh air so much that I thought I'd come back up and enjoy it," he replied.

"Please come with me," she beckoned. "Your friend, the one you arrived with, is looking for you."

Marshal followed her back down the stairs. Instead of going to the lobby where the other guests were visiting, she took him to a separate waiting room.

Seeing Marshal, his guard stood up quickly. "Hey, boss, sorry I didn't wait for you in the lobby. When those rich muthers showed up, they asked me to come in here." Then sitting back down on the sofa, he continued, "I guess they don't want us *nobodies* spoiling the evening."

Marshal found a sofa across from his guard, and thanked the lady. As soon as she was gone, he leaned forward and began to speak to his companion. "I think my fears are justified. My *other* briefcase is in place, so after dinner, I think it best that you grab your duffel bag in the taxi also."

The man smiled back at Marshal. His bleached white teeth almost glowed against his dark-brown skin. "Yeah, I think this party needs a little excitement, anyway."

Chapter 17

Dusty crouched behind a tall prickly hedge just inside the courtyard of Marshal's complex. She'd spent months working out of this complex. It was a crude compound, but mandated by Marshal's financier.

The rotting cinder-block buildings fit in perfectly with the surrounding neighborhood. She had walked these grounds countless times, but now found herself hiding next to a Filipino who she thought had been blown up in Egypt.

"I'm sorry, Gual," she said. A futile atonement for abandoning him.

Gual looked at Dusty with sympathetic eyes and said, "You okay fine. You not the bad. Other man is the bad."

"I know," Dusty said. "But I didn't try hard

enough to stop him from hurting you guys.”

“Good that G.I. Joe Flint save us,” Gual said with a smile.

Dusty already knew that Flint wasn’t with the military. She also knew that Gual didn’t think so either. She’d spent enough time around here to know that most Filipinos referred to Americans as Joe. She guessed it had to do with their military presence during World War II.

Dusty nodded but said nothing.

“So,” Gual mentioned slowly. “Flint very-very *guapo*. You very-very pretty, too.”

Dusty looked into Gual’s face to see what he was driving at.

“You and Flint maybe boyfriend, maybe girl-friend?” he asked.

“Are you kidding me?” Dusty said with a blush. “I just barely met the guy. Even then, I didn’t make a good first impression.”

“Aeh.” Gual shrugged his shoulders. “He come for help you. I see you look at him, soft eyes.” Gual then did his best impression of a love-struck woman.

Dusty allowed a small laugh.

Gual put his finger to his mouth to shush her. She went quiet. They both heard footsteps approaching.

Dusty and Gual remained hidden as four tall men passed by. Dusty was able to sneak a peek, but she didn’t recognize any of them. She did, however, notice that each one was carrying a pistol.

“We need to warn Flint and his friend,” Dusty whispered to Gual.

Gual pulled her back down as she was starting to get up. “No,” he whispered. “You stay.”

Dusty obeyed, even though it pained her to do

so. Her heart pounded, and she willed it to slow down. She was sure that Gual could even hear it, and maybe even the men who'd just passed by. Still, she risked another look. The men had stopped only ten feet beyond the hedge where she and Gual were concealed.

The four men were whispering to themselves then suddenly, they stopped. One of them pointed toward the shack that Flint had gone into. From her vantage point, Dusty couldn't see the shed, but she had a fairly clear view of the space just in front of it. The direction the new men were pointing revealed a man she remembered as Ham. He was pushing Philip with the tip of a rifle into where the shed would be.

With the four other men distracted, Dusty crawled a little farther out so she could see the shed and what was happening there.

Ham had stopped just outside the door and Dusty assumed he was talking to Flint. Ham then raised his gun to shoot, but then one of the tall men from behind stepped up and shot twice.

Ham fell forward.

Dusty turned to Gual. "Those guys just shot the last mercenary!"

Chapter 18

Flint opened his eyes, slowly at first, then he dared himself to focus. He looked at the two men on the ground. One was the mercenary. The other was Philip. The mercenary had two small slugs buried in his back. The impact of the bullets had knocked him forward, causing him to fall into Philip.

Philip also looked surprised to be alive.

Coming to his senses, Flint looked out to see who the shooter was. With the sun at his back, Flint couldn't make out any figure. "Hey Monk, since when did you decide to play with guns?" Flint said, then bent down for his AK-47.

"I wouldn't do that if I were you," said a stern voice from outside the shed.

The voice was obviously not from Monk. Flint paused to watch as a tall silhouette moved into the doorway.

The man continued, "If you want to end up like your friend, just try and pick up your gun."

Flint put his hands above his head, and took a step away from the gun. "Who are you?"

The tall man motioned for him to get out, as he ordered, "Come outside, and if you try anything funny, I'll put a few holes in your chest, also."

Flint walked outside and saw four men. Two of them were scanning their surroundings. The speaker then directed one of his men to check on the prisoner.

Coming back out, he reported, "Their prisoner is in bad shape, but I think he'll live."

"I think it's time you give us that package," the man told Flint.

Dusty looked at Gual to see if he recognized the tall men who shot Ham.

Gual evidently didn't know them. He asked, "They good or bad?"

"I don't know," Dusty replied, her eyes deep with concern. "But I can't stand here any longer and watch."

Dusty got up to creep closer when she heard footsteps behind her. Without looking back she whispered, "I didn't think you were going to come."

The voice that replied wasn't from Gual. "I'm not here for long. I just need to grab something, then I'm heading over to Bohol."

Dusty knew the voice. It was the one man she loathed even more than Marshal. Turning around she stood face to face with the animal Sperl. He put his arm around her shoulder and asked, "What happened to your knight in shining armor?"

Dusty looked over toward the shed in time to see

Flint step out with his hands up. "They followed him there. Are they with you?"

Sperl stared hard for a minute then said, "Nope, but it looks like they're about to tie up one loose end for me. Come on, I need something."

Sperl pulled Dusty toward one of the buildings that was used for the mercenaries' quarters. When inside, he pulled out a duffel bag and put a MAC-10 machine pistol with several clips inside it. Then he added a sniper rifle that disassembled into two pieces. He added one box of large shells for the massive gun and zipped it up.

"Whaddaya say we go visit the romantic beaches of Bohol, honey?" Sperl said, with a twisted grin that sent a chill over Dusty's body.

Mustering her courage, she replied, "I don't think you're my type."

Sperl faked a hurt look, then forced a kiss on Dusty. She squirmed back and slapped the man hard. Sperl wasn't even affected. He just stepped closer and with a grin showed her how hard he could return her slap in the face. The impact of his open palm drove her to the ground.

"Maybe we'll meet up again sometime under different circumstances," Sperl said with his usual demonic grin.

Two more shots rang through the air. Stepping out the door, Sperl looked back toward the shed. One of the tall men was on the ground and the other three had run for cover. Standing behind Flint was the driver of the Mercedes that had left the airport ahead of everyone else.

"Way to go, Hammy," Sperl said, just loud enough for Dusty to hear. Then he casually walked out of the compound with the duffel bag across his shoulders.

Several more shots rang out, and Dusty sat on

the floor sobbing. "I hate you," she wanted to scream, but her voice only came out in a small, wispy whimper. She clenched her hands and sank lower on the floor. She waited for some minutes, not daring to look out the window to see Ham standing over the dying man she'd suddenly discovered a fondness for.

###

"Package?" Flint had asked. "I don't have any package. What are you talking about?"

The tall man scowled. "Don't play stupid with me. We've been following you, and we know that you have it. Now give it—"

He was cut short by the thunder of two more shots. Everyone dove for cover, except for the tall man and Flint. The tall man did an almost graceful spin before falling to the ground. Flint stood motionless as the mercenary stepped out of the shed.

The tall man looked up in horror as the mercenary stepped out with a rifle in his hands. He peppered the spots where the others had dived. He didn't hit anyone, but he kept them in hiding. Then he looked at Flint as he tore his shirt down a little, revealing a bulletproof vest. It appeared to be of the same make as the vest he'd swiped back in Egypt from the dead soldier. Yet another reminder that he was dealing with serious professionals.

"Never leave home without it," he said. "Now where were we? Oh yeah, I remember." He centered the barrel of the gun right on Flint's forehead.

Flint smiled and said, "It's been nice meeting you. Too bad we started off on the wrong foot."

The mercenary wrinkled his brow at the comment, but he never fired. He just stood frozen in place. A four-foot-long piece of rebar suddenly entered the soft part of his shoulder, near his neck, though only the top foot of it now showed.

Flint gave a salute to Monk, who was standing on top of the shed. Monk then turned around and disappeared again. Following this, Flint knelt down as he returned his attention to the tall man on the ground. He barely heard the mercenary's body fall to the ground as the other men rushed over.

"Troy!" one of them shouted. Followed by another asking, "How bad is it?"

Flint was gently examining the wound. He looked up at the others, who seemed unsure about what to do with their guns. Before they had a chance to threaten Flint again, he said to them, "Your friend here looks like he'll make it. Only one of the bullets caught him, and even at that, it just sliced through some of the meat on his shoulder."

Troy tried to get up, but labored under the pain that coursed through him. Had the inertia from the bullet not thrown him to the ground, he might not have known he was shot. But now the stinging sensation looked as if it had spread through his whole body. His suffering was clear as he looked at Flint and asked, "You don't have the plates, do you?"

"Sorry, pal," he replied. "I don't even know what you're talking about."

"But we followed you. Aren't you the one who stole our jet to get here?" Troy asked.

"Well, we did steal a jet that shot us down. We just thought it was these murderers." Flint gestured at the impaled mercenary. "We had no idea there were two groups of killers on the loose."

Troy just grunted in reply.

"So . . ." Flint hesitated. "Is anyone going to tell me who you are, and why everyone seems to want me dead?"

One of the other men chimed in, "We thought you were working for Shen Mao. We had to stop you."

"By the way," another man asked, "if you don't work for Mao, or Marshal, what are you doing here?"

"First off," Flint replied, "my name is Flint. Second, I don't know either of those men. I just came here to help out a girl, and to rescue my friend, which reminds me . . ."

Flint turned around to check on Philip, only to see him leaning up against Monk. His arm draped loosely around Monk's neck. "Thanks again," Flint said to Monk." Then, turning back around, Flint raised his voice. "Third, will somebody please explain what kind of hornet's nest I've gotten my head stuck in?"

The men helped Troy to his feet. As soon as he was standing, he said, "As you may have gathered, my name is Troy. We're part of a group that has been around since before the days of Moses. Shen Mao learned of us many years ago. He was able to steal an ancient record that was copied out of some sort of golden book of engravings. This record also contained some very important information, among which was the location of the original gold plates."

"A lot of violence for a little record. Maybe you ought to talk to the Mormons, don't they know something about gold plates?" Flint said.

"You don't understand," Troy continued. "Those engravings aren't just historically important, but dangerous. The book also contains important technological information. Plus, the site that he took it from may have had a working prototype of this technology."

Flint shook his head in disbelief. "So you're telling me that all this killing is to learn how some ancient civilization discovered the wheel? I can't believe this."

Then for the first time, Philip weakly interrupted.

"Flint, you should listen to them. They aren't talking about a bunch of Bedouin nomads, they're talking about a spaceship crashing here from Mars thousands of years ago."

"So that thing they blew up really was a spaceship?" Flint asked.

"You know, then?" Troy pried.

"I don't know anything," Flint responded. "All I know is that I was out for a hike when I stumbled upon a bunch of Filipinos about to be blown up in something they called a spaceship. I saw a pretty girl being forced into a helicopter, and then they took my friend here. That's all I know."

Troy still appeared skeptical, but said, "Okay, Flint. Let's say I believe you. Would you help us find Shen Mao?"

"Sorry, friend," Flint said. "I've just about died enough times in the last couple days. Besides, this is your fight, not mine."

Then he went over to Monk. Helping support Philip, he asked, "So, have you had enough fun for one week Phil?"

To which Philip replied, "If you want to play hero ever again, I'll kill you myself."

Monk chimed in, "And Saul also went home to Gibeah; and there went with him a band of men, whose hearts God had touched.' 1 Samuel 10:26."

As they were walking away, Troy shouted, "It's not just our war."

Flint ignored him. But Troy's next few words stopped him dead in his tracks.

Monk also stopped and quietly quoted 1 Samuel 18:2: "And Saul took him that day, and would let him go no more home to his father's house."

Chapter 19

Flint stood still for a moment, then let Monk retake the main support of Philip. He was turning around to face Troy when he heard footsteps racing toward him. Instinctively he reached for his rifle, only to remember he'd left it in the shed.

Instead of a threat from another mercenary or gang of killers, he found a threat of a different kind. Dusty dashed up to him, as if she were going to throw herself on him. Instead, she stopped just in front of him.

They stared at each other for a moment. Dusty had an awkward look that suggested she felt stupid and embarrassed. Flint also felt a little off ease. He then noticed the wet circles in Dusty's eyes.

"Are you okay?" he asked.

Dusty didn't say anything. She just trembled in

place. Flint stepped forward and cradled her in his arms. No sooner had he put his arms around her than she began to soak his shirt with tears.

Flint tried his best to comfort, but Troy's words were still too fresh to focus solely on the distraught woman.

"I was afraid for you," she sobbed. "And then Sperl came back, and then I thought they killed you, and—"

Flint tightened his grip on her and soothed, "It's okay Dusty. Nobody will hurt you. And who is Sperl?"

Philip spoke. "Imagine if a great white ape, okay. Now combine that with a Nazi and breed it with a rottweiler and you'll get Sperl."

Dusty brought Flint's attention back to her. "Sperl is the one who was beating you before your friend there showed up," she explained, referring to Monk's save earlier at the airport.

Flint jumped alert again and let go of Dusty. "Where is he?"

"He's gone now," Dusty replied. "He said that he had to run off to Bohol."

"That's it!" Troy shouted. "He's headed out to Shen Mao's place."

Something inside Flint snapped. A primal growl started in his diaphragm and crawled its way up. Troy's comment had been turning in Flint's mind while he tried to comfort Dusty. He turned around and stared hard at Troy, "Tell me everything! First you try to kill me, and then you beg me to help you. Then you drop this bombshell on me, something about how he might destroy the whole Earth. What is going on?"

At this, Dusty stood back. She looked puzzled and asked, "Destroy the Earth? We haven't been doing anything that could destroy the world."

"I don't expect you would know about it," Troy said as he stepped forward. "All right, here's the story. Around 3000 B.C., there was a thriving people who lived on the planet Mars. This, I suspect, you might already have figured out. Anyhow, these people were highly advanced; enough so to create a spaceship that was able to utilize a propulsion drive similar to a theorized method referred to here on Earth as an Alcubierre drive."

Troy paused and watched Flint and Dusty for any sign of recognition. They just shrugged, so he continued.

"The theory behind an Alcubierre drive is that you can bend space and slide along it as if you were surfing. Therefore, you don't have to use a rocket to propel your craft. The Martian people made this theory work. However, to bend space, they had to create a bubble of space around their ship that would help them slip along this distortion.

"This is where they ran into problems. When that bubble is initially formed, it creates a hard break between the normal space and the space around the ship. It's like slicing space with a butcher knife. The bubble was supposed to be tight with the exterior of the ship. But it seems that a perfectly tight separation might be impossible, because there was obviously enough of a gap that some full nitrogen atoms were split.

"The atmosphere of Mars at the time was similar to ours. This meant it was mostly made of nitrogen. When the one atom split, it caused a chain reaction. I wouldn't call it a nuclear explosion. It was more like a nuclear ignition. The entire atmosphere of Mars was incinerated with temperatures thousands of degrees hotter than anything a habitable planet could withstand.

It turned Mars's atmosphere to plasma. All life was destroyed and it could happen here if they attempt to re-create a spaceship. Nothing would be able to survive above or below ground."

Everyone stood motionless for a minute. Flint was still digesting the idea when Dusty spoke up. "So the part we took from the excavation site was part of the propulsion drive? It was so old. They'll never get it working."

"That's where you're wrong," Troy said. "We've learned that Shen Mao, the one who financed your dig, is having a private bidding tonight. At that bidding, he promised a demonstration. We know that he has a record already that would give him sufficient knowledge to build a ship. Now with the golden record, he may have the remaining secrets needed to build that propulsion drive."

"But we just found it," Dusty protested. "There's no way they could build anything fast enough to demonstrate tonight."

Flint then asked, "Did you see the device?"

Dusty nodded her head. "Yes, but it's ancient. It wouldn't be able to work."

"What did it look like?" he asked.

"Well, it was black, and round, and . . ."

Flint cut her off and rephrased, "I don't mean its shape. Did it look solid, rusted—what was the overall condition of it?"

"Well, I didn't know what I was looking at," Dusty said. "But still, it's over five thousand years old."

Troy then reminded, "It doesn't matter. Mao is going to try to use it tonight. If there's any chance it can be used for even a moment, we might all be in trouble."

"And this Shen Mao guy, he doesn't know about the risks?" Philip asked.

"We're not sure," Troy admitted. "In the records he obtained from us several years ago, it does offer a warning. If he knows about it, then the only way he'll be able to activate it without igniting the atmosphere would be to do so in a vacuum."

Troy expounded, "They would need some way of sucking all air away from the ship before it creates the initial space bubble. If they're able to actually start it safely, then the possibilities would be great; it could be the ultimate spaceship. Conversely, it could be used as the ultimate bomb delivery system. Since its pocket of space would be separate from ours, the ship would in theory become invisible and immune from any defense or attack. It could even fly through solid stone without disturbing a single pebble. The device would simply bend everything in normal space around the ship."

"So do we know who's invited to this party of Shen's?" Flint asked.

Troy shrugged his shoulders. "We have a general idea of parties who are invited, but no specific names. You can bet they won't be the most reputable group of people."

"Well, why are we standing around in committee here?" Flint declared. "Let's do this. Are you in, Monk?"

"'A dog is not considered a good dog because he is a good barker. A man is not considered a good man because he is a good talker,'" Monk replied. Then continued, "'I do not believe in a fate that falls on men however they act; but I do believe in a fate that falls on them unless they act.'"

Flint smiled and said, "Good, we'll need every bit of help we can get. By the way, where's that in the Bible?"

Monk shook his head and replied, "Buddha."

"Ah." Flint smiled. "China is already rubbing off on you. I like it. Let me go grab my guns, and we can head out."

Returning with his AK-47 and his cash lined backpack, Flint jogged up to the hedges and called, "Gual, are you still here?"

Gual popped his head up and said, "You okay?"

"Yeah, we're okay. Listen, I need a favor."

"Okay, boss," Gual replied.

"I need you to take my friend Philip here, and get him to a hospital, and—"

Philip interrupted, "Like hell. I know what hospitals are like around here. I'll be safer coming with you."

Flint turned around to protest, but Philip just raised a weak hand and said, "I'm bruised and broken, but I ain't dying. Besides, if you screw this one up, we may all die, anyway."

Flint couldn't argue with that. So he asked Troy, "Do you know how to get to Bohol?"

"My plan was to stop you and get the artifacts before you ever went to Mao," Troy said. "I don't know enough about this area to get us anywhere."

"Okay, Gual," Flint said. "I just need your help getting to Bohol."

Gual looked nervous. Half raising an eyebrow he asked, "I go with?"

Flint could see the hesitation, so he said, "No, you don't have to come with, but could you help us get there?"

Relief flushed across Gual's face. "Yes-yes. No problem, boss. You need SuperCat. I help you find."

Flint tried not to let skepticism show on his face. He didn't know who or what SuperCat was, but Gual couldn't possibly be suggesting a feline super hero. Not unless Flint had totally miss-judged Gual's character.

Since Sperl had taken the Mercedes, and the taxi driver was gone, they all rushed back to the jeepney. It was the only vehicle that could fit all of them in one trip.

Gual again sat up front, with Flint and Troy about to join him. The others piled in back and sat on the narrow benches which were small, even for a Filipino. Watching three men over seven feet tall trying to sit comfortably on them was the first real laugh Dusty seemed to have had enjoyed in a long time.

Dusty sat next to Monk and Philip, preferring the strangers more closely associated with Flint. "So, Monk, is it? What's your story? How do you know Flint?"

Monk replied, "A man void of understanding striketh hands, and becometh surety in the presence of his friend.' Proverbs 17:18."

Dusty looked hard at Monk. "I don't think I understand."

"Oh, I think I do," one of the tall men replied. "My cousin is autistic, and Monk reminds me of him. Is that Flint guy related to you?"

To which Monk replied, "A man that hath friends shew himself friendly: and there is a friend that sticketh closer than a brother.' Proverbs 18:24."

"So Flint isn't related, but he's just a good friend?" Dusty asked.

Monk simply nodded. Another one of the men asked, "Do you always talk like this?"

Monk didn't even look at the man, and his expression didn't change. All he said was, "The words of wise men are heard in quiet more than the cry of him that ruleth among fools.' Ecclesiastes 9:17."

The men laughed and poked each other in playful accusation.

Up in the front, Flint was following Gual's directions and learning more about Troy. "So you're saying you're a descendant of the men from Mars?" Flint asked.

"Yes, though I must admit there is far more human blood in me than Martian," Troy began. "In fact, every man with me right now is of an order that was established around 2500 B.C., formed to preserve the history of our ancestors. We've gone by different names, but currently we call ourselves GRIP."

"Why GRIP?" Flint asked. "It sounds sinister."

"It stands for Global Representatives for International Progress. But really it's just a name to make us look like one of those NGOs, you know, like Greenpeace. We found that people pay less attention to us when we say that we're just a group of tree huggers."

"You look pretty normal to me," Flint said.

"Well, the Martian people were almost identical to the men from Earth, save one important difference. They were much taller."

"I see," Flint replied. "That's why your men are all so tall."

"Yes. But we are only a shadow of what they used to be. Have you ever read the Bible?"

"Just snippets here and there," Flint admitted. "I read it a little more when my wife was around, but lately I haven't picked it up. Most of what I know, I hear from Monk."

Troy leaned over as if to give a secret. "In the Old Testament, there're several accounts of the men running into giants. The most notable example is in Genesis 6:4. It says: 'There were giants in the earth in those days; and also after that, when the sons of

God came in unto the daughters of men, and they bare children to them, the same became mighty men which were of old, men of renown.'

"Those sons of God are the ones who were the giants. The daughters of men were the men of Earth. They eventually mixed together, and their offspring were called Nephilim. This created a group of people that were very mighty, as the scriptures mentioned."

Flint thought for a moment. "So how tall were the men from Mars?"

"Most of them were around nine feet tall, give or take a foot. Their DNA has been so intermingled with those of this world that it's very likely a good quarter of the world's population now has some Martian blood in it. I wouldn't be surprised if you have some in you, too."

"Turn here, turn here," Gual said suddenly, breaking the awkward tension that was creeping into Flint's mind.

Making the sharp turn, he sensed the discomfort of the passengers in back. This was confirmed a moment later when he heard a fist pounding on the metal fender behind the cab. "Whoops, maybe our passengers would prefer a little more warning next time, Gual," Flint hinted, with a tinge of mischief in his voice.

It didn't take long for them to arrive at the port for the SuperCat ferry. The next ferry to Bohol was scheduled to leave in ten minutes. They hurried, bought their tickets, and boarded. By the time they found their seats, a video screen came alive with a preparatory safety video.

At the conclusion of the video, a recorded prayer was played, blessing the voyage. The screens then went blank. After about two minutes, they flickered back on to display an FBI and Interpol warning for pirating DVDs. The warning was immediately followed by a pirated copy of *The Mummy 3*, starring Brendan Fraser.

The movie was the last thing that Flint wanted to see, so he looked at the people he was traveling with. His muscles tightened as his gaze landed on a man sitting ten seats over and three rows forward. It was the man who'd nearly beat him at the airport—Sperl.

Chapter 20

The jet's passenger phone just rang and rang. It had been a couple of hours since Lydia had last talked to Troy. He should of had enough time to locate the plates. She hoped he was okay. After getting no answer, she replaced the phone into its seat-back cradle.

"No luck?" Grisha asked.

"I should be there," Lydia sighed in frustration. "I don't think Troy and his men even know how to shoot a gun."

"You just need to trust him," Grisha said. "I'm sure they'll be able to handle things just fine."

"I swear, I'm going to kill those men who stole our jet!" Lydia vented.

"Don't forget me," Grisha said, motioning to his head. "I too have a score to settle."

Lydia shook her head. "I guess I hope it doesn't come to that. I'd rather just put this one behind me. Something about it just doesn't seem right."

"I don't understand," Grisha replied. "They've managed to out-pace us for the last two years. Maybe next time we'll catch them off guard."

"We came so close this time!" Lydia sighed again, wondering if she was getting any closer to her end goal or if Shen Mao was just toying with her. "I just want this to be finished."

Grisha looked at her with understanding. "I know it's been difficult for you, but if we fail, we fail the whole world. I wish it didn't have to be this way either."

Lydia looked at Grisha. She knew he'd already sacrificed so much for this cause. "Don't worry, my friend," she said. "I'm not giving up. Not now that the plates've been found. This time we pull out all the stops. We won't fail."

Her second in command firmed up his shoulders. A faint smile, less with his lips than with his softening eyes and relaxed forehead, seemed to approve her resolution. As Grisha reclined in his seat, Lydia could feel some of her own agitation melting away. Grisha was a welcome companion, even with his quirks.

The Russian gave up using ice to reduce the swelling of his face. Having already considered using some painkillers, he opted instead to let it continue throbbing, as if he felt that the pain was deserved. He'd been beaten and lost their jet because of it. The pain was the cost of failure to him, and in a weird sort of way, it was also a source of strength. Grisha would allow the anger to run deep until he could again confront the men who'd humiliated him; especially that smug American who'd stolen the jet from under his nose.

Lydia sat upright next to Grisha. She didn't fully approve of his method of dealing with failure, but at the same time, she couldn't complain. It seemed to work for him. Right now, that was all that mattered.

As she willed the aircraft to go faster, her mind trailed back to the past. She'd been close and she knew it. She wanted so badly for this chapter of her life to end. She would see this through.

She didn't believe in karma. She didn't even think anyone would ever know of the good she was doing. She desperately dreamed that someday, *he* might be able to forgive her.

But no. Lydia couldn't accept that. How could he ever tolerate looking on her again?

Chapter 21

"Welcome, Mr. Pruitt," Mao said as the last guest arrived. "Please come in and make yourself comfortable."

The blond Brussels man was one of only two guests who held an air of honesty about him. He was also the only one from Western Europe. His company had been a major advocate of the privatization of space travel. His rival was an American, who also had been lobbying for the same.

James Pruitt walked over to his American competitor and extended his hand. "I suppose I should have expected to see you here, Amelia."

Amelia Zimmerman stood up and shook his hand with the fire of an independent feminist. He suspected this was just a ruse, planned and executed time and again to throw off her male counterparts. In an industry full of men, it helped to level the playing field.

"I'm glad to see you here too, my friend," Amelia said. "I don't think you've had the pleasure of meeting all of the other guests yet, but I think you and I are the only ones who haven't committed acts of terrorism, genocide, or been an evil dictator of a small country."

"Speak for yourself," James replied. He forced a straight face, but his beaming blue eyes gave him away before his smile cracked back into place.

"Come on in, James." Amelia put her hand on his back as she guided him into the lobby. "And let us toast to the hope that my checkbook is larger than yours."

They entered the room and James leaned over to Amelia. "I think I see what you mean." In the room there were men who looked to be high ranking in their countries of origin. They were dressed in starched, fully decorated uniforms. Each man had at least one guard with him at all times. Pruitt noticed a few from the Arab countries who looked like they were a product of the rich oil fields. He also saw a few others from various parts of the world. Most of the globe had their representatives, but Amelia was the only female, aside from one of the ladies serving drinks.

Though James didn't like the idea that he would be bidding against Amelia, he was glad to have her here with him. She was a headstrong woman and he'd always admired her, in spite of their competitive businesses.

Amelia was named after Amelia Earhart. Amelia's parents wanted their little girl to be inspired to reach higher, even if it meant breaking a few social molds.

James had learned of Amelia's past some time ago. Even though her family had a passion for flying, they hadn't done much of it since her grandfather's days in Germany. Not being a pilot but still having a love of flight, had brought Amelia into upper management of one of the few privately owned aviation companies. Her main responsibility was lobbying the government to allow private industry the rights of space exploration programs. Until recently, the idea of allowing individuals or private companies to capitalize on space travel was a touchy subject. Lately, her activities had been stretching beyond congressional lobbying. She was focused on securing contracts and deals for when the government gave its official stamp of approval.

James knew Amelia was a good woman, and pleasant to be around. He also knew that she was smart and shrewd. During her career she had developed a reputation for being able to get the job done.

Taking another look around the building, he knew this would prove to be a very interesting night. The Chinese serving woman brought over a couple of glasses, and James offered a toast. "To my inadequate pocketbook," he said as he raised his glass to Amelia's.

"May it never stand in my way," she replied.

The two clinked glasses. As they were drawing their beverages to their lips, Mao entered the room. A hush fell, and Mao addressed the guests. "Good evening everyone. It brings me great pleasure to see you all here. I anticipate that you will enjoy yourselves tonight. To start off, I have arranged for an authentic Filipino performance, which will last one hour. Refreshments will be available during this time. After which, dinner will be served in the main dining room. Following dinner, we will arrive at the pinnacle of the evening. I will demonstrate to you all why you should generously impart your money to me."

A chuckle arose from one of the North Koreans. "You have promised much, but told us little. This demonstration better be worth the investment that you told us to prepare."

Mao took a slight bow. "I assure you, you will not be disappointed. Now please, if you will follow me, I will direct you to my outdoor amphitheater."

"So, Amelia, what do you make of this?" James asked.

"I don't know. I was told there would be a demonstration that would basically make the space shuttle look like a square wheel."

"Do you think we can trust this guy, Shen Mao?" he asked.

Amelia looked at him with a playful grin. "Not a chance. I chose a driver with a cell phone in case I need to bail at a moment's notice. This whole thing looks pretty shady."

"Just a thought," James pried. "But if this turns out to be as revolutionary as Shen makes it out to be, I'm wondering if you'd be willing to join forces."

Amelia's face went serious. "What do you mean by that?"

"Well," James started, "I have a feeling that, if this thing is for real, some of the men here will have no problem outbidding us. I worry about what would happen if any one of them were to actually get their hands on something as disruptive as Shen makes this out to be."

"You're thinking they might become the leaders in space exploration?" Amelia asked.

"Worse. I recognize some faces here, and rocket technology and weapons technology often go hand in hand."

Amelia nodded in understanding, "I don't know if I have the authority to partner with anyone on this."

James put his hand on her shoulder. "Amelia, we can't let anyone walk out of here with something that could tip the world powers into the hands of a terrorist—or worse. I actually go golfing a few times each year with your CEO. Together, I'm sure we can work out the business end of it later. Please, consider it."

Amelia shook her head. "I'll think about it. But I want to see exactly what it is they're selling before I make any commitments."

James's smile returned to his face. "Until then, how about we enjoy the evening?"

He extended his elbow and Amelia linked her arm through his. With a light, almost carefree stride, they joined the rest of the guests as several young women performed in the center of the amphitheater, dancing in circles with candles balanced on their heads.

Chapter 22

Dusty leaned slightly into Flint, hoping he might take a hint.

The SuperCat ferry glided across the sea. Its gentle rocking betrayed its true speed as it raced from the island of Cebu to Bohol. All around, conversations in foreign tongues were drowned out by the speakers as the front screens played a movie that Flint suspected was only meant to keep passengers' minds distracted from thoughts of sea-sickness. Flint didn't need any movie to distract him from the rolling vessel.

Dusty whispered int his ear, "I've never been a big fan of this movie, have you?"

Flint looked at Dusty. He knew she'd been through a lot. She was mixed in with a bad crowd, but looked honest in her desire to be rid of them.

Flint also had to admit that she possessed a certain country-spunk charm. Like his wife, she had long smooth hair. The biggest difference was in color. While Lydia's hair was blonde, Dusty's was dark and silky. How he'd confused Dusty for Lydia in Egypt, Flint might never fully know. Perhaps it was because of the dark of night.

True, Dusty did have the same build as Lydia. She was thin, but not anemic. Her arms and legs had a healthy tone. She was an attractive woman. Not many women would be able to pull off a khaki button-up safari shirt like she wore, but she was the type of woman who could wear a potato sack and still look amazing.

Flint gave her a half smile and she blushed a little.

"You know," he started. "I've never liked the *Mummy* series either, but maybe being in good company will make all the difference." Flint threaded his arm down her side, until it slid comfortably into her hand.

Dusty allowed herself to melt into his shoulder. She cocked her head up to look at him with pensive eyes. "I think I'll enjoy this movie a lot more this time around, also."

With his free hand, Flint stroked her hair. His concentration, though, was not solely on the beautiful woman in his arms. Instead his focus was on the large man sitting too close to him for comfort.

At least the man they called Sperl seemed engrossed in the movie playing on the front screen. He had no reason to suspect that he was being watched like a hawk from just a few rows back.

Flint looked over to Philip, who was struggling to find a comfortable position. His bruises and broken bones would need real medical attention, but he wasn't about to sit completely on the sidelines. When Philip noticed Flint's gaze on him, Flint did a little head nod, pointing with his lips in the direction of Sperl.

Philip looked over, and after a moment recognized the threat in front of him. Philip's expression turned from discomfort to worry. Flint put a finger to his lips. He wasn't quite ready to get Dusty riled up over it. He'd seen how distraught she'd gotten after encountering Sperl a little while ago.

Within a short time, Flint had everyone in his party, except Dusty, aware that Sperl was on the same ferry. Troy switched seats to be by Flint. With Dusty on the opposite side, Troy whispered in Flint's ear, "This might be a good thing."

Flint glanced over at him with a questioning look.

Troy expounded, "We know that Mao is on the island of Bohol and that his mansion is in some small coastal town, but we don't know how to get there. I bet we can follow him straight to it."

"The trick is to not let him catch us following him," Flint whispered back.

"So, any good ideas?" Troy inquired.

"Yep. He knows my face now, and he's very familiar with Dusty, but I doubt that he got a good look at your men. Maybe try to have a couple of them follow him discreetly, then we'll follow them a little farther behind."

"*Discretely* is not an easy proposition for a bunch of tall white men in a short Filipino crowd," Troy reminded.

"That's why I said *try,*" Flint reminded. Besides, white Mormon missionaries are all over the place, not to mention a bunch of dirty old men from the States hitting on young ladies. Maybe your guys can try striking up a conversation with some of the locals." But even as Flint said this, he realized the difficulty of the proposition.

Dusty then stirred. "What did you say, Flint?"

"Nothing much," he replied. "I just told Troy here that I think I'll take you to the back of the ferry, maybe find a little more privacy in the back row."

Dusty smiled again. She didn't seem like the type to be afraid of what others thought of her, but she clearly wanted Flint to feel comfortable snuggling up to her.

Flint wondered if she felt a little silly, since they'd just met. He felt she was getting comfortable a little faster than he was accustomed to. She appeared to feel strongly for him, like she hadn't been around a good man in years. Perhaps she hadn't. Flint wondered if she liked him for this reason, or if she had some other motive. He found it difficult to imagine why else she'd be so quick to warm up to him.

He admitted to himself that her affection might be because he was a strong, ambitious man. He even imagined that he carried a soft but mysterious look. He had no way of telling if she'd allow her feelings to continue after this was all over with, but for now, if she needed a man, why shouldn't he be the knight in shining armor to comfort her? He'd risked a lot to help her in the first place. Why not enjoy her affection for a little while?

He stood and ushered Dusty in front of him. Troy later related that Sperl had noticed some movement, and instinctively turned around in his seat. All he could see was Flint's back and the faint outline of a woman in front of him as they were walking away. Since he didn't recognize them from behind, he seemed to dismiss them and refocused his attention on the movie.

Ten minutes after Flint and Dusty moved to the

back, Troy joined them and explained how he'd been watching carefully. He even debated in his mind what to do if Sperl did take notice of Flint and Dusty. On one hand, Sperl was the only chance Troy had of finding Shen Mao. On the other hand, he knew that Flint would be useful when they arrived at Mao's mansion. If it came down to it, though—and he hadn't hesitated in telling Flint this—finding Mao was more important to him than saving Flint and his new girlfriend.

Flint wasn't sure how he felt about Troy insinuating that Dusty was a girlfriend, or that they could easily be classified as collateral damage, but he dismissed arguing the point. Luckily, Troy never had to make the decision he'd been pondering.

By now Troy had visited with all of his men, and the plan was in place. He, one of his men, and Philip, had gotten up and joined Flint at the back of the ferry. Monk and the other two men remained up front to keep an eye on Sperl.

Flint and Dusty both watched as the two men came over and sat down. Dusty seemed afraid that Flint would feel uncomfortable holding her in their presence. She let out a small sigh of disappointment as they approached. Then, looking up into Flint's eyes, she gave a longing puppy-dog pout.

Flint simply smiled and squeezed her hand.

"We're all ready now," Troy said as they took a seat next to him. "Your friend and two of my guys'll follow Sperl. We'll be just behind them."

At the mention of Sperl, Dusty dropped Flint's hand and sat erect. "What's this about Sperl?"

"Don't worry about him," Flint said. "He doesn't know we're here. We're going to follow him to this Chinese guy's house."

"He's not human, you know," Dusty warned.

"What, you mean he's like Martian or something?" Flint asked.

"No." Dusty sighed. "He's just, I don't know, evil. They all are. Marshal, Sperl; they kill for pleasure, but they find even more fun in causing pain. Sperl is the most sadistic of them all. Be careful around him. He's not just mean, he's also cunning. Don't underestimate him."

"Good to know," Troy acknowledged. "But for now his attention is focused on the movie."

"He doesn't watch movies," Dusty warned. "He might look like he does, but his attention is never on them. He's always on the alert."

Troy briefly repeated his observations of Sperl before they all fell silent in contemplation. The dull humming of the SuperCat's engines droned on. Flint was sure that Dusty wanted to sink back into his arms, but she was still a little annoyed that he hadn't told her that Sperl was on board, so he'd just have to wait until she forgave him.

Being completely honest with himself, Flint admitted that he'd been enjoying the comfort of Dusty's arms earlier. It had been a couple of years since he'd held another woman. After his son had died and his wife disappeared, he hadn't been on a single date. Technically he was still married, because Lydia's body had never turned up. She could still be alive somewhere. Everyone suspected her to be dead, but what if she wasn't?

Having a woman close to him again, he remembered the feelings that a good woman could provoke and he longed to hold her tight. However, since she seemed to have given up her desire to be held at the moment, he decided not to push things. Instead he mentally inventoried his weapons and ammunition.

He'd already gone through his weaponry on the

plane trip over. Since anything could happen on the next leg of this trip, reviewing everything was the only way to settle his mind about the upcoming confrontation. Then he remembered something Monk had mentioned in the terminal, just prior to boarding the SuperCat. He'd quoted the fifth-century B.C. Chinese general Sun Tzu, "Hence the skillful fighter puts himself into a position which makes defeat impossible, and does not miss the moment for defeating the enemy. Thus it is that in war the victorious strategist only seeks battle after the victory has been won, whereas he who is destined to defeat first fights and afterwards looks for victory."

Flint mulled over this for a few minutes. How could he prepare for a battle when he didn't know what to expect? The thought scared him a little, but at least he knew of one advantage—they would not be expecting him.

Chapter 23

Sperl's gaze was locked on the movie screen when it abruptly stopped. "Right at the good spot," he muttered, even though his mind had been elsewhere the entire time. Rather than paying attention to the movie, he'd been trying to focus on the reflection on the television's screen. He couldn't be sure, but he thought he could make out some tall Caucasians in the glare. If this were the case, then GRIP truly might be following him. He planned to exercise caution.

An attendant's voice came over the loudspeaker and announced their arrival at Bohol. Sperl looked out the window and searched the shore as they approached the pier. The voyage was shorter than he'd anticipated, but he wasn't disappointed. The next leg of the trip would be far less interesting.

The SuperCat docked and an announcement was made, first in Tagalog, then in English. They would pause here for only ten minutes before continuing their voyage to Negros, the next island on their itinerary.

Sperl waited for disembarking passengers to go ahead. He then followed, carrying the duffel bag of weapons. After getting off, Sperl paused for a moment to see if anyone else got off behind him. He noticed two tall white men coming down the ramp before turning to walk the other way.

He maintained a paranoid vigilance about everybody, but decided to be extra cautious about these two. He continued on a little ways, while discreetly checking over his shoulder. They didn't seem to take any notice of him, but he still didn't want to risk anything.

He moved around the corner of a building and paused for a minute. This test could prove whether they were following him or if it was just his normal paranoia. If the little maneuver worked, he could immediately expose them. Then he'd be forced to kill or be killed. Sperl knew he could handle them, there was no reason to fear. The biggest problem was the attention it would draw, which is why he hoped it didn't come to that.

When he turned back to expose himself, he found that they were still paying no heed to him. Instead they were busy by the roadside, trying to negotiate or get directions from a jeepney driver. Feeling a little more comfortable, he decided not to pay any further attention to the two men. They were most likely businessmen or Christian missionaries.

Upon arriving at the taxis, he found a driver willing to make the long road trip to Jagna. The taxi driver was just about to shift into gear when some stubby guy in a full-brimmed hat stepped in and asked, "Jagna?"

The driver nodded, "Jagna, oo-yes."

Sperl protested, "I don't need company, let's just get going."

But the other Filipino man was insistent. Sperl realized that he must not understand English, because without any change in the man's face, he sat down next to Sperl, and handed the driver an extra wad of bills.

Sperl, frustrated, just turned away. He wanted to shove the other Filipino out and put his gun to the driver's head, but since he wasn't being followed, now didn't feel like the time to draw attention to himself. He'd have to suffer carpooling with another man for the next couple hours.

Sperl decided to make the most of his trip. He slouched back in the seat, and attempted to sleep. Something, however, bothered him about the man sitting next to him. He looked familiar, but Sperl couldn't place him.

The headache he had from earlier was now throbbing again. Silently he fumed over Flint for besting him at the Lapu-Lapu airport. He gained some satisfaction from knowing that Hammy had probably killed the pesky visitor by now. Sperl's comrade Ham had never fully cared for the slower pace at which Sperl preferred to kill his victims. Ham was more of a get-it-over-with kind of guy.

Sperl watched as the man rolled down the window and waved good-bye to somebody. Already he was debating the idea of killing him at Jagna. While pointless, it would provide Sperl with a little entertainment, even if it did complicate things a bit. True, he might find enough excitement at Shen Mao's place, but the night was still young.

Within ten minutes of being on the road, Sperl's eyes felt heavy. The harder he tried to stay awake, the more difficult the task became. After all, he was a professional. He couldn't let his guard down, especially considering his unexpected traveling companion.

Looking over at the darker skinned man next to him, he tried to remember if he'd seen the face. As Sperl studied the man digging through a faded fanny pack that belonged to the 1980's, the man grabbed at something that was stuck inside. Though the stranger's face remained impassive, his elbow drifted a little close to Sperl's own face as he tried to yank a particular item free.

With one eye on the struggling man next to him, Sperl wondered if his headache meant he'd received a concussion at the airport. "The airport," Sperl whispered to himself. Was that where'd he'd seen the face before? With a slight turn of his head, he wanted to study the man next to him more carefully again, but right as he did so, the struggling passenger's hand yanked free of the fanny pack. The unrestrained momentum of the man's pull sent his elbow crashing hard into Sperl's face. The blow, compounded with the already drowsy and most likely concussion stressed brain sent Sperl into a helpless sleep. The only sound he heard as his world went dark was the hypnotic humming of tires on the road as the taxi exited the city limits.

Chapter 24

Flint forced a path through the traffic of boarding passengers. Dusty, Troy, and one of Troy's men followed close behind. They'd waited as long as they dared before giving chase. Troy's nerves were beginning to show when he couldn't spot any of his men. In the event that they needed to give chase, Flint could see that finding a ride would not be hard. The moment they were on solid ground, they were bombarded by jeepney and taxi drivers. Flint was a little frustrated and tried to find his way past them when another jeepney pulled alongside.

"Hurry up, get in, get in!" one of Troy's men yelled from inside the vehicle.

They all piled into the elongated cab. Without further explanation, they were off. Sperl apparently had gotten a small head start, but the driver of the jeepney was more than happy to impress the Americans with his almost reckless driving abilities. It wasn't long before they came up behind the taxi carrying Sperl.

"Don't get too close," Flint warned the driver. The taxi was taking a beach-side road that led around the southern half of Bohol. They were leaving the city of Tagbilaran, and the countryside was becoming scarcely populated.

"What cities lie up ahead?" Troy asked the driver.

The driver casually replied, "Loay, Lila, Dimiao, Valencia, Jagna, Duero."

"How far are they from here?" Troy inquired.

"Maybe few minutes, maybe few hours. Where we going?"

Troy replied with a hint of edginess, "I don't know. Just stay behind that taxi, and we'll pay you double the going rate."

"Okay, boss," the driver stated, seemingly unworried that they might follow the taxi for hours. Carrying a truck full of Americans was a rare treat for the drivers. They were usually able to charge more and the Americans would never notice. Neither Flint nor Troy seemed to mind, Flint because he had recently come into a good deal of money from the jet, which he was still reluctant to give back to Troy, and Troy for his concern over the use of the technology that Mao was about to unleash.

Flint started looking around and noticed that Monk wasn't in the jeepney with them. Leaning over to the two men who'd procured their ride, he grabbed their shirtsleeves to get their attention.

"Hey, where's my buddy Monk?" Flint grilled sharply.

"I was just about to mention that," one of them said. "Monk stole my hat so Sperl wouldn't notice him. Then when we got off the boat, Sperl must have found our presence odd. He was watching us very closely. We didn't know what to do. We stuck out like a sore thumb and his eyes were right on us.

"Monk, however, left us without any warning and started toward Sperl. He may be Hispanic, but he sure blends in here a lot better than we do. Good thing, too; we might have lost Sperl if he didn't. I don't know where you found that guy, but he is one gutsy dude. He opened the door to Sperl's taxi and stepped in with him. It caused a little delay, which was long enough for us to find a jeepney driver willing to carry us all, and to follow the taxi.

"You guys almost took too long getting off the boat. We lost him for a moment, but right before we picked you up, we saw Monk wave at us from out the window of his taxi as he was pulling away. Seriously, any longer to get off, and we would've lost them for good."

Dusty put her head in her hands. "That was so stupid. Sperl's going to kill Monk!"

Flint just shook his head and laughed.

"How can you laugh at that?" Dusty demanded.

Even Troy and the others were surprised. Flint countered with a smirk, "I'm not worried one bit. Monk can handle himself pretty well." Flint laughed again. "Actually, it's Sperl who has another thing coming to him. Monk may be different, but he doesn't lack in personality. He has his own brand of humor. I think Sperl is the one who got the short end of the stick this time. Besides, Monk doesn't just quote the scriptures, he firmly believes them. It may sound odd, but I get the feeling that he's in really good standing with God, and that His grace goes with Monk more than we might normally consider possible."

"For his sake, I really hope so," Dusty said.

Chapter 25

The aroma of dinner in the other room was almost more than Marshal could bear. He'd been politely escorted with his bodyguard to a different room. Mao didn't want to risk letting him ruin the atmosphere that was being created with the other guests, and though he was offered something to eat, at the time his stomach wouldn't allow it.

"I'm telling ya, Marshal," his bodyguard said. "This food is amazing. You should have taken them up on the offer to eat."

"Food is *not* important right now," Marshal rebuked his mercenary. " Listen, Karl, when Mao takes those people upstairs, we need to be ready to move. And where is Sperl? He should have caught up to us by now."

"I'm not too worried," the mercenary replied. "I

was scouting around, and security seems pretty minimal. This Mao guy has got way too much trust in his guests."

"I wouldn't be too sure about that," Marshal countered. "A guy like that doesn't leave much up to chance. For all we know, the cooking staff could really be the muscle behind Mao's fortress tonight. Mao is all about show, and tonight, his security is probably the last people we'd expect them to be."

Karl finished his last bite of Visayan manok, a famous rotisserie-style chicken. He savored it for a moment and sighed. "Maybe I should do another walk around, see if there is anything I overlooked."

Marshal nodded. "Good. And if Sperl doesn't show up, I want you to get set up. I doubt we have more than half an hour before Mao starts taking everyone upstairs."

"You got it, boss," Karl affirmed. He then stood and left the room. Marshal remained to stew over his plan until the demonstration started.

Karl, once out of the room, took a quick stroll outside. He went over to the taxi and retrieved his weapons. He looked down the street and wondered if Sperl would actually show up. This should work, even if he was on his own, but he wouldn't mind the backup.

Contrary to what he'd told Marshal, he didn't scour the mansion to assess any further threats. Everything except for himself and Sperl were where they needed to be, and with any luck, Sperl would soon be there to fill in his part. Leaving the street, Karl started back to the mansion. He needed to be in place before dinner was over if everything was to go according to plan. He was almost through the gate when he heard a familiar voice call out to him.

Chapter 26

The taxi driver looked in the rearview mirror and snorted a little laugh. He'd managed to double his fare by adding another passenger. The fact that he didn't understand English was no problem because his passengers weren't too keen on talking. While the money was good, he hoped silently that the two men in the backseat were the friendly sort. If not, then hopefully the large white man would at least be okay with the other passenger, or else the guy might get angry and deny him his fare.

The taxi driver didn't pay much heed to the jeepney that was tailing them, nor did he focus a lot of attention on the road ahead of him, at least not much more than he absolutely had to. His passengers were quickly becoming far too entertaining to ignore.

The second man to enter, though darker in complexion, was clearly not a Filipino. He was wearing a blue fanny pack, the type that few people dared wear in public anymore. His other passenger, Sperm, or Sperl, or something like that, had just been accidentally knocked unconscious when the mystery passenger unzipped the unfashionable fanny pack and pulled out a permanent marker.

The passenger poked at Sperl a few times, finding the large man to be out cold. With very delicate brushes of the pen, so as not to wake his slumbering companion, he began to create a work of art on Sperl's face.

He first drew an outline of a doll on the man's face, careful not to tickle his five o'clock shadow. It was complete with heart-shaped cheeks, freckles, stitches, lips, eyelashes, and a button nose.

By the time he was finished, Sperl looked almost like a Raggedy Ann doll. He then colored all of Sperl's fingernails black. Once he'd finished with that, he put the cap on his pen and waited for half an hour while the ink dried on his skin more effectively.

During this time, the driver occasionally administered a look of concern about his passenger's future temperament, at the same time trying to repress himself from laughing out loud. His pranking passenger didn't seem to care one bit about the deed he'd just done. Even when making eye contact via the rearview mirror with this stranger, the man seemed unwilling to exchange any nonverbal signs of mischief. He wondered if the man had fully finished with his prank and he couldn't wait for Sperl to wake up and see the transformation that his friend had imposed upon him.

The driver was still worried, but also delighted when the man continued to play with the sleeping passenger. He started off by finding and withdrawing one of Sperl's sheath knives from its scabbard. It was a nice blade and very well taken care of. The driver wondered why anyone would carry such a blade, but didn't dwell on it. He watched as his playful guest tested the edge, and upon finding it to be almost razor sharp, he set to work on his next step of the joke.

Careful not to wake the man, he glided the knife around Sperl's lower chest, cutting off the bottom layer of his shirt. Sperl's back was more difficult, and he had to wait for Sperl to shift slightly before he could finish cutting the shirt entirely off. When he finished, the man was left wearing only the top half of his shirt, so that he looked like he was wearing a fat teenage girl's belly shirt.

How long could Sperl remain unconscious? the driver wondered. But the shorter man seemed confident that his subject wouldn't wake while he continued with the pant legs, turning them into high cutoff jeans. The driver struggled seeing this, but a quick look over the cushion confirmed his suspicion. It was a slow and tedious project, but by the time he was finished, the large doll-faced American now sported a new and more feminine wardrobe.

Pleased with his creation, the passenger then tucked the knife and extra cloth under the seat of the taxi. Crossing his legs and sitting Indian-style on the backseat, he pursed his lips to make an annoying humming noise.

The man did this for almost a full minute before realizing that Sperl was still fast asleep. So he reached over and flicked Sperl's ear with his finger, then immediately resuming his humming.

Sperl only stirred for a moment, but did not wake up. The man repeated this twice more before Sperl started to regain consciousness. As if planned, the first thing Sperl noticed was that the man sitting next to him was making an awful humming noise.

"What, are you meditating?" Sperl mumbled. When no response was uttered, Sperl tapped him on the shoulder and said, "Hey, buddy, will you tune it down a bit."

As he was doing this, he noticed the black fingernails. The fog must have lifted from his head, because he also noticed a mild draft. A quick glance down revealed his hairy belly protruding from the bottom of his newly shortened shirt. His legs also were completely exposed from the thigh down.

The driver suppressed another laugh and waited with tense anticipation. The American jumped in his seat. The taxi heaved under his weight. Then, glaring at his bench mate, he gave him a hard shove into the door. "You must really want to die!"

The man just continued to hum and stare straight ahead.

"Hey, I'm talking to you," Sperl growled as he reached over to grab him by the neck.

To the driver's surprise, the man shot his arm up in time to catch the reaching palm and twisted it into an inconvenient position. Sperl was caught off guard and in the confined space of the taxi, he had no room to maneuver his bulky body.

The driver watched it all through his rearview mirror, realizing that he'd allowed a complete stranger to harass and humiliate his passenger. What first appeared to be a fun joke was now a worst-possible scenario. Sperl had a pained expression on his face, but the permanent marker makeup told a different story. His pained look now made him look like a comically sad circus clown.

The cab driver was glad that the darker-skinned

passenger had paid in advance and he hoped that Sperl wouldn't forgo his fare because of the incident. If so, the entertainment would almost be worth it. He managed a strained smile for no other reason except that he couldn't think of any other way to respond. Looking back, he found that the perpetrator was still sitting like before, humming. The cab driver shrugged, unsure of what to make of it all, but at least the arguing had ceased.

Since his mirror didn't show the lower half of the two passengers, the driver wondered if something more sinister was happening. The one called Sperl, though quiet, still looked blood red with anger. Unsure of whether or not he dared look, the driver risked turning around. Astonished, he found that Sperl was actually struggling to keep his shoulder from being dislocated and the small guy, casually and effortlessly, was pinching the man's arm behind his back. The driver regretted not knowing enough English to understand them, because he was certain the few words that were exchanged might shed some light on the whole spectacle.

Since he couldn't think of anything to do, the driver considered his own safety for the first time. They had just recently passed Valencia, which meant that they were only about fifteen minutes away from Jagna. The driver felt relieved knowing they were almost there. He'd seen too many simple fights grow to be violent, even deadly. No entertainment was worth making a widow of his wife if this thing escalated that far. He debated stopping the taxi and forcing the two to get along, but he feared that things had already intensified beyond that point. He needed to get them where they were going and be done with them. His foot pressed the accelerator pedal deeper.

###

Monk's perfectly calm expression mirrored his inner feelings of serenity. Sperl, on the other hand, was fuming. His cheeks turned bright red, nicely filling in the hearts that Monk had drawn on him. "Whoever you are, you can be sure that once this taxi stops, you're a dead—"

Monk cut him off by applying a quick pinch of pressure on Sperl's arm. Then every time Sperl opened his mouth, Monk twisted even harder. Sperl was forced to endure the humiliation in silence for the duration of the trip.

As he observed Sperl's face, Monk thought he could see the mercenary debating the idea of allowing his shoulder to dislocate. This would give him enough freedom to attempt an attack. It was what Monk would have done in his place, but Sperl must have thought better of it since he didn't attempt anything.

Monk also guessed from Sperl's angry and bewildered expression that the man had never been so easily handled in his life. Though fear may have stopped him, the possibility of not performing some future job could have also kept the man from dislocating his shoulder.

Monk wondered if it would be better to completely subdue this soldier of fortune now, so as to prevent the likelihood of dealing with him later. Killing was something that Monk preferred to do as a last resort. Maybe this guy wouldn't be a problem if he was let go. A lot was at stake tonight, but Monk decided to wait on killing Sperl until he actually presented a real threat. He also wondered how much Sperl was getting paid for his part in the whole set of events. Possibly this little incident might help to lessen Sperl's resolve of risking life for his employer tonight. Then again, Sperl might not think like that.

Most people would shy away from a fight when they already had been beaten once by the same combatant. Sperl was more likely the type to hold a grudge.

Monk thought this silly, since his little prank was so harmless, but the world was full of weird people.

Monk was well aware that his humming was annoying Sperl; he suspected it might annoy the driver, also. He kept it up for sheer pleasure and the psychological effect it might have on his enemy.

They soon entered the town, and the driver called out, "Oy, Jagna."

Monk lightened up on Sperl's arm long enough to let him know that he was free to direct the taxi driver the rest of the way. So with a free arm, Sperl pointed down the road, and directed for a few minutes until they were close to a large fancy home. It was the only such home in the entire town.

Sperl then opened the door as they were coming to a stop, even with Monk keeping his hold. The driver then said, "Four hundred peso."

Sperl scowled in return. "I ain't paying a single peso for this bull—"

Monk twisted his arm to shut him up again. But Sperl gave out an angry growl. Monk slid over in the seat and pushed the brute out the door with his feet, simultaneously letting go with his hands. At the same time he reached into the back pocket of Sperl's new cutoff jeans and plucked out the mercenary's wallet.

Once out of the car, Monk slammed the door and locked himself in with the driver. If Sperl noticed the missing wallet, he didn't try to retrieve it. Rather, he ran around to the back and pounded on the trunk, denting it in the process. The driver pulled the release and the trunk popped open. Sperl grabbed his bag and began to unzip it. Before Sperl was able to retrieve his gun, Monk paid the driver with Sperl's money and motioned to leave quickly.

The driver sensed the urgency and drove off with the trunk still flapping open. Only when they turned a corner did the driver get out and close the trunk.

As the driver was closing the trunk, he side-stepped into the street to see the American he just left behind. Sperl wasn't hard to miss; he was the only white man in cutoff jeans and a belly shirt. What stood out most to the driver wasn't the silly outfit, it was the large machine pistol drooping from one hand. Only now did he fully realize how close his wife had come to being a widow.

Returning to the car, but with a little more caution this time, the driver headed back to the main road. Once there, his other passenger stopped him again and handed him the rest of the money from Sperl's wallet. It was four times the taxi driver's normal fare. The man got out and tipped his full-brimmed felt hat in appreciation.

Only after the driver was alone, did he realize he was shaking. He took a couple calming breaths, then smiled so big it hurt.

The taxi driver pulled away and started home. He could almost smell the extra cash. It smelled good. He'd had one of the most interesting drives of his career, not to mention one of the most profitable ones. Even with the adrenaline rush still clouding his better judgment, he knew this would be a great story for his buddies, just not his wife.

Chapter 27

"Sperl, I was just about to give up on you—aah, hey!" Karl dropped his jaw to laugh. "What on earth happened to you?"

"I had a bad trip up here," Sperl said. As he approached, he pointed a finger. "And if you say one more thing about how I'm dressed, you won't live past the night."

Karl just laughed. "Well, in that case, I'll ignore your fancy outfit and just admire that sweet Cabbage Patch face of yours."

"What are you talking about?" Sperl frowned.

"You mean you don't know?" Karl snorted with mirth. "I look forward to hearing all about this. Anyhow, Mao's about to start the demonstration now. We need to get set up. Marshal is going to make a move very soon. Frankly, I was getting worried that you were going to skip out and let me have all the fun."

Sperl followed him inside the mansion and down the hall. Before they separated, he caught a glimpse of himself in a decorative mirror that was hanging on the wall. The blood in his veins boiled, and he punched the mirror hard enough that it not only shattered, but also cracked the plaster on the wall behind it.

"Easy there, Sperl," his companion rebuked. "We got a job to do. You can vent afterward."

They went over the plan once before parting. Sperl's knuckles dripped blood as he ran outside to take his post before the excitement began. He was just taking up his position when the lights on the mansion's upper patio illuminated the platform.

At this same moment a light bulb flickered inside his own head, and he realized why the man in the taxi looked so familiar. He clenched his fists. He didn't have time to warn Karl that Flint and his little bald friend from the airport might join them later. He did take some pleasure in knowing that before the night was over, he would slowly crush the short bald man's head with his own bare hands. As for Flint, Sperl was sure he'd find an entertaining way of extinguishing his life, also.

Chapter 28

Mao's party was going smoothly. All political discussion took a backseat for the evening. There was an indisputable tension in the air, but the guests were all attempting to make the best of the situation. They came from different backgrounds, some of the representatives' political and national affiliations being in direct conflict of rival guests. Everyone knew that when the real action started, money would be their only friend or foe.

During the many courses served at the dinner, Mao entertained his powerful guests with stories. First of how he'd chosen to settle in this small obscure town, known only for it's illegal stingray fishing. Then he slowly steered the conversation into how he'd come into the relevant technology that would be the highlight of the evening. His real strength, however, was in the way that he always pushed the conversation toward the individual members of the group. Mao knew how to play the soon-to-be bidders. While he wanted to give them a little taste of the prize, he wanted to hold back just enough to keep them guessing.

When the Chinese entrepreneur had initially invited everyone, he'd made it clear that the items for auction would change the course of the world forever. He had also informed them that the items were uniquely suited to the guests' personal and professional interests. To preserve secrecy, he'd made it clear that nobody would know exactly what he was offering unless they showed up to the auction.

The goal now was to sell them before they even knew what they were buying. He'd them riveted on the story of how he had obtained the items. But since he kept changing the subject by diverting the stories to individual guests, he was able to familiarize each guest with the others. This slyly executed effect was not just painting a picture of the importance of the items being auctioned, but the importance of each party outbidding the other guests at the table.

Oswaldov Escalona from Venezuela was just finishing a pompous bit of self-flattery. He ran a cooperative weapons development company that worked closely with the Venezuelan government. His specialty was developing weapons delivery systems. In no small part was he responsible for the assassination of half a dozen political figures and hundreds more that had come about during government protests and riots.

His company was first established in the early 1950s with the help of Pérez Jiménez, who was the military dictator at the time. Since then, Oswaldov had been successful keeping in good standings with

the various Venezuelan leaders. He would do anything, or kill anyone, to guarantee his own personal
success.

Though Oswaldov had few financial problems, he
was facing harsh competition from other weapons
manufacturers. Even if he was as ruthless as the
dictator who'd given him his start, his delivery systems were outdated by international standards. He
was hungry for the next best thing. As Mao listened
to him rant, it became clear that Oswaldov considered himself a saint. In the man's own opinion of
himself, chaos would be rampant in his country,
and Venezuela would have likely fallen long ago.

Regardless of how much Oswaldov embellished
his accomplishments and honors, few men at the
table were able to sympathize with the tyrant. His
pomp served Mao's purpose perfectly, causing many
of the guests to hate the arrogant killer, even when
most of them had committed similar, or worse of-
fenses. Ironically, while everyone viewed the others
as despicable, not one of them fathomed their own
inhumane characteristics as being deplorable. Mao
took great pleasure in knowing the whole room was
filled with these people who repulsed one another.

From the Venezuelan arms dealer to the Russian
cosmonauts, as far as Mao was concerned, whoever
won the bid, would eventually leak the tech to the
rest of the world. The global espionage network was
too good to ensure exclusive rights for long. Soon,
fear of this technology would inspire world peace.

Mao had no problem making a fortune on world
peace, and what a fortune was expecting. Not one
group here likely sympathized with the other parties'
motives. They were almost fully primed and ready to
outbid one another for mere spite now.

Mao was especially pleased to notice that two

guests from the private sector of commercial enterprise were getting into the spirit of the game. If one of them managed to win the bidding, Mao would feel even better about his evening. He didn't really care, but a little less bloodshed on the horizon couldn't be all bad.

Besides, for Mao it really was a game. He had played it many times before, but never on such a grand scale. "My esteemed guests," he said, as Oswaldov finished bragging about his own mansion back home, "I thank you all for attending. I hope the food and entertainment have been satisfactory. I know you're all anxious for the climax of our evening. I must excuse myself for just a minute or two. I can see that you are almost finished with your desserts. If you would like tea, you are free to it. When I return, we'll go to our demonstration."

Mao gracefully alighted from his chair and exited. He passed his lovely Chinese assistant on the way as she reentered the room with a large steaming kettle. Down the hallway, he ducked into his office and shut the door.

Unlike the rest of the house, Mao's office resembled that of a CEO in a large corporation. The desk was made of thick, rich mahogany with solid wood bookcases lining most of the walls. The floor was the only carpeted surface in the mansion besides his own bedroom. The carpet's extra-plush texture was softer than most beds in the little town of Jagna.

Mao took only a few steps into the room. The sun had gone down, leaving only a little light to filter in through the panoramic windows. At the other end of the office, Mao saw the outline of a man sitting on his large and expensive sofa.

"What is your appraisal of the situation?" Mao asked.

The man in the shadow responded, "As you suspected, Marshal is not to be trusted. As for your other guests, most of them are armed, but we don't see them as posing any threats. Just in case anything gets out of hand, we have a sniper moving into position right now."

"Very good," Mao said as he turned back toward the door. He lifted his hand to the doorknob and paused. "I am putting a lot of faith in you to make sure that this evening concludes without any major problems. If all goes well, you will be handsomely rewarded."

"Understood," the man replied.

After a brief stop at the restroom, Mao returned to the dining room. "You have all been very patient," he addressed his guests with a bow. "If you will follow me, we will not delay our demonstration any further." Mao then started up the stairs to the top-floor balcony. The others eased out of their chairs and followed him.

Chapter 29

More homes emerged along the side of the road again. The jeepney was rattling by as fast as it could go. The smaller car they were following was better suited for speed than the clunky jeepney. The car would often be out of sight, only to appear again when it got stuck behind a bus or another jeepney.

Since leaving the main populated portion of the town of Valencia, they hadn't seen any sign of the taxi that Monk and Sperl were in. Looking ahead for the cab, Flint hoped that in this new town of Jagna he might catch up to them again. Flint nearly missed it, but one of Troy's men recognized the man in the trilby.

"Whoa, whoa, that was Monk!"

The driver braked. They'd passed Monk by only a few hundred meters when the jeepney stopped. Flint jumped out and cried, "Hey, Monk—over here!"

Monk turned to see Flint and walked over to meet him. Flint jogged the gap, and when he reached his old friend, he slapped his arm around the guy's shoulder and turned back to the jeepney.

"You had us worried for a minute there, we almost passed you right by," Flint told him. "So where do we go from here?"

Monk pointed up a small dirt road and said, "So likewise ye, when ye shall see all these things, know that it is near, even at the doors.' Matthew 24:33."

"Do we walk or drive?" Flint asked.

Monk didn't answer; he just hopped into the jeepney. Once inside, he attempted to return the hat he'd borrowed from Troy's man, but the original owner thought it looked better on Monk. He urged Monk to keep it. Monk didn't mind, and he turned his attention to directing the driver up the road to where the mansion waited.

Flint didn't have to guess hard at which building belonged to Shen Mao. There was only one mansion in the whole town that boasted a tall cinder-block fence with a guard tower on one end. Flint was staring at the large estate moments before Monk had the driver stop the jeepney.

"Good idea, Monk," Flint commented. "We'll walk from here."

They paid the driver and let him go. "What do we do now?" Troy asked, looking at Flint.

"I thought you were running this show." Flint balked.

"I'm a scientist, Flint," Troy shot back. "You seem to be more qualified than me when it comes to launching an assault."

Flint was flattered by Troy's show of confidence, but he still felt it was a little undeserved.

Nearing the property, they observed the only part of the fence that wasn't made of twelve-foot-high cinder block. The tall metal gate was the only access point to the inner grounds. From the shadows surrounding the spear-like balusters, Flint found a good view of the massive house. Lights were on everywhere, but the ones that caught Flint's eye were on top of the building. He'd been looking at the house for less than a minute when those lights turned on.

"I bet you anything that they're on top of the roof," Flint suggested to the others. "I think that's where the demonstration is going to take place."

Taking one last look around, Flint tried to study the small guard tower built into the side of the property. It was obviously used for security purposes, but there were no lights on in it. Sure that it was occupied, he continued to stare until he noticed a slight movement at the top.

"That security tower over there," Flint quietly warned the others. "Somebody's moving around in it. Lets not give whoever is there a clear line of sight to our raid."

"Are you sure? I don't see anyone," Troy said.

"Pretty sure," Flint replied. "What do you make of it, Monk?"

"Psalms 10:9. He lieth in wait secretly as a lion in his den: he lieth in wait to catch the poor: he doth catch the poor, when he draweth him into his net.'"

"I think you're right," Flint said. "They probably wouldn't have a big to-do like this without a few security precautions. Come on, I have an idea."

Flint led them around to the end of the property, opposite Mao's watchtower. "If we can get over here, I doubt they'll be able to see us from the tower. The house should block their view, and if not, the lights of the house should at least make it harder to see us.”

Flint decided not to mention that the building likely had security cameras catching all angles of the mansion. The tower’s main purpose would, therefore, be to service a sniper. Rather than risk frightening everyone, he kept this part to himself, and hoped for a little more luck.

“How do we get over the fence?” Dusty asked.

The moon was just starting to rise, and as it dimly lit the evening, Flint cast his eyes in and around the wall, looking for something to stand on. His eyes rested on his new seven-foot-tall friends. “We break one of your backs,” Flint said, hinting at Troy’s men.

“Come again?” one of them said.

“I’ll get on one of your shoulders, and we’ll climb over,” Flint explained. “The last one remaining can keep Dusty and Philip company outside here.”

“Oh, no you don’t!” Dusty protested. “I’m not about to sit idle while you boys are off acting macho. I can be useful, too.”

Flint leaned over, gently wrapped his palm around the back of her neck. “Dusty, I flew a quarter of the way around the world and was nearly killed several times to save you. Stay here so I don’t have to worry about you in there. I’d hate to have come this far to lose you now.”

Dusty blushed, though it was only mildly apparent in the cool shade of night. She did want to help, that much was clear. At the same time, she must have realized that she would only get in the way. “Okay, but Flint—”

“Yes?” Flint asked as she pulled him closer.

“You’ve come all this way to help me already,” she whispered. “Be careful. I really don’t think I’d like losing you, either.”

Flint leaned in and planted a soft kiss on her

pouting lips, and for a moment the world seemed to slow. "I'll be back. Don't go anywhere." He then winked, and started over to the fence, his mind more on that kiss than where it needed to be.

Climbing over the wall quickly proved more challenging than he'd anticipated. On the top were thousands of broken bottles that had been cemented into the crown of the barrier. This created a razor-sharp environment to navigate as they pulled themselves up and over. Large shrubs broke their fall and their skin as they dropped from the wall into Mao's yard.

Flint and Monk made it over without any problems. Troy sliced a finger. One of his men tore his hands completely open and was unable to cross the fence. Not only did this elect him to be the one staying behind with Dusty and Philip, it also landed him the job of footstool for the last of Troy's men. They made it over without any problem.

"Okay, here's the plan," Flint told the small crouching group while surveying the lawn that stretched between themselves and the house. "Monk, you go secure that guard tower. Troy, take your guy and sweep the inside of the house. I'll head for the roof."

They all nodded. Troy and his man moved to the side of the house where they were able to force their way in through a window. If there was a security monitor in place, it was silent. Monk kept to the shadows as he snuck up on the security tower. Flint was about to go through the window behind Troy when he noticed the side of the house had a decorative brick pattern. It alternated between flush bricks and others that marginally popped out. For many men it wouldn't mean much, but for Flint, it might just provide another way up. The closer he examined the bricks, the more they reminded him of the church walls he used to scale as a kid. This wall might be just as good as any ladder to him.

Flint's rifle banged against the brick wall as he started climbing. He came down and readjusted the sling strapped around his back. Then he scaled the wall. The first story was easy. The second story—not so much. His fingers were getting tired, and his already fatigued body was beginning to protest.

He was running out of strength, and was unable to stop the pistol in the back of his pants from slipping out and falling to the ground. This left him without a backup firearm, only now he was too high to safely climb back down and retrieve it. The only way to go was up. He'd have to make do with just his rifle and a sheath knife that he'd strapped to his belt on the trip over.

Flint was relieved to find that the bricks weren't covered in bird poop. Most of the birds in the area must have already been hunted down and eaten by the people. It was a sad reality, but it served Flint for the time being. Climbing the last few feet, he found a small ledge right below a concrete railing. Fat stone balusters supported the bench-like railing that surrounded the rooftop balcony.

The ledge was large enough that he was able to sit on it and rest. His fingers were stuck at a ninety-degree angle from the pressure of the climb. As he massaged his joints back to functionality, he gazed to the side of him and noticed a metal briefcase. It looked professional, and he knew that it must be related to tonight's event in some way.

He could now hear voices on the other side of the rail. At first he heard many people talking among themselves. Then it went quiet. One man with a Chinese accent was speaking. Flint repositioned himself to hear better with out being discovered.

Chapter 30

The room was dark and empty. The glass in the window hadn't made enough noise to attract any attention when Troy and his two companions broke in. Slowly sneaking into the hallway, they checked every room. When they found nothing of importance, they moved up to the next floor.

On the second floor, Troy found a kitchen with two cooks who were working fervently to clean up after the feast they'd just provided. They were fully occupied and Troy left them alone. He checked the other rooms on that floor. Nobody remained. Apparently Flint was right. They were all up on the roof.

The last room Troy checked turned out to be Mao's office. Troy didn't know how much time he had left until the demonstration began, but he couldn't resist the unguarded room. Careful not to alert anyone of his presence, he opted not to turn on the light. If there were guards around the house, they would immediately be alerted by the light appearing in the window.

Instead, he used the dim screen on his smartphone to provide the minimal illumination he needed. The filing cabinets revealed little of importance.

His shortest companion went directly to Mao's computer. Instead of trying to get past any security passwords, he expertly pulled the housing off the computer. After quickly locating the hard drives, he removed them and shoved them into his pocket.

Troy was getting frustrated at not finding anything he was looking for. As he was about to give up, he walked over to a plush sofa on the side of the room. Next to it was a small cabinet, again containing nothing of any importance. He was tempted to slump down onto the couch, but right in front of him on the coffee table, in plain sight, was the very thing Troy had been digging for: a folder containing a copy of Mao's research into the calibrations for the Martian technology that would make the ship operate correctly.

Troy picked it up and leafed through, noticing the detail and pains that must have gone into not only translating the language, but also deciphering the advanced mathematics necessary to make the machine work. Mao must have used the papyrus he'd stolen from Troy years ago to begin with, but the rest of this would have had to come through a lot of extra work and research.

The papyrus that Mao had taken from Troy had a jumbled mix of the Martian, Middle and Old Egyptian, even some Demotic, Coptic, and Arabic writings. An incomplete hodge-podge of writings passed down and translated from generation to generation.

The golden record, which Troy suspected was up on the deck about to be auctioned, would contain only Martian writings. It would have a full accounting of the technology and many other things that had since been lost to the ages. This manuscript from the coffee table, with all of Mao's notes and translations, would still prove enlightening, especially if he failed to retrieve the actual golden record.

Even with this little treasure, the one thing he wanted more than the stolen manuscript or golden plates was upstairs about to be activated after millennia of dormancy. Troy still needed to secure that propulsion device.

"Come on," he said. "I don't think there's anything more for us here."

They carefully let themselves out the door. "Let's go see how Flint is doing," he whispered as they headed for the only staircase leading up.

Chapter 31

James Pruitt fiddled with his fingers as he watched with quiet anticipation. Mao finally opened his mouth and the guests immediately hushed. During dinner, James had noticed the expert salesmanship of his host. He could see that his audience was being built up and pinned against one another as they dined. Yet even though he could see it happening, he knew it was working on himself, too. He sensed that even Amelia was getting anxious.

The flat rooftop where everyone was crowded now served as the platform for the demonstration. The doorway at the top of the staircase was surrounded by an eight-foot wall, extending a good fifteen feet in each direction. Since the patio-roof was only about thirty feet square, the otherwise spacious area felt a little cramped, or at least given the company. Surrounding the area was a short concrete baluster rail, with the house diving down two stories from there. James kept Amelia close. Mao was just beginning his presentation and if an alliance between himself and his American competitor was to happen, it would soon be the time to decide.

"My dear friends," Mao began, "I have spoken to you tonight concerning adventures and buried treasures. Within my possession are two artifacts from history. However, it is not our history to which they belong. We may be alone in our galaxy, but many thousands of years ago this was not the case. Our own neighboring planet, Mars, once carried an advanced civilization."

With the mention of this, the guests standing in a half circle around Mao began to murmur. One of the men from North Korea suggested, "You have brought us here as a big joke, I think."

Mao continued, as if he hadn't been interrupted, "Everything I have told you tonight is the truth. Before you now, I present two objects. The first lies within this briefcase. It is a record of a group of men from Mars who crashed-landed on our planet around the year 3000 B.C. This record is engraved on many thin plates of gold."

James watched as Mao walked over to the large machine in the center of the balcony. Sidestepping a little to get a better view, he listened as Mao continued explaining.

"This other device is what I have brought you all here to witness. We haven't had a chance to try it out until tonight, as the main component of it didn't arrive until just before you all did. My friends, within this chamber is the most state-of-the-art craft that has ever been assembled on this world. I present to you the next leap in space travel."

He opened a hatch on top and invited everyone to step up and take a look at the floating pod inside. James and Amelia waited as Oswaldov finished his observation.

"It is so small," Oswaldov stated. "You mean to say that this capsule can fly into space?"

"Not only can it fly in space," Mao said proudly, "but it can fly faster than the speed of light."

"Not to put a canker in your little demonstration here," Amelia blurted, "but any idiot can see that this thing is just floating because of a bunch of well-placed magnets."

This comment got everyone stirring a bit, yet James noticed that Mao wasn't fazed at all. "Please," he petitioned softly as the group settled down. "I do not suppose you all to be so naive. That capsule is in fact a spaceship. It is suspended by magnets in preparation for its initial launch."

He then invited everyone to sit down as he pulled out a remote controller. With a single click, he activated a projector that was sitting on the same table as the nickel briefcase. The shadowed wall next to the stairs they had recently ascended lit up with a slide presentation.

James sat down on one of the fold-out chairs that had been conveniently placed to watch the display. Slides with pictures were provided in succession. Most were of the excavation site from where the items had been retrieved. Mao was brief in his narration, only slowing down once he got to the diagrams of the so-called ship that now floated in the magnetic field near them.

"In a record we have of the men from Mars, we learned that they destroyed their atmosphere, vaporizing all that was on Mars when they launched the ship that crashed here on Earth. The reason for this is that they failed to launch their ship within a vacuum."

The next slide showed a diagram of what looked like a pointed lemon around the ship. "Their means of propulsion is not at all similar to ours. This diagram depicts a ship within two curved lines. These lines represent the fabric of space. The ship creates a bubble around itself, then inserts itself between the fabric of space. The ship is then moved along by bending normal space around the ship, not dissimilar to squeezing the last bit of toothpaste from the bottom of the tube to the top. It is a very effective way to move, and allows them to travel great distances with little effort.

However, when the men from Mars attempted this with their ship, they did not do so within a vacuum. When the initial bubble of space was formed around the ship, it not only split the fabric of space, but also any atoms that were present at that split. This mistake turned their nitrogen-rich atmosphere into a raging furnace. Nothing survived the fireball that engulfed their planet. Nothing, that is, except the ship that crashed here."

"So why didn't the ship get destroyed when the atmosphere ignited?" one of the men asked.

"From what we understand," Mao explained, "the bubble they created around their ship was disengaged almost immediately after it was created. In that split second, the ship had already made its way out of the planet's atmosphere. The vacuum of space then diffused any further heat damage that could have destroyed the ship from within its little pocket of space. After all, splitting nitrogen atoms is different from splitting say, plutonium. Where the plutonium would explode, the nitrogen would create more of a fire or plasma that would simply incinerate everything. Theoretically the pocket of space they were in would also have offered protection from the burning atmosphere below."

James couldn't believe what he was hearing. "You mean to tell me then, that this ship you have here could destroy our planet if launched?"

"A very good question, Mr. Pruitt," Mao said. "And a very important point. To use a cliché, yes, I am selling you something that could be considered a doomsday device, but only if it is not handled properly. That is why my ship is so small. It can only hold one person. This is done so that it can float within the chamber before you. The chamber is a vacuum. When we begin the demonstration, we will pull all the air from within the chamber so the ship may launch safely.

"Once it is launched, it can travel through our atmosphere, and even through solid matter, without hurting anything. We will not be able to see the ship because everything in our space will bend around it. It could even safely travel straight through your body without your being aware."

Mao gave this a minute to sink into everybody's minds. James, however, realized the insinuations immediately. He turned to Amelia and whispered, "That's it. That's why we're here, but also why he's invited weapon developers from all over the world. Can you image the implications for weapons delivery systems?"

Amelia looked at James, her face going white. "A perfectly undetectable missile! Nobody could stop such a weapon if launched."

"Let's pray that this is all a big hoax," James said.

Amelia lifted half her lip in disapproval. "I don't think we'll be that lucky." She motioned to Mao, who was walking back to the machine.

"Now that you have an idea of what this little ship is capable of, I thought we might see if the five-thousand-year-old part we excavated from the initial wreck still works," Mao said, making sure that he included his little disclaimer.

"So you're actually going to use one of the old parts from the Martian ship in that thing?" James asked. "I mean, this thing destroyed a world, and now it's thousands of years old. Is that really a good idea?"

Mao smiled and bowed. "My dear friends, we have examined the device very carefully. It seems to have held up well over the millennia. We believe that it is safe and that it will function either perfectly, or not at all. We have taken all precautions necessary to ensure that if it does work tonight, it will operate safely."

Mao then motioned for someone to come up. The man who appeared was dressed in tight white clothing. He had a pair of goggles in one hand that were extremely tinted.

"My friends," Mao introduced, "this is Jung Ho. He has been my head scientific researcher on this project. He designed and created this ship. He will now attempt to pilot the vessel to the moon and back tonight. You will notice that he is carrying in one hand a video camera. He will send us live feedback of the entire voyage. Please gather around as we make history tonight."

Everyone gathered in close to watch Mr. Ho climb into the cramped vessel. Once inside he connected the camera to the main panel before him. He then switched his electrical systems on and pointed the camera out the hatch. Mao pushed a button on his remote, and the projector behind them displayed his audience looking on at Mr. Ho.

"The connection is working, Mr. Ho," Mao stated. "Let us proceed."

Jung Ho pulled the camera inside and mounted it forward. The only thing it was able to record was the black interior of the chamber where the craft was suspended. He then pulled the hatch closed and sealed himself inside.

As soon as Ho was secure, Mao closed the hatch on the vacuum chamber and turned the locking wheel until it was also sealed. On the projector they saw a dark picture of Jung Ho turning the camera toward himself and giving a thumbs-up before returning the camera to its forward position.

Mao went over to a small control box on the side of the chamber and flipped a switch. The watchers heard diesel motors roaring to life around the perimeter of the house as the air was sucked out of the chamber.

It took a few minutes for the vacuum to fully stabilize. Once the meter registered empty, Mao pulled out a small transmitter and spoke to the pilot. "You are ready to launch."

James, along with the other guests, kept shifting between watching the chamber and the projector. The projector also went fuzzy as the signal was cut. All were silent.

For those who had been watching the chamber when it happened, they thought they imagined a slight ripple around the chamber. James, however, believed their minds were just playing tricks on them.

Mao flipped the switched off for the vacuum chamber and air returned again to fill the void. Then unscrewing the hatch, he looked inside. "My friends," he announced. "If you would like to view inside, you'll notice that the chamber is now empty."

James didn't get a chance to look inside, though he knew by the reaction of the others that it was as Mao had stated. After all, the chamber was suspended several centimeters above the floor. No smoke and mirrors here. Before he could even witness its absence with his own eyes, the projector flickered back on. They were now staring at the moon. The camera was shifted to show that it was indeed Jung Ho filming it. He then pointed the camera at Earth. He even took his ballpoint pen out and filmed it floating in the cramped cockpit of the vessel.

"If you would still like to examine the chamber, you have only a few minutes left," Mao declared. "I have instructed Jung Ho to remain in space for only five minutes. Because we were forced to keep the size of his ship small, he doesn't have any reserve oxygen. He won't last much longer if we let him stay up there."

James and Amelia humored Mao as they examined what they already knew to be true. The chamber was indeed empty, and there was no way that the ship could have been removed unless it had performed as described.

"So much for a hoax," James said to Amelia.

She looked him in the eyes and nodded. "I'm with you. If we don't combine our resources, there's no way we'll get this."

"I'd like to own this tech, also," James replied. "But right now my only concern is keeping it out of the hands of some of these guys here." They both looked around, and could see the glint of greed and power in each of the men's eyes.

"What if we can't get it?" Amelia asked with a shake in her voice.

It was the first time that James had ever heard Amelia sound truly worried. "I don't know. Let's pray it doesn't come to that."

After they all backed away from the chamber, one of the men asked, "Aren't you going to seal it off again for reentry?"

Mao calmly replied, "There is no need. The danger is in the initial launch. The traveling portion of the trip and the reentry phase do not pose any risk."

Mao then looked at his watch. "It would seem that we have only thirty seconds until Mr. Jung Ho returns."

They all returned their gaze to the projector. Jung Ho could be seen filming himself as he played with his saliva, letting it float out of his mouth. He was able to move it about by fanning it with his free hand and by blowing on it. Ho then looked at his wrist-watch, and put the camera back to a forward-looking position. A few seconds later, the projector went fuzzy again.

"It would appear that when the ship is traveling in its own bubble of space, it is unable to send out its communication signal," Mao remarked.

It took a few seconds from that time until Jung Ho returned. His return left no doubt in anybody's mind. The massive sonic boom jarred everyone's hearing and balance. The open chamber erupted, spewing an enraged mist of humid air through the man-hole as the ship's reappearance displaced the surrounding air at speeds far beyond the speed of sound.

The blast was enough to drill a hole through any man if they happened to be laying over the hole when it happened. The fact that the metal chamber itself was still intact was astonishing. Jung Ho then stepped out, rubbing his own ears in a dazed show of surprise. Then regaining composure after having been in the heart of that monstrous drum, he gave a small pained bow before stepping away, probably to cry.

They all looked back inside the chamber, only to find the vessel once again floating as calmly as before. Mao said, "When you are satisfied, we will begin the bidding at five billion American dollars."

James swallowed hard. A quick estimation put his and Amelia's combined recourses at a top bid of only fifteen billion dollars. That would not likely be enough.

Chapter 32

Dusty heard the diesel engines roar to life on the other side of the gate, fresh with terror and anxiety. Philip must have been just as worried, but decided to ease his personal tension by taking a short walk to a more private shadow to relieve his bladder. She didn't know what the ship would sound like as it was taking off, but she knew something was starting to happen.

"I'm not waiting another minute," Dusty asserted, quietly enough to only risk objection from Guy, Troy's man, and not Philip also. "Help me over the wall!"

"I don't know," Guy replied. "Your boyfriend told us to wait here."

She wanted to say that Flint barely even knew her and that she was capable of handling herself.

Of course, to say that would make her sound easy. Guy had witnessed how warmly she'd been treating Flint. "Something is happening in there and we haven't heard anything to suggest they're going to be able to stop the flight."

"I just don't feel good about it," he said. He looked nervous, and was clearly conflicted.

Dusty pounced on his indecision. "If this thing takes off, it could kill everyone on the planet. Are you seriously willing to risk a little chivalry for the sake of the entire world?"

"If you get hurt," he clarified, "then I'm telling your boyfriend that I tried to stop you, and you ran away, and found your own way in."

"Fine by me," she said. "Now help me up."

The man squatted down as low as he could. Dusty mounted his shoulders, her knees jabbing him hard in the back. She could hear him grunt, but was too concerned for Flint and the ship to worry much about this man's comfort. Once she had her feet on his shoulders, he slowly stood up. Dusty walked her hands up the wall for balance until she was able to grab the ledge.

The climb over the top was harder than she'd imagined. The shards of broken glass cemented into the top proved almost impossible to avoid. Once on top, she carefully maneuvered around, and began to let herself down the other side. Glass dug into her legs and palms.

The pain and worry about her small wounds were quickly overshadowed by the realization that she was still dangling pretty high. With her arms stretched up to the top of the wall, her feet still hung a good six or seven feet above the ground. She wanted to change her mind, but knew that even if she could muster the strength to pull herself back up, she would just feel like a worthless coward.

When she finally let go, the soles of her feet were stabbed with fleeting pain. She then examined herself, but the darkness made it impossible to see the extent of her injuries. Wiping her hands against her pants in an attempt to dispel some of the sting, she jogged toward the sound of the motors in the yard. They weren't hard to find. Four large motors with heavy steel pipes leading up the side of the building were straining at high rpm.

Dusty wasn't sure what their function was; only that it was likely part of the launching system. She looked around to find some way of shutting them off, but the bulky machines had no obvious control panels. It seemed her best option would be to damage the things.

Glancing around, she found the maintenance shed attached to the side wall of the mansion. Even under the eve, hanging on the outside wall of the shed was a token of the city's shady heritage. Though she'd never seen one before, she'd heard rumors of people keeping dried stingray tails as weapons. While interesting, it was irrelevant. Either Mao or one of his workers was proud of the memento, but Dusty wasn't looking for pieces of a long dead fish. She brushed by it and entered the unlocked shed where she found a toolbox and grabbed the object of her necessity, a large crescent wrench.

Back at the engines, she located a few nuts that seemed important, and fitted the wrench, loosening them one at a time. After she removed three nuts on one of the engines and started on a fourth, the engines began to cough. Then all four engines died at the same time.

Dusty looked around, and decided that they must have some sensor connecting them all together. Feeling proud of herself, she dropped the wrench. As she walked away, she changed her mind, not wanting to be completely unarmed. She went back and picked up the wrench. It wouldn't be much help against anyone with a gun, but it still gave her some comfort.

Walking toward the building, she found the broken window. After ducking through it, she made her way to the top floor. For a moment she thought she heard somebody down the hall. A quick turn revealed nothing. Proceeding up the last flight of stairs, she peered onto the patio-styled roof. A large boom that sounded like an explosion nearly sent her stumbling back down the stairs.

Scared and confused, she again looked over the patio. Dusty couldn't see any sign of Flint, Troy, or Monk. What she noticed was a large crowd of mostly men. Obviously nobody had been hurt, but she still couldn't explain what just happened. Their attention was fixed on some sort of large metal container. Also on a table nearby was a brushed nickel briefcase. She recognized the briefcase as the one Marshal used for carrying the golden plates and the propulsion device. She hoped that both artifacts were still inside it. Then, still not wanting to give up the wrench, she slipped the handle along with her hand into her pants pocket. Concealing the top end of the tool with her shirt, she casually walked out onto the patio.

She spotted Marshal and slowly made her way to where he was standing. Nobody had yet to pay her any attention. Mao finished explaining how the auction would work. Dusty found herself standing behind her former partner. She realized that she didn't know what her next move would be. Her fist tightened around the hidden wrench, and she waited, hoping that Flint or Troy was about ready to make a move of their own.

Chapter 33

The demonstration had gone off without a hitch. Marshal was now fully aware of how the ship operated. The actual controls within the ship were still a mystery, but he hoped they wouldn't be too difficult to figure out. He leaned over to Karl, who'd met up with him only a few minutes ago. "Did Sperl ever show up?"

"Yes, he is in position," the mercenary whispered back.

"Well, no time like the present," Marshal said.

"So what's the plan?" a female voice asked from behind.

Marshal and his guard spun around to see Dusty standing tall with a grin, her hands at her sides. "How'd you get here?" Marshal asked.

"How else?" she replied. "I came with Sperl."

"He never mentioned you when I saw him," Karl pried.

"Do you think I would actually ride in the same car as him? No, I was more of just following him," she confessed. "What do you expect, that I'd let you collect my share of the money and then be gone? I may not get my way with where the artifacts end up, but I'm sure not going to walk away from all those years completely empty-handed."

"My dear, sweet Dusty," Marshal said as he gently put his arm around her shoulder. "I knew you'd eventually come around and see things my way. Unfortunately, you decided too late."

Then, tightening his grip around her shoulders, he threw her into the crowd and shouted, "We have an intruder!"

Dusty fell to the ground. When she looked up, several guns looked back. Marshal used the distraction to fade back into the crowd. He motioned for his guard to follow him over to the table where the golden plates were waiting to be auctioned off.

"Explain yourself!" Mao demanded.

Dusty didn't stand a chance. Marshal snuck over to the ship with the briefcase. From somewhere a voice called out, "Someone is stealing the ship!"

Immediately all eyes were turned back to Marshal, who by this time reached the ship with a pistol in his hand. His mercenary friend stood between him and Mao with a MAC-10 machine pistol at the ready.

"I'm sorry to ruin your evening," Marshal announced to the guests. "But I was made promises that were never meant to be kept. If we're all honest men, this would still belong to me, anyway."

Mao stepped forward to confront Marshal head on. He was unarmed but showed no fear. Marshal seemed surprised at his gall.

"You are making a foolish mistake, Mr. Steel. I told you that you would be handsomely rewarded for your efforts. Now you choose to throw that all away. You will not survive if you do not back down now."

With his mercenary on point, Marshal started to climb up to the vacuum chamber's opening. "I'm tired of listening to this clown," he said to his guard. "How about you put a bullet in his thick head?"

Marshal paused as he watched the mercenary step away from him. He leveled his gun at Mao's head and paused.

"Do it!" Marshal demanded. The guests looked on with their guns pointed at the mercenary. It appeared to be a standoff, but he'd anticipated that something like this might happen. Frustrated, he looked into the crowd, then pulled out a remote dead-man trigger and announced, "Hidden on this deck is enough nerve agent to turn everyone's blood to stone. If you kill us, you die also!"

The guests lowered their weapons and Marshal commanded his mercenary again. "You're good, now let's finish this." Karl remained still. Dusty wondered if Marshal noticed how Mao was staring directly at the mercenary, calm as could be. Mao gave a slight nod, and the mercenary turned and leveled his gun at Marshal.

"This is your last chance to stand down, Mr. Steel," Mao informed him. "If not, I will be forced to end you."

"Kill me, and you all die," Marshal said holding up the trigger.

Mao laughed. "With what, this?" He then held up a defused canister of the gas that had previously been in the silver case. "You see, Mr. Steel, your guards work for me. We have already disarmed your bomb."

Marshal looked at Karl, the man he'd thought was his guard, who was now returning a sadistic smile. "Sorry, Marshal, but don't you like surprise endings? I do, especially when they pay really good."

Karl was about to pull the trigger when one of Troy's companions tripped on the top stair as they were coming up to the patio. The distraction gave Marshal the second he needed to pull his gun up and squeeze off a couple shots at his former guard. No sooner had he done this than a bullet from a sniper rifle in the security tower ripped through his bicep and skinned his chest.

Marshal gasped. Adrenaline kept the pain to a minimum. He'd been standing with his side to the sniper. The bullet had hit his bone but deflected enough to avoid passing through his core, narrowly saving his life. The impact still caused him to be thrown off the chamber's ladder.

The sniper kept shooting at Marshal. Karl got back to his feet. Marshal's 9mm slugs couldn't penetrate his protective vest. The impact momentary dazed the mercenary, but when he got up, other men had appeared in the stairway to hold his attention.

Marshal, crawled around the vacuum chamber with his one good arm. The sniper continued to bounce bullets off the chamber. Some of them came too close. At least he was now hidden on the opposite side of the vacuum chamber.

Marshal's guards had turned against him. His only hope now was the arrival of those other tall, uninvited guests. He wondered how long before the sniper would run out of ammo but knew better than to wait for that moment. After all, Sperl was an expert. If he did run low on ammunition, he'd make sure the last few bullets counted.

Marshal felt reasonably safe for the moment, or at least until Sperl sent a bullet ricocheting off the patio floor underneath the vacuum chamber, branding a streak across Marshal's calf muscle. His adrenaline was wearing down and the pain would soon be crippling.

The vacuum chamber was suspended only a few inches off the floor, but Marshal had to reposition himself so as not to get hit again by a bouncing bullet. He could hear the report of gunfire all across the patio.

When the sniper fire stopped, Marshal realized that if he was to make a move, now was his opportunity. Struggling to his feet, he sprinted around the chamber and slammed his good hand across the control panel, re-activating the diesel pumps. Then, struggling up the ladder, he nearly fell into the ship as another volley of sniper shots pelted the chamber within inches of him.

Once he was inside, the pressure reduction made his ears pop. The engines strained to suck the air out of the still open chamber, and Marshal began to reposition himself. Finagling both ship and vacuum chamber hatches, he managed to pull them down and seal them from inside. Since the vacuums had already pulled some of his breathing air out before the ship was sealed, he guessed he had less than a minute before he ran out of oxygen. He knew he'd only get this one chance of getting through this alive.

Chapter 34

The demonstration was brief and incredibly interesting. From his position behind the railings, Flint was able to stay hidden, but still witnessed all that transpired on the rooftop patio. He wasn't sure if Monk had been successful in taking out the man in the guard tower, but he didn't dare expose himself yet.

Flint had decided not to intervene the demonstration for three reasons. First to give Monk more time in securing that guard tower. Second, he realized that Mao was aware of the destruction that would follow by improperly launching the vessel and had taken the necessary precautions. Last, he was curious as to whether the ship would really work.

From his vantage point, he couldn't see the projector displaying the flight. The reaction of those watching was proof enough. To say that he wasn't impressed would have been lying. At least now he knew the world wasn't about to come to an end tonight. Since Earth was temporarily safe, there seemed to be no sense in storming the patio, guns ablaze. This afforded Flint a little more time to make a good plan of action.

Unfortunately, just as he was starting to collect his senses, the patio thundered. The noisy return of the ship wasn't what rocked Flint, it was the arrival of Dusty at that same moment.

He gripped his AK-47 tightly and watched as she talked to a man in his late thirties to early forties. The guy was something of a pretty-boy type, and Flint assumed this was Marshal. Then the whole situation began to explode before his eyes. The man Dusty was talking to suddenly went wild.

Within a tense minute, Troy ascended the stairs also and the whole rooftop patio thundered with gunfire. In the chaos, men were scrambling everywhere.

Flint was glad he hadn't charged onto the patio earlier. Several high-powered rifle shots smashed into and around the chamber where Marshal Steel, if indeed it was Marshal, was taking cover.

He saw that Dusty had dropped to the ground and was clutching something in her hands. Mao's guests were running around trying to get off the roof, only nobody knew who his enemy was anymore. Everyone was fending for themselves.

Troy and his tall minion seemed to be handling themselves well, better than Flint thought a couple of scientists should be able to. Troy, however, was the least of his concerns. Flint turned his attention back to Marshal, he noticed that Marshal vanished from his defensive spot behind the chamber. A hollow feeling imploded Flint's chest as he heard the diesel motors revving up again.

Everyone else was preoccupied with one another on the patio and Marshal was jumping down into the small space vessel. Flint quickly stood and fired two rounds at him. He missed. The sniper then resumed firing at the chamber, but only succeeded in making the metal cylinder gong with eerie discomfort.

The thought that terrified Flint more than Marshal stealing the technology was something he couldn't hide and hope away. That high-powered rifle had delivered several direct shots into the front of the vacuum chamber. If any of those penetrated, the Earth would erupt into an all-engulfing ball of plasma when the ship launched.

"Monk," he said to himself, "I hope you get rid of that sniper quick!" Then he jumped over the rail and sprinted toward the ship.

Chapter 35

"Hello, sweetheart," Sperl had said as he scoped the rooftop. "You came back to me. We'll have to meet up after this is all over." He moved his sights from Dusty to Marshal.

It would've been easy to take Marshal out then, and he probably should have, but he was curious to see how his boss would try to steal everything.

There was little risk. Karl had disarmed Marshal's gas bomb earlier in the evening. Sperl couldn't wait to see Marshals surprise. Maybe he'd have another trick up his sleeve.

Sperl grinned as he saw the surprise on Marshal's face when Karl turned on him. "Okay, now try to blow them up, Marshal," he said. "I think you'll be in for another surprise."

Just as Sperl predicted, the frustrated Marshal

threw the remote for the bomb on the ground. *Wait, what was this?* Another three men came running up the stairs. Their arrival brought on a few gunshots. Marshal too began to raise his gun at Karl.

"Sorry, Marshal," Sperl said, ignoring the other two men. "I meant to give you my two weeks' notice a little earlier." He pulled the trigger on the long-range rifle. Marshal gave an unexpected twist on the ladder and Sperl's bullet didn't hit as true as he had hoped.

Marshal, for being wounded, proved to be surprisingly quick on his feet. He managed to scurry around the chamber before Sperl could get a clear bead on him.

"So it's like that, eh? I always did like shooting at jackrabbits." He squeezed off several more rounds. When he couldn't see Marshal anymore, he tried bouncing a few bullets under the metal chamber. Then he shot a few more rounds near the three men who'd come up the stairs. He didn't hit anything with the first two shots, but could have sworn that his third shot went true. He then took a second to aim a little better. As the crosshairs centered over the man's face, he recognized him as one of the tall men who had been holding a gun on Flint earlier.

"You got the better of Ham," he said in disgust. "Well, I'll give you one for him." He pulled the trigger. The hammer fell on an empty chamber.

"Aagghh!" Sperl growled as he switched out the clips in his gun. His frustration peaked not only because of the empty gun, but also for the mystery of where Flint and that bald-headed freak of his were at, also. He had expected two men; now he had five to find and deal with.

Bringing the scope back up to his eye, Sperl noticed Marshal making a dash for the top of the machine again. The pumps in the yard had just fired to life when Sperl resumed shooting. In his haste to change the spent clip, he'd accidentally strengthened the power on his scope. Though he would've been able to read the label on Marshal's shirt, he wouldn't even know whose shirt he was looking at unless he zoomed out the lens on his scope. *If only I hadn't met that bald guy*, he thought. *I can't even think straight.*

Abandoning it, he lifted his head and began to shoot at Marshal without the precision instrument. He could see the sparks of his bullets as they hit the chamber, and he used that as a reference, slowly drawing a line of sparks across the chamber until he closed the gap between his first shot and his mark. Marshal was lucky enough to jump through the hatch half a second before Sperl's last bullet had a chance to pop him in the head.

Hissing and spitting, Sperl readjusted his scope and tried to fire a shot or two into the chamber, to no avail. Then he noticed another man running toward the chamber. He drew the crosshairs on Flint with immediate recognition and squeezed the trigger.

The gun blasted, but not before a flood of cold water found its way down his back. His sudden flinch sent the bullet off target. Then Sperl rolled and aimed the rifle in the direction of the water. The vase that had held the water flew into his face, shattering against the Cabbage Patch canvas in a shower of blood and porcelain.

Sperl blindly fired the gun at random into the small room of the security tower. He then grabbed the searing-hot barrel of the gun and began swinging the butt wildly. He hit nothing, and the hot barrel was burning deep red marks in his hands. Throwing the gun in the direction of the ladder, he tried to clear some of the blood away from his face. His vision was fuzzy when the light in the small guard tower turned on.

Sperl blinked hard a couple of times until he was able to see a figure walking up to him. The first thing he recognized was the full-brimmed hat. It was the same guy he'd shared the taxi with only half an hour ago; the same one who'd foiled his attempt at Flint earlier at the airport, and spoiled his whole focus for the evening. "You!" he declared with all the hatred of his soul. "I was looking forward to finding you again."

The man before him calmly quoted from the Bible: "And the revenger of blood find him without the borders of the city of his refuge, and the revenger of blood kill the slayer; he shall not be guilty of blood.' Numbers 35:27."

"Good luck, pipsqueak. You make me to look like a fool, now you'll learn what pain is!" Sperl charged the small man.

However, the man was quick on his feet, quicker than Sperl had anticipated, fighting with surprisingly good skill. Sperl had no sooner reached him, intending to plow him over, when the man did a quick side step and bent over. His hand snaked around Sperl's, and before Sperl could react, he was in the air. The momentum of his body carried him hard into the upper tower wall and he fell down, bending his head and smashing his neck and shoulders on the bamboo floor.

His adversary then quoted another scripture, though Sperl didn't recognize the source, "'Fools mock, but they shall mourn.' Ether 12:26."

Sperl leapt back to his feet, slightly disoriented. He had figured that this foe would go down easily. Now he began to exercise more caution. "It's been awhile since I met a man who could really fight," he said to his opponent as they matched side steps, circling each other. "This will be good."

Sperl's next attack was better planned. He launched his fist at the Bible thumper, and as he expected, the man tried to grab Sperl's arm and use his momentum against him. Having planned this, Sperl caught his opponent off guard by redirecting the momentum enough to avoid a classic jujitsu reprise.

Instead of letting the man get the best of him, Sperl dove into him while locking his arm around the other guy's arm. With a roll, he tumbled to the ground, rolling like a two-man wheel. Just as Sperl was about to roll to the up side, he kicked the smaller man into the opening of the room where the ladder was mounted.

Bible Baldy fell down to the ground floor of the tower, leaving his nice hat in the lookout room above.

Sperl rushed to the ladder and looked down. At the bottom, he saw his foe trying to stand up. Not wanting to let the taxi beautician get back on his feet, Sperl grabbed the ladder. Instead of climbing down it, he applied pressure on the sides of the rails and slid down like a fireman's pole. When he was no less than four feet away, he let go to land square on the man's back.

Instead, the injured body below him flipped onto his back and arched so that he was upside-down, resting on his shoulders. A single leg shot up between Sperl's own legs and the master mercenary started seeing stars.

The smaller guy's foot completely halted the full weight of Sperl's momentum as he hung in the air for a moment, suspended by his crotch over the unkindly placed fulcrum.

Falling to his side, Sperl instinctively reached for his groin, folding into the fetal position as Bible Baldy rolled away. Sperl knew he was at a disadvantage and forced himself back onto his feet. He relied on adrenaline to help him ignore the splitting pain.

While Sperl labored back to his feet, he realized that Teeter Taughter was actually letting him get up. "Well, aren't you the cocky one," Sperl accused.

Staggering toward the man, he was beginning to recognize the pattern of his opponent's fighting. Bible Baldy seemed most comfortable fighting on the defensive side. Part of Sperl's training had been in defensive tactics, and though he preferred to fight offensively, he also knew how to counter defensive strategies.

Stepping up to Baldy, Sperl threw a fake punch, followed by a quick knee to the man's side. He was surprised at how quickly the man reacted and adapted, and for a full thirty seconds, Sperl threw several combinations of punches and kicks. A few of them were good solid hits, but his opponent was successful in blocking most of them. As the deadly dance progressed, they found themselves outside in the relatively open battlefield of the mansion's yard.

Sperl stepped back for a moment to catch his breath and like before, the man stood still and stared at him. He didn't make a single facial expression, or any advance toward him. Sperl fought off a chill. This man was starting to worry him. He was small, but very skilled. Most of all, it was his passive expression that made Sperl most uncomfortable.

"Come on," he beckoned, as he waved the man in. "You've come to fight, let's see what you got."

Baldy stared him down a moment longer, so Sperl repeated, "Bring it on!" He then hocked and spat a juicy loogie at the man's face. Baldy simply tipped his head to the side as it sailed past. Sperl then positioned his feet as his rival took a step toward him. Sperl wasn't one to be fearful, but his concern for the outcome of the fight was confirmed when he found himself dodging several open-palmed punches.

Unlike most men, who tended to ball up their firsts when they fought, a trained killer relied more on the open palm. This method was less likely to break the bones in his hand when he punched. Even if a bone got broken, the open palm could still be used effectively as weapon, albeit painfully.

Sperl's adversary relied heavily on this style of fighting, throwing open punches more than kicking, since punches were faster and more lethal than kicks. Sperl recognized this deadly way of fighting because he had been required to learn it once upon a time. Naturally he didn't like it, because the style was only for killers who cared little for the fun of a fight. One good thing about this style of fighting was that Sperl could focus less on Baldy's lower half.

Sperl had never encountered a fighter with superior training, but this shorty was very quick and knew how to handle his punches better than any man Sperl had fought before.

Sperl realized that he had no upper hand. The man had caught him by surprise twice already. The next time would likely be fatal. Sperl needed to throw something his opponent would not expect.

Forcing himself to recall the layout of the yard, Sperl got an idea. Maneuvering so that he could fight and feign, he lead his man toward the diesel engines.

Chapter 36

James looked down at Amelia. Her face was pale. When the shooting had erupted, he'd tackled her with the hope of keeping her safe from any stray bullets. However, when he lifted himself off her, he could see the telltale sign.

Her shirt was covered in red. He could even feel the warm liquid on his own stomach. A wave of guilt passed over him and he felt light-headed. "I'm so sorry Amelia, I'll get you to a hospital. You'll be all right, I swear."

Amelia looked up into his eyes with a pained tear. "James—"

James wouldn't have any of it. "Don't talk," he said as he tried to soothe her. "We'll wait for the shooting to blow over, then we'll get you out of here. I won't let you down." James feared the worst. There was a lot of blood, and he doubted she really would make it. He'd never been so close to having someone traumatically die in his hands before, but he was surprised by his own difficulty in keeping from shaking.

He remembered that pressure should be applied to help stem bleeding, so he started to look for the entry wound. Amelia resisted and tried to say something, but James continued to shush her as he looked for the bullet hole. It felt like he was in a dream, albeit a bad one. "Just relax, I'll take care of you."

Amelia grabbed his wrist with one arm, the strength of her grip surprised him. "No," she said firmly. She then moved his hand to his own belly. Following her movement with his eyes, he noticed his mistake. It wasn't her blood at all; it was his own.

Instantly his whole stomach began to burn with pain. Looking hard at Amelia, he stood erect on his knees and said, "I'm glad you're all right." Then, clutching his stomach, he cradled himself to the ground.

He stared over the deck; the guests from the party were scattered. Some were dead, a few were wounded, but most of them had gotten off the roof. The only ones left were himself, Amelia, an unfamiliar tall guy or two, Shen Mao, and his guard. Even the guard was now nursing a wound in his own leg. James then saw another man running toward the ship. He wondered if Mao would be able or even willing to provide help now that the party was ruined.

James continued to watch as bullets sparked against the chamber. Someone was racing up the ladder and James realized that this Marshal guy was trying to escape in the ship. "Stop him," James choked as he staggered to his feet. The burning in his stomach reminded him of all the blood he'd lost, and how dire his own situation was. He was struggling to keep conscious as he lurched forward in what felt like a vain attempt to halt the man.

Amelia reached out and put a hand on James. He shrugged it off. Whether from shock or something else, she didn't try to stop him again.

The tall man raced ahead of James, but was intercepted by a tough-looking bodyguard—the same one who'd been with Marshal before siding with Mao. A swift elbow to the face from the beefy black man, and the tall guy was out cold. Then the guard started toward the chamber. All James knew now was that he would die tonight and he wasn't going to die feeling sorry for himself. He wanted to go out by making a difference.

As James continued toward the chamber, he watched the guard grab another younger man from the ladder, and repeatedly punch him. James's vision was fuzzy, but he could tell that the man getting hit wasn't Marshal, there was something nobler about him.

Either because of blood loss or just his better judgment, James felt that the younger man was also trying to stop Marshal.

The younger man seemed to put up a good fight. He even dealt a smart blow across the guard's face with his rifle. But as James watched, the guard tore the gun from the younger man's hands and threw it away. The gun skidded across the floor and landed just a few feet away from James.

As James tried to bend over, he completely lost his balance and fell to the floor. The pain spread throughout his entire body and he strained to keep his eyes open. Slowly getting back to his knees, he pushed himself up. Below him lay the rifle.

The gun was unlike any that James had ever fired before. It looked similar to the guns used by terrorists on TV when they depicted Middle Eastern fighters. Raising the firearm, he tried to aim it at the guard, but his eyes were too blurry to tell which was which. Instead he used the gun as a crutch and pushed himself back to his feet.

When he reached where the two men were fighting, he again raised the gun and pulled the trigger. A flame shooting from the barrel surprised him, as did the realization that he could only hear a dull bang instead of the usual sharp crack of the AK-47. The last thing he saw before his world went black and he fell to the ground was the guard yanking the gun from his hands.

Chapter 37

Flint had run to the side of the chamber to turn off the vacuum. He hoped if he could do that, then Marshal would not try activating the ship. Unfortunately a stray bullet had already destroyed the control panel. His only option was to stop Marshal from the top.

He started climbing the ladder, but someone grabbed him from behind. Flint swung his gun around, driving the wooden stock into Marshal's former bodyguard. The more highly trained combatant unleashed a volley of punches, and Flint only managed to swing the gun into the man's face once more before the guard disarmed him. He flung the AK-47 at the feet of one of the European guests, who looked to be in worse shape than any of the other people still standing on the rooftop.

Flint tried every trick he'd ever learned from Monk, but the mercenary was able to defend and deal more harshly. One of his punches knocked Flint against the chamber right as a shot was fired. The bullet nearly grazed both men. The mercenary fell back a moment to pull Flint's rifle from the dying European. This gave Flint a moment to unsheathe his knife.

Before he could do any good with it, the mercenary turned around, AK47 in hand. He looked Flint in the eye and said, "Sorry, pal, not your lucky day."

The guard raised the gun, Flint remained motionless. There was no place to run. No time to attack. He could try throwing the knife, but he lacked the skill to make it stick. Flint knew he was about to be shot by his own gun—but then a crescent wrench came flying through the air and pegged the guard right in the temple.

He roared like a bear and spun around with the AK-47, ready to level the entire deck. Flint took the opportunity and lurched toward the mercenary's back, shoving his knife up under the man's bullet-proof vest and burying it to the hilt with a sharp twist. As the hot warm blood streaked down his hand, Flint pulled the knife out. The sound of flesh ripping along the blade's edge was lost in the penetrating eyes of the mercenary as he collapsed to the floor.

Flint dropped the blood soaked knife in disgust and took back his rifle, searching for the source of the flying wrench. Dusty was standing about ten feet away. Relief and worry flooded him. He was glad to have any allies possible, but her disobedience had put herself in danger. *As if I didn't have enough to worry about*, he thought to himself. Still grateful, he gave her a smile and a wink. Then, turning back toward the chamber, he watched as the hatch slammed shut. Flint raced back up the ladder and grabbed the locking wheel to pull the hatch back open. It wouldn't budge.

Though Marshal was unable to lock it from inside, the suction from the vacuum helped to seal the heavy metal door shut. As the pressure increased, Flint heard a crash from somewhere outside and risked a look down into the yard. One of the large diesel engines was smoking.

"I think that's one of the pumps," Dusty said from the bottom of the ladder. She was about to climb it to meet Flint on top of the chamber. "I tried disabling it earlier." Her voice held a hint of pride.

"I don't think you understand," Flint said. "That suction pump is all that's keeping our world from burning like Mars did. If there's any air left in this chamber when Marshal launches, it'll destroy the whole atmosphere. I was afraid of a bullet puncturing the tank, but now that your pump is out, there's no way it'll suck all the air out of the chamber."

Like a slow motion horror film, Dusty went from looking proud, to stupid, to terrified in two seconds. "Wa-wa-what can I do?"

Flint pointed at the dead mercenary. "My knife, quick!"

Dusty bent over to grab the blood-soaked knife. She nearly gagged as she put her fingers around the slippery handle. Then she ran back to the ladder and handed the knife to Flint.

He was less concerned about the blood. He simply took the knife and shoved it between the joint of the chamber and its hatch.

When he managed to get the edge of his blade under the seal, he pushed down on the handle to pry the thing open. A small whistle seeped through the door. No sooner did he hear it than the tip of his knife broke off and the hatch slammed back down.

Frustrated, Flint studied the iron seal. The bulky round door recessed into the chamber opening and sat flush with the exterior of the metal container. The thin gap around the hatch went down half an inch before it ended in a thick rubber seal. With no easy way to proceed, Flint attempted to slide the knife under again, but it kept slipping around. Momentarily abandoning the attempt, he wiped the blade dry on his jeans then stabbed it into the seal and pried once more.

This time he straddled the hatch, pulling on the locking wheel with his hands, while pressing down on the knife with the heal of his shoe. Holding his breath in the effort, the hatch whistled open. He almost lost his balance as the hatch suddenly swung free. The suction from within the chamber made a loud hiss as it equalized. It was followed by the dull ear-popping pressure, or lack thereof, as the vacuum struggled to consume the atmosphere within the chamber.

Unlike the chamber's hatch, the hatch to the ship was sealed from inside. Flint banged the butt of his rifle on it, but as he expected, it didn't give way. "Sorry, Marshal," he said as he turned the rifle around in his hands. "I hoped it wouldn't come to this." Leaning back to avoid ricochets, he stretched his AK-47 over the side and aimed the best he could without seeing.

After expelling five rounds, Flint leaned back over to see the damage. Three of the five shots had hit the hatch; the other two hit just to the side of it. None of them had penetrated the hull of the submersible-shaped capsule. With the hull metal being too thick, and the gap between the chamber and the vessel too small, Flint realized he wouldn't be able to reach the glass porthole in front.

Looking over the rest of the floating ship for vulnerability, he noticed a small panel behind the ship's entrance. The panel was about one square foot, with four screws holding it down. "Let's hope you're important," he said to the panel and rammed the butt of his gun into it. Nothing budged. He would need to either find a screwdriver, or shoot the panel off. Since he didn't have a screwdriver, the gun would have to do.

"Please work, please work," he said to himself as he again took aim, leaned away from the chamber, and pulled the trigger.

The patio was still in some turmoil as the last of the guests made their escapes. Somewhere in that panic, Flint suspected that Dusty was watching his back. He had larger concerns preventing him from taking much notice.

Looking back inside, he could see that his bullet had punctured the thinner metal panel. At this same time he heard a few clicks and the small humming of electronics. That told him Marshal was beginning to power up the ship.

Marshal was apparently beyond reason, since he would have to know that the chamber was no longer under vacuum.

Flint had only seconds to act. Less cautious this time of a ricocheting bullet, he took careful aim and fired four more shots into the corners of the panel.

With the screws broken, he leaned into the chamber and pried again with his knife at the edges of the panel. It popped off easily and revealed a simple cubby.

In the cubby a few prongs held a black orb in place. Flint had no idea what it meant, only that it looked important. Raising his gun, he took careful aim at the orb and shot. A single bullet shattered the relic piece of technology. Black shards spewed up and scattered.

Flint grabbed one of the pieces. It was as smooth as a polished magnet. On the inside was a tangled mess of metal, fiber optics, glass, and some form of black material holding it all together. It was unlike any technology Flint had seen before, yet it somehow reminded him of a computer chip, only much more complex.

As he examined the piece of material, a small shower of sparks emanated from the cubby where the orb had been. Flint laughed with relief as he found his way back down the ladder. Dusty was waiting with worried anticipation. "Well?" she asked.

"I don't think he'll be getting very far in that thing today," Flint replied.

Troy joined them. "Where's the record?"

"What record?" Flint asked.

"The one that tells how to build another device like it."

Flint remembered now, and pointed at the chamber. "Well, when Marshal went into the ship, he had a metal briefcase, could that have been it?"

Instead of Troy answering, another voice butted in, "That briefcase does indeed have the golden record."

Flint watched Troy turn around, then side step a little to reveal Shen Mao holding a pistol at them. "Hello, Mr. Troy Malko. It has been some time."

In the back of Flint's mind, the name Malko triggered a memory. It seemed important, but in the tension of the moment, he couldn't recall why.

"Shen Mao," Troy snarled. "You backstabbing coward."

"Ha, ha," Mao replied. "You come here and ruin my party, destroy my ship, and now you stand helpless before me. Yet you still have the nerve to insult me? Is it any wonder that I would not work with one such as yourself?"

"What's he talking about?" Flint asked. "I thought you didn't know him."

Mao interrupted before Troy could explain. "I know who Ms. Dusty is, however, I do not believe I know who you are. Are you with Troy's little band of giants? You don't look that tall."

"The name is Flint, and to be completely honest, I just happened to be in the wrong place at the right time."

Mao looked puzzled. "So Mr. Flint, you mean to tell me that you don't know these two?" He pointed to Troy and Dusty.

"Just met them today," he replied.

"Very interesting," Mao continued. "I must ask though, since I do not know you either, to please place your weapon on the ground."

Flint complied. Mao had his gun pointed directly at him. Flint was sure that he wouldn't be able to draw his own quickly enough to defend himself. Flint discreetly gazed over the deck looking for anything to distract Mao with. All he needed was a couple of seconds to pick up the gun and take the upper hand.

"Thank you," Mao said. Then without any warning, he fired a single shot directly at the center of Flint's chest.

Flint could see the flash of the barrel, and he found himself being propelled backward. The world went black, and he never felt the floor as he hit it.

Chapter 38

Philip stood outside the fence as the guests came crashing through the gate. When the gunshots began, he looked up and saw flashes from both the rooftop and the guard tower. He went through Flint's backpack and found a grenade. It was the only weapon left in the pack. It would have to do.

As the last man exited the gate and Philip realized that Flint wasn't among them. He grew worried. "Screw this," he said. With a hobble and a limp, he inched towards the gate by himself.

"Hey, not you, too?" Guy exclaimed.

Philip just brushed Troy's man aside and limped on toward the mansion without any further opposition. His face was still swollen, but his vision had improved in the past hour. The front door was wide open and he walked right in with a determined stride, or at what passed for a stride in his condition.

He pulled the pin to the grenade just in case, but was careful not to let go of the triggering lever. There were no signs of anybody inside the house, so he climbed up the stairs to the roof. He arrived just in time to see Flint fall.

His teeth protested as he clenched his jaw in horror. Winding up his arm to throw the grenade at the shooter, he paused long enough to see Dusty on the rooftop not far away. The hope that she might survive kept him from throwing it.

He watched as a Chinese man walked over to a large metal tank and slammed the lid shut. He tried to lock the hatch down, but it seemed he was struggling against an opposing force from within the tank.

Philip watched with uncharacteristic indecision. The hatch sprang open. It hit the Chinese man in the face. He fell off the tank and an obviously wounded man struggled to make his way out.

Instead of climbing down the ladder, he let himself fall to the ground, cushioned by landing on the dazed Chinese man. The injured man then kicked the gun away from the human pillow. Nursing his arm, which was wrapped with a shredded piece of what might have been a very nice shirt, the man stumbled for the stairs where Philip was standing.

The man walked backward, making sure that nobody pursued him. Something about him seemed familiar to Philip, even from the back. As the man neared, Philip's eyes were able to focus more clearly. It was the same pretty boy who'd commanded Sperl to soften him up. "Marshal Steel," Philip whispered to himself.

Marshal was nearing the stairs when Philip silently stepped forward. When Marshal was about to run into him, Philip cheerfully said, "Good evening, ma'am."

Marshal spun around, only to be met by the hardest punch Philip had ever thrown. "That's how you punch a man, Marshal!"

Marshal hit the floor hard. Philip screamed and hopped with pain inside his head. On the outside, he barely maintained a tough posture. He folded his arms, carefully stuffing his broken hand into his armpit. Fingers that hadn't previously been broken by Sperl, now were definitely shattered.

Marshal fumbled with his one good arm to push himself up, at the same time trying not to let go of a metal briefcase he was carrying. Once Marshal regained his balance, he swung the heavy case at Philip, who dodged it by a hair.

Choking down the throbbing pain in his right hand, Philip stretched out his other arm and held the grenade in front of Marshal's face. "Try anything again, and we both die," he warned.

Marshal struggled to regain his composure as he stood up to face the old man. The corner of his eye was oozing blood and beginning to swell shut. "You're bluffing."

Philip muted a painful cough and then spit a bloody loogie on Marshal's beautiful Italian shoe. "Because of you," he said as he wiped his lips, "I'm going to die anyway."

Marshal looked worried. Philip added, "You were right to suspect me when you first kidnapped me," he lied. "But you should've killed me when you had the chance."

"Kill me and you kill your friends," Marshal said, trying to appeal to Philip's good nature.

Philip let out a pained laugh right before he began to cough again. Then, spitting out another mouthful of blood, he said, "You obviously don't understand us very well. We're all ready to die. Are you?"

Marshal looked around him at the carnage. Philip followed his gaze as he noticed who lay among the dead and injured. Burning with hatred again upon seeing Flint's motionless corpse, Philip forgot all about his pain. He wanted revenge and Marshal was right in front of him.

The only source of hesitation now came as Philip noticed the briefcase, which contained instructions for creating the world's biggest catastrophe. "I'd suggest you drop the briefcase now," he said with spite.

"Yes, Mr. Steel, drop the case."

Philip looked behind Marshal to see that the Chinese man, whom he now suspected to be Shen Mao, had gotten back on his feet. Shen had recovered his weapon and was leaning against the end of the large metal tank for support. Philip made sure that Mao could see the grenade by holding it up high.

Mao responded, "I do not doubt your resolve to end your life, but let me help you see the situation more clearly." He stepped forward, advancing near Flint's body, which he chose not to notice.

"That grenade may stop anyone here from obtaining the record in that briefcase, but it is highly unlikely that it would destroy the record itself. It will find its way into some other person's possession, whereby you will have failed to secure the contents."

Philip was conflicted. The man made a valid argument. "So what you're saying is, we have ourselves a standoff."

Mao gave a slight bow in confirmation, or he was just hunching over because of his injuries. Mao then stood erect again, and began to take a small step forward. Just then a foot shot up from the corpse next to him.

Philip's heart skipped a beat, causing his chest

to ache as he watched Flint roll over and kick-trip the Chinese man.

Mao stumbled forward but didn't fall. In that moment he accidentally fired his gun, the bullet embedding itself in the stair wall behind Philip.

The distraction gave Marshal the upper hand, and he swung the briefcase at Philip. The case hit Philip in the stomach, and he folded to the ground. The grenade rolled out of his hand as Marshal jumped over him and charged down the stairway.

Mao took cover behind the thick steel of the vacuum chamber, but Philip had no place to run. He closed his eyes, waiting for the fuse on the grenade to end.

He had failed. His young friend Flint, who he thought was dead, would truly die now because of his actions. The technology to destroy the world would end up back in the hands of a sociopath. Philip's family wouldn't even know how he died.

As these last thoughts of regret were coursing through his mind, he hoped as much, as he wondered, if Hell reserved a little spot for screw-ups like himself.

Chapter 39

The grenade was on the floor, with only a couple of seconds to go.

Moments before, Amelia had just found her way over to James when a man showed up holding the grenade. Ignoring him briefly, she checked on her friend and found a weak pulse. He was shot, and the whole time he'd been thinking of her safety. Reaching for any solution, Amelia came up blank. She needed to get him to a hospital fast, but lacked the ability to move him.

She knew one thing she knew for certain. With the arrival of this grenade-wielding fool, things could only get worse.

Fighting back her fear for James's life, Amelia knew that retrieving the briefcase was more important. She looked around but couldn't find a gun close enough to grab without being noticed. Without a weapon, she realized, somebody else would have to make a move before she could.

She noticed the other woman on the patio. This woman, Dusty, was the same one Marshal had used as a distraction earlier. She now seemed to care for the man she called Flint. Amelia remembered the moment he'd been shot, and how Dusty had instantly reacted. Now her face didn't show the same hurt and despair. In its stead was a face brimming with some determined calculation.

Feeling guilty for ignoring James in his hurt condition, Amelia still forced herself into a crouch. The man with the briefcase wasn't armed, and she figured that she would be able to knock him over if she caught him by surprise. Waiting for her moment, she kept the corner of her eye on Flint and Dusty.

Her chance came just as she figured it would, but even as she sprinted, she knew she was too late.

There was no time to run away. Her only option was clear. She bent over and scooped up the grenade. She didn't know how long before it would blow up, but she didn't care to hold on to it any longer than absolutely necessary. The second it was in her hand, she did a spinning jump and tried to launch the grenade over the rail.

The grenade didn't clear the railing. It bounced back onto the patio. She gasped at her clumsiness, but found a little hope as the grenade skidded to the other side of the spaceship.

Every muscle in her body tensed as she turned away from the blast. When it came, it was loud. Never before had she ever felt, nor did she know she could feel like all her internal organs were bursting.

Suddenly, her whole body was the extension of a large sub-woofer at full volume. Bits of debris show-ered down, but were almost irrelevant next to the jarring concussion.

Relieved to find she wasn't hurt, she made a quick search of her surroundings. Clarity being more easy to come by than she would have thought possible under the circumstances, she found that she'd succeeded in keeping everyone alive on her side of the ship. Mao, having run to the other side, was the only person directly exposed to the blast.

The briefcase was gone, but at least one more disaster had been averted. Now she wondered if the men standing in front of her could be trusted. Knowing nothing about them, she decided to risk a show of good will and hopefully keep them from turning into her enemy. Quickly bending over, she helped the older man who'd dropped the grenade.

Philip, as she later learned, looked up at her and said with a puzzled expression, "For going to Hell, I'd have to say, the angels here sure look pretty."

She smiled and blushed. "Here, let me help you up."

As soon as he was standing, his expression changed to one of concern. "Flint!"

Amelia followed as Philip hobbled over to where Flint was getting up.

"I thought you were a goner," Philip said. "You really shouldn't be scaring me like this."

Flint looked up and said, "Philip, if you'd stayed where I left you—"

Amelia cut him off. "I could have sworn I saw you get shot."

"I did," Flint replied. He then pulled his shirt down a little to reveal a Kevlar vest. "Compliments of one of Marshal's men from back in Egypt. By the way, I saw what you did there. I'd say we all owe you one. Do you have a name?"

"Amelia and that's my friend James Pruitt." She pointed to the man crumpled up on the ground. "He's been shot, and I really need to get him to a hospital."

"Yeah, I remember him," Flint said. "He tried to help me when I was fighting that one guy. Oh hey, Troy."

The tall man approached. "Where's Marshal and Mao?"

Philip lifted his arm. "Marshal took off down the stairs. The Chinaman ran behind that big metal container."

Without a word Troy ran behind the chamber and began searching for Mao. The blast had torn away a section of the deck, but hadn't blown a hole completely through the floor. Nobody could see Mao anywhere.

Amelia looked around puzzled. She didn't think a grenade could completely disintegrate the man. Focusing her eyes near the railing, she spotted a bloody arm between the concrete balusters. She said nothing; a simple point of her finger was all that was needed.

Everyone rushed forward, but Amelia held back. She wasn't enthusiastic to see if anybody was still connected to the appendage.

Troy was the first to reach the railing. He leaned over and found Mao alive. "Shen Mao," she overheard him say. "Isn't this an awkward position to be in?"

Amelia took a step forward but stopped, remembering that Mao might be an ugly sight. Unfortunately she wasn't able to turn away in time to avoid witnessing the ruthless way the tall man smashed the heel of his shoe into the already mangled arm. The arm released its tentative grip on the baluster.

Amelia squealed in protest as she turned her face. She knew Shen Mao was falling. *Maybe I shouldn't trust these people after all.* The two story drop would be painful and possibly lethal. She could feel her stomach clawing for her throat.

A comforting arm slid around her. She looked up to see Philip. He looked like he'd been through a lot. Still, he maintained that trustable air of comfort that Amelia found common in older men. "Come on, let's take care of your friend," he said in a soothing voice.

Even while he labored under his own pain, he appeared to be more concerned with everyone else around him. Amelia was touched. In a way, he reminded her of her own father. She couldn't help but trust him.

Helping him more than he was helping her, they returned to James.

Flint joined them, suddenly stopping to ask. "What about Marshal? He still has that record."

"Hey, Troy," Philip called out. "Why don't you go chase him down? This wasn't our fight to begin with."

Troy picked up Flint's AK-47. "I need to borrow this," he said as he ran down the stairs.

Amelia and Dusty grabbed James's legs, Flint looked hurt, but managed to put his arms under the dying man's shoulders. She only hoped there was a good enough medical facility in this podunk town to save him.

Chapter 40

Monk pursued Sperl. It was a well matched fight, For the moment, Monk knew that he'd gained the upper hand. Sperl was still in the fight, but both men were getting clumsy. One wrong move on either man's part could spell death.

Monk took confidence as Sperl kept backing up. He'd prefer if Sperl would simply give up or run away. Still, Monk didn't dare let him go, especially since he might continue to prove harmful to Flint.

Though the fighting was tense, Monk still found it entertaining to watch Sperl fight. The big mercenary looked extraordinarily silly in his cutoff jeans, belly shirt, and doll face.

They fought for several minutes. Monk would engage Sperl, who would defend himself, and retreat a little farther back. They were nearing the diesel motors now, but skirting close to the mansion walls.

Monk found some allure using his skills against an opponent of similar ability, but he was ready to end the engagement. Once he had Sperl pinned against the mansion wall, he knew the end would be quick. Sperl no longer had any room to retreat, and Monk was determined to finish the fight.

Regrettably, he didn't anticipate Sperl's next move. Hanging on the wall, partially hidden by shadows, was a whip. Something about it seemed odd to him. Sperl was quick to swing the stiff whip at Monk. It was only about seven feet long, but it gave Sperl an edge that Monk didn't know how to defend against.

"I've enjoyed this," Sperl said. "Now I think I'll end your life. Don't worry, I'll make it nice and slow. I think I owe you that much."

The whip was too stiff to snap and Sperl swung it in more of a flogging manner. With each swing, Monk managed to dodge it. Luckily, Sperl wasn't as good with a whip as some Monk had seen. Even if he was, this was no ordinary whip. Unlike a bull-whip that had a flexible end and could wrap around an object, or snap it in half, this one held a rigid shape, even after being flung. It was meant to be used for flogging. Or was it?

"You're puzzled by my new weapon?" Sperl snarled. "Did you by chance know that the venom in a stingray's tail remains, even after the animal's dead?"

Monk was unfamiliar with stingrays, but he didn't doubt what Sperl was telling him.

"This stingray tail only needs to hit you to give enough of a powerful neurotoxin to make you very ill. As soon as it's allowed into your bloodstream, it's over for you. How do chill, fever, vomiting, and paralysis sound? I think I'll paralyze you, then give you a little taste of your own medicine." He waved his free hand around his face, referring to the artwork that Monk had previously done on him. "Only I think I'll use my knife, or maybe a sharp stick to carve the features into your face. I'll then give you enough lashings with this whip to ensure you die a very slow and bitter death."

Monk knew better than to suspect the man's words. He'd been led here on purpose just so Sperl could snag the venomous whip. Monk's mind turned to the only source of strength he could find in this new challenge: the Bible.

Though his face might not show it, he was struggling to believe in the words as they left his mouth, hoping with all his heart that his faith in God would sustain him. "Behold, I give unto you the power to tread on serpents and scorpions, and over all the power of the enemy: and nothing shall by any means hurt you.' Luke 10:19."

Sperl let out a caustic laugh. "An invisible, uninvolved God won't save you from the reality of what I'm going to do to you."

Monk then looked around for anything to defend himself with. He found nothing. Taking a deep breath, he stepped up to face Sperl. He dodged the first whip strike, and while Sperl was winding up for another attempt, Monk lashed out with a quick fist combo to the larger man's chest.

Sperl absorbed the well-placed punches, and before Monk could retreat to a safe distance, Sperl got his other hand around the tip of the whip and looped it around Monk's neck.

Monk felt the scaly texture of the dried tail as Sperl positioned himself behind Monk and gave a strong jerk on both ends of the whip. The tail rubbed chunks of skin away from his neck, depositing its toxin within the new gouge around his whole neck.

Instead of placing his hands between the dark scaled tail and the soft brown and red flesh of his own neck, Monk thought of a better way to loosen the grip of the cartilaginous appendage. If he were to attempt loosening it with his hands, the only result would be a loss of precious mobility by also trapping his hand. Instead, he backed himself closer to Sperl, making it difficult for the aggressor to strangle him outright. Monk then delivered several quick jabs at the man's torso with his elbows.

Sperl kept a grip on the whip during Monk's backward advance and countered by jumping up and planting his knees into Monk's back. Monk struggled to remain standing as his larger and more weighty opponent extended his powerful legs, effectively standing horizontal on Monk's lighter frame.

Like an evil version of Davy Crockett, Sperl wrangled the ferocious bear with his own bear hands, holding tightly to the reins as the beast reared its powerful mass. The rough whip tore a deeper ring around Monk's neck as he lost balance. Both men fell backward.

Sperl let the whip slide out of one hand, gripping more of Monk's flesh as it passed under his collar. Once Monk was on the ground, Sperl rolled out from under him and brought the tail of the whip down hard on his chest. Monk could feel tissue being torn away along with bits and pieces of his shirt.

Monk rolled away and began to stand up. A wicked grin ran across Sperl's face. "Any second now, and you'll be mine."

Monk just stood. Aside from the sting of the lacerations, he could feel no effects of the poison. Sperl took a step closer, ready to raise the whip, but it dropped from his hands. He looked down at them in bewilderment. His hands had gone numb. Monk could see a sore where Sperl's hands had been rubbed raw by the rough texture of the tail. The poison must have rubbed into Sperl's palms, causing his hands to stop functioning correctly. As Sperl looked down in confusion, Monk took the opportunity and attacked with a quick series of punches meant to break Sperl's ribs, and hopefully puncture his lungs.

Sperl staggered back until he hit the wall where the whip had hung. He coughed a little blood, and his eyes went dark with hatred. A sudden explosion on the rooftop above seemed to accent Sperl's newfound power, as though his emotions were manifesting in pure destructive force.

Monk knew at that moment the Devil must be real, as no man could look so evil on his own. Even during his time in prison, Monk had never seen anybody look so malevolently monomaniacal as Sperl did at that moment. It was the eeriest feeling he'd ever experienced. Monk retreated a couple of paces as this unforgiving squall advanced.

Monk hoped that it was just his mind playing a trick on him, but the man had clearly left all remnants of humanity behind. Monk's rib-shattering punches had worked, and he knew that Sperl's lungs were filling with blood. Still, this grizzly-bear had not only turned into the walking dead, but also into an unstoppable murderer. Sperl grabbed Monk's neck and held him above the ground. Monk let fly a few well-placed jabs at some pressure points, but Sperl wasn't at all fazed; he'd moved beyond feeling. Consumed by fury, he simply stared at Monk, eye to eye, looking for any sign of fear. Monk returned his stare with his usual undaunted expression.

Sperl heaved Monk to the ground, and while Monk knew that Sperl only had about ten minutes before the blood seeping into his lungs drowned him.

Monk wasn't going to survive the fight that long, yet staring up at the demonic figure looming above him, he wasn't afraid of death. Monk had always been different from everyone else. He would've loved to fit in, but never understood how. Instead, he devoted his life to learning the gospel, from not only the Bible, but as many religions as he could. His studies had given him a certain faith in God that warranted peace of mind in the face of death. Inaudibly he quoted his Savior, '*Into your hands I commend my spirit.*'

Now, lying on the ground before Sperl, Monk closed his eyes to his murderer. Sperl had the moment's advantage. Monk had no escape. With this knowledge, he waited with curious anticipation to see what the great mystery of death would reveal to him.

Monk cringed when he heard a hard thud, along with the muted sound of bones snapping below sinew. He'd only heard a sound like that once before and it had sent him to prison. Now he was hearing it again, but found it odd that he couldn't feel a thing. He wondered if the poison from the whip was dulling his senses and he thanked God for the blessing of not having to actually feel that bitter sting of death.

After a moment, he realized he was still conscious. A cool night's breeze wisped over him, and he opened his eyes. To his surprise he was very much alive and well. Even the poison from the whip seemed to have had little if any effect on him. He stood up and looked at a crumpled heap of flesh. Sperl's neck was bent at an awkward angle, clearly broken when the back of a Chinese man falling from above had snapped over Sperl's head.

The calm resignation Monk had succumbed to was instantly replaced with elation for the two miracles that had happened that night, each of them saving his life. Obviously he would never forget them, but these two miracles would be especially sacred to him.

First was the protection from the stingray tail; second was the convenient, if not unusual, death of Sperl. Monk collapsed to the ground in self-compulsory thanksgiving as he offered a silent prayer to that God who is anything but *invisible* and *uninvolved*.

As he walked around the home, he was debating whether or not he should go into the house or outside the gate when he heard some noises coming from within the massive structure. He looked on as Philip opened the front door. Dusty and another girl were carrying the legs of a wounded man and Flint was at the head. Monk walked over to help.

Chapter 41

He skipped down the stairs two at a time. Nearly tripping as he went, Marshal felt victorious. He hit the main floor and raced toward the door. Nobody was behind him when the grenade went off. He hoped that if it didn't kill the men up there, then at the very least they might be distracted while he made his exit.

The gate to the mansion was open so he darted through it. The first thing Marshal recognized was another of the tall men. He was standing on the roof of a jeepney trying to get a good look at the aftermath from the grenade. Marshal halted his dash, and silently sneaked past the jeepney without the man noticing. Then, turning onto a small driveway, he found the taxi that he'd arrived in. Without hesitation, he opened the driver's side door and took a seat.

Before turning the key in the ignition or even shutting the door, he lifted the briefcase onto his lap. The heavy nickel case reflected a dull shine as the moonlight bounced off it. It was a consolation prize. Even if it wasn't the ship, its value was immense. He flipped open the latches to examine his golden treasure. The lid resisted at first, but with a pop like a burst of bubble wrap, it swung open.

A flimsy bag pulled apart. TA gush of shiny liquid made Marshal flinch in horror. It was the same toxic substance he'd almost touched in the mansion's fountain just a few hours ago. Now as the mercury soaked into his clothes, his mind flipped into survival mode.

Marshal dropped the briefcase out the door and ignored the idea of returning for the golden plates. His only thought was to clean himself before the mercury fully soaked into his skin and the gashes he'd received from the sniper bullet. Before he had a chance to unbuckle his belt or pull off his shirt, he heard another familiar click that froze him in place. The cold steel of a gun barrel touched his neck.

Looking in the rearview mirror, he saw a uniformed man. "Police?" he asked cautiously.

"Maybe police, and maybe not," the voice behind the gun said. "You think nobody notice your guns? Police here are not many and they fear. We are many and we have men that are police." He lifted a badge so Marshal could see it in the mirror.

"I don't think I follow you, but I have a real problem here," Marshal said as he tried to explain the mercury on his clothes.

The man cut him off. "Yes, you have a big problem. Police fear to come here, but I am not here as police."

Marshal was getting anxious. "Well, who are you, then and are you going to kill me or not?"

"I come to see what happened here, then I see dead man in car. I wait and you come into the car. Now, you visit NPA. There you will stay."

Marshal had heard of the NPA, or New People's Army. They were guerrilla rebels and the main source of unrest in the Philippines. Keeping mostly to themselves, they sometimes ventured out and were known to kidnap Americans for ransom.

Though they could be ruthless, their primary goal was for governmental change. At their heart they believed that what they were doing was right for their people. Marshal knew that having the NPA find a dead Filipino in his car would cast immediate judgment against himself. He also knew that he would not escape alive.

"What do you want? I have money, I'll pay you," he begged.

The guerrilla soldier wouldn't hear of it. "You drive now. We go into mountains and you say goodbye to your old life forever."

Marshal swallowed hard. He'd heard of the conditions the NPA put prisoners in and he hoped the mercury would kill him quickly.

###

Flint was sure that the jeepney ride would offer only a slight amount of relief. He wondered how awkward the ride with Troy would be. Ever since the despicable manner in which Troy had knocked Mao off the roof, Flint found it hard to respect the man. Mao had been hurt and unarmed, no longer posing a threat, but what was done was done.

Now the more pressing matter was to get this other man to a hospital. Amelia said that his name was James, and she briefly explained who they were and why they were at Mao's auction.

Flint's muscles were wasted with fatigue. They had only stopped shaking a little after the long haul of getting James from the rooftop down to the jeepney. Flint had been close to forty-eight hours without sleep, and the strain of events was taking a large toll on him. When he finally did let go of James, he gladly let Troy's other men move the dying man onto the floor of their rented jeepney.

With the burden of carrying James's body and the weight of the world finally being alleviated, Flint rested against the side of the vehicle as a wave of dizziness swept over him.

Dusty must have noticed because she put his arm around her shoulder. Flint was glad to have her there. Just after she tried supporting him, a last burst of energy surged through him, "Monk—" he started.

"He's here," Dusty soothed.

Philip added, "The driver's helping Monk wrap up a few cuts right now."

No sooner had she relieved him of his worry than Flint's energy tanked again. "I think I need to sit down," he explained to her.

The hard, homemade seat cushion of the jeepney felt like heaven. He rested his head against the back-rest, and closed his eyes. He had no doubt that Troy would be able to stop Marshal. Right now, he just wanted to sleep. And sleep he did.

Chapter 42

Once inside the kitchen, the Chinese hostess walked to the side of the room. Next to a large built-in freezer were two doors. One was to a deep pantry, the other was to a tiny office. The area outside it was small enough that she had to close the pantry door before being able to open the office door. Inside the closet-sized office, she seated herself in a hard swivel-chair by the computer. The office generally served three purposes: one to manage the kitchen, one to keep tabs on household responsibilities, and one to monitor security.

In order to fully serve the guests and Mao, the surveillance system had been wired to his office and this room. It allowed the Chinese lady to see where everyone was, so she could anticipate their needs. Since every camera was also attached to a motion sensor, and that camera image could be forwarded to her personal smartphone, she wasn't required to be in the room at all times to monitor outside threats.

This was a complicated evening, and she was well aware of the outside intrusions from the beginning, but for now it served her purposes. For the last several minutes, instead of planning how to serve Mao's guests, she watched from the safety of the cameras in the small office as the demonstration turned to chaos.

She was glad that Mao hadn't opened the briefcase before launching the spaceship. She knew he'd wanted to keep the golden plates for later. If the ship failed to launch, he would still be able to redirect the auction to the priceless golden treasure.

If, however, he had opened the case, he wouldn't have found his precious artifact. Earlier, when everyone was dining, she'd escorted Marshal's bodyguard to the roof where they had found the gas bomb that Marshal had placed. Moving things around, they disarmed it and secured the roof once more. Once she was free of the bodyguard, she returned to the roof with a zip lock bag.

She'd filled the bag with mercury, the same heavy liquid metal from Mao's prized fountain. She'd then covered the bag in glue before placing it in the briefcase. This was to ensure that a large, dangerous mess would result if either Mao or Marshal were to open it. The bag of mercury wasn't necessary, but she'd hoped it would add enough weight to the case to make it feel as though the gold plates were still there. It also might provide a suitable distraction for her to get away with the actual ancient records.

Now as she sat down in the small office, she punched up the cameras to replay the moment when the ship had been disabled. She wasn't at all surprised by the extra company who stormed the rooftop. In fact she'd been expecting them the whole time.

To her pleasure, Marshal was about to escape with the mercury-filled briefcase. In her mind there weren't many men more deserving of the poisonous trick.

Replaying one of the videos, she zoomed in on the vacuum chamber to get a better look as the one man worked to stop Marshal from taking off in the ship. Since she already knew the outcome, she could focus more on the details and less on the suspense. The moment came that she was most interested in.

After the man destroyed the ancient device that propelled the ship, she watched as he examined a small portion of the shattered orb. Her biggest concern was that the device might still be salvaged. Not only had the man averted the potential disaster, but it appeared that she wouldn't have to worry about cleaning up the pieces after all. From her camera angle, the device looked sufficiently demolished. Maybe when things had settled down more, she'd return for a more thorough inspection, and if necessary, clean up.

Before leaving the computer, the Chinese women typed and sent an encrypted e-mail message.

The device has been destroyed. As you predicted, Troy did show up. The golden record is in my possession. I will be delivering it shortly. By the way, before the device was destroyed, it was successful in launching Mao's ship.

After sending the message, she checked the current surveillance one last time. The small standoff taking place on the roof had just turned sour, and the only men left outside the house were still fighting. She turned the computer off and picked up her own briefcase before she left the room. Two of the cooks gave her pleading stares. They were sitting in a corner, frightened by the gunfire overhead.

"Don't worry," she said to them. "Mao has taken precautions in case of disruptions such as this. Everything will be fine."

"Where you go?" one of them asked her.

"I'm going to find some medical supplies in case any of our guests are hurt," she replied.

Then she left the kitchen, closing the door behind. She watched patiently as Marshal charged through the front door. Casually, she followed him. She flinched as a grenade blew up on the roof. Shaking her head, she walked out of the mansion.

Once outside the gate, she continued walking across the street. Undetected by Marshal or the men at the jeepney, she entered a small shack and took the plates out of her worn leather briefcase.

She hefted them into a small compartment below the seat of her 150cc scooter. Then, after changing into something more fitting for a long drive, she looked out a hole in the wall that served as a window for the shanty garage. A few men and women were carrying a man out of the mansion and loading themselves into the parked jeepney. Within several minutes they were gone. She buckled on a helmet, fired up the little scooter, and drove out the front door of the shanty.

She didn't look back. She had been masquerading, serving Mao as his house servant for the last five years, secretly waiting for this very moment. She was relieved that everything had worked out well. The years were long and she had remained patient.

Finally she knew the record would be safe.

Chapter 43

August 3

When Flint opened his eyes, he was clearly not in the jeepney. The sky was dark, but the sun was just licking the horizon. Flint looked around, not recognizing the area. He was lying on a bamboo bench near a littered park, with Dusty curled up next to him. She was sleeping with her arm around his waist, her head leaning into his stomach. There was a bench across from him where he saw his autistic companion. Monk was sitting Indian-style, looking out over the ocean. Flint could see that he had some gauze wrapped around his neck, and a few red spots seeping through.

Flint couldn't see Amelia, or her friend James anywhere. Troy was pacing up and down the concrete walk, his face wrinkled in consternation. A quick glance around told Flint that the rest of Troy's men were elsewhere.

Sliding out from Dusty's grasp and careful not to wake her, Flint stood up in the crisp morning air. The smell of the ocean mingled with the smells of the city, creating a unique calming odor. It wasn't unlike waking up on a farm to the familiar smells of the fields mixing with the animals. He knew that in an hour the sun would be up and it would feel like high noon in the humid climate. Stepping forward, his muscles protesting with every move, Flint made his way to Troy.

"Good morning," Flint said as he stretched. Unusual sleeping positions went unnoticed through the wake-less night, but he was quickly learning that no casual stretching would undo the stiff knots that punished him now. He was also bitter about last night's treatment of Shen Mao, but decided not to dwell on it. He then studied Troy's face and added, "By the look on your face, it might not be a good morning after all."

"Did you have to destroy the artifact?" Troy suddenly accused.

Flint was taken aback. "I thought the whole idea was to keep it from ever being used!"

"I'm sorry," Troy apologized as he continued pacing. "I'm just a little upset at having lost both that and the record."

"Come again?" Flint pried. "I must have slept through that part of the evening. You didn't catch Marshal?"

"No. I got outside just in time to see him pull out in a car."

Flint thought for a second, then ventured, "So Marshal still has the record and you need to get it?"

"No," Troy replied again. "He doesn't have it, either. When I got to where his car had been parked, I found the briefcase that he'd taken. It was drenched in mercury. Somebody there had been playing him or Mao, or maybe even both of them."

"So what now?" Flint asked.

Troy looked up and gazed across the sea. "I think this is where we part ways. When we get back to the airport, I can take you as far as Hong Kong, but then you're on your own." He paused and added, "That is, as long as you're content with not stealing our jet again."

Flint laughed. "You know what? Saving the world is tough business. I think I'm ready to spend the rest of my vacation not getting shot at."

Troy let out a courtesy chuckle. "So what's your plan?"

"I think as long as I'm here, I'll see a few of the sights," he replied. "Besides, before I get Philip onto a plane, I want to make sure he'll survive the trip."

"The islands can be very beautiful," Dusty said, as she broke into the conversation, her arms finding their way around Flint's waist. "Especially if you're in good company."

"Well, good morning, sunshine," Flint said as he turned around and gave her a sweet kiss on the cheek.

"What do you say we check out the local bakeries?" Troy suggested. "After all, we should have about an hour before the ticket office opens for the ferry to Cebu."

Flint smiled. "Sounds like a great idea. My stomach feels like my throat has been cut. I think only Monk can relate right now. By the way, what happened to that other girl and her friend? Did he make it?"

"I think he'll be fine," Dusty said. "He was in tough shape, and had lost a lot of blood by the time we got him to the hospital, but they said he should recover. His lady friend happened to be the same blood type and was able to stay with him and donate."

By now Flint could see that Philip was beginning to stir awake. "Hey, Philip, did the hospital check you out too?"

"I don't need their doctors examining me," he replied groggily. "They'd probably just poke me with a rusty needle, anyway."

"Back at Shen Mao's place you sounded like you were dying from internal bleeding," Flint reminded.

"Ha," was his reply. "That was nothing. I just loosened a blood clot where they knocked one of my teeth out. You have to admit, though, I did have them going. Nah, I think I have a few broken bones, but I'll get that fixed back home."

"Just so you know," Dusty said, "you can still get some pretty serious painkillers here without a prescription. I think you can even find some over-the-counter meds here that would normally be illegal back in the States."

"Shoot, that sounds better than breakfast," he replied. "Please lead the way, my dear."

"I saw a bake shop just around the corner here," Troy said pointing to a little market area. "We'll meet up with you there in a few minutes."

Dusty took Philip by the arm and hobbled along, looking for a pharmacy.

"I'm sorry that your record got lost," Flint said to Troy as they left.

"It's all right," Troy replied. "From what I understand, it was written in the Martian language. If anyone tries to translate it, they'll pop up on our radar again somewhere."

The trip back to Cebu was relaxing. Flint gave Troy his weapons, including his prized AK-47. He knew that he'd have a hard time smuggling them back to the United States anyway. "I think we'll go back to Marshal's compound for a few minutes, gather up Dusty's belongings, then go island hopping for a week."

"Sounds fun," Troy said as he extended his hand.

Flint shook it, then watched as Troy and his remaining two men caught a taxi for the airport. "I'll be seeing you around!" he shouted to Flint as the taxi pulled away.

"I hope not!" Flint shouted back, and waved goodbye. When the taxi was out of sight, Flint looked at Philip and Monk. "You're both welcome to spend a week playing here with us if you like."

"Do you still have that satellite phone I gave you?" Philip asked.

Flint took it out and handed it to Philip. "You need to make a call?"

"No," Philip replied. "I need to do this." He then threw it into the street as a large bus came by. The phone was pulverized.

Flint looked at Philip with shock in his eyes. Philip then told him, "If you get in trouble again, you're on your own. I'm going home. I'll see you in a couple of weeks."

Monk came to Flint and said, "Confucius says: Wheresoever you go, go with all your heart. And 1 Thessalonians 4:3: For this is the will of God, even your sanctification, that ye should abstain from fornication."

Flint gave Monk a pat on the back. "Thanks, buddy. Am I to guess that you're going back to study in China?"

Monk replied, "Confucius says: He who learns but does not think, is lost. He who thinks but does not learn is in great danger."

"I'll take that as a yes," Flint said. "Thank you again for your help. It couldn't have been done without you."

Monk gave Flint his first smile since arriving. Flint knew that expression was unnatural. Monk did it for the effect it communicated, because that's what friends do. After a tense two seconds, his expression returned to normal. Instead of finding a taxi to the airport, Monk decided to walk back. Flint watched as he disappeared down the street.

"Shall we?" Flint invited Dusty, holding out his elbow. She linked her arm in his and they walked out to the street to hail a taxi.

Once in the taxi, Dusty leaned over and snuggled up to Flint. He quickly repelled her as he was jabbed by something hard and uncomfortable. She questioned him with a muddled grin. Flint shot her back his own quizzical expression before understanding what just happened. Looking down, they both noticed the large bulge in the side of his hip.

Flint laughed, then reached into his pocket and pulled out a large wad of bills. "I forgot that I had this. I should have given it back to Troy. We kind of borrowed it from his plane. I hope he doesn't get mad when he can't find it."

Dusty leaned into him and said, "Don't you think you deserve some compensation for helping save the world?"

"You didn't hear me complaining, did you?" Flint replied, then leaned over and kissed her.

Chapter 44

"Troy was unsuccessful at retrieving the arti-facts," came the explanation from the strict woman on the phone. "You might as well come back. Nobody is likely to return to the compound, especially any-one who might know where the artifact is. Besides, we still have the other matter to take care of."

"I understand," Lydia replied to the woman. She then hung up her phone. She sighed and turned to Grisha. "It sounds like Troy is waiting for us at the airport. He recovered our jet, but the book has dis-appeared."

Grisha put down his binoculars. "One wild goose chased down, one more to go."

"I sure hope not," Lydia replied. "I'm ready for something to work out for a change."

They headed back out to the street where their

taxi driver was sleeping. They woke him up as they loaded their gear back in. "To the airport," Lydia ordered. The driver shifted into first gear and started rolling out.

They hadn't gone one block when Grisha yelled, "Stop, stop—that's him!"

The confused driver slowed down, not knowing what the matter was.

Before the car came to a complete stop, Grisha was opening his door to step out. Lydia looked at her comrade with intensity. "What did you see?"

"The—the man," he stammered. "It was the man from Egypt, the one that stole our plane!"

Lydia's eyes went wide as she grabbed her duffel bag and opened her door. "We'll be right back," she told the driver. "Wait here."

The driver shrugged his shoulders and turned the car off again. As soon as Grisha was out, the driver reclined his seat again to finish his nap. Lydia followed quickly behind her Russian companion.

They stood outside Marshal's old compound, not wanting to alert the man inside of their presence. Lydia took a quick look around and told Grisha, "You're clear, but hurry up."

Grisha had already unzipped the duffel bag. With the speed of a man who'd done it a thousand times, Grisha assembled a collapsible rifle, the scope being the last thing to go on. Lydia hung a pair of binoculars around her neck, then checked her pistol. "All right, let's go."

They entered the compound. Grisha was first with his rifle up to his shoulder, followed by Lydia with both hands on her pistol. They got in just in time to see the door shut to one of the buildings. Grisha motioned with his rifle at the building and Lydia acknowledged with a simple nod.

They ran around to the side of the main building, then crouched and waited. Grisha leaned his body against the exterior wall with Lydia just behind him and to the side. She lifted her binoculars and began to glass the building. She could sense movement within, but the windows were too dirty to see inside.

Grisha never took his eyes away from the scope on his gun and asked, "Do you think we dare move in?"

"No," she replied. "He got the better of you once, I'd rather not underestimate him. Besides, he has to come out sometime and he doesn't know we're here."

"Do you think we'll find that book?"

"That'd be nice," she replied, her eyes fixated on the building.

They kneeled on the ground for ten minutes before they started getting antsy. Lydia's knees were aching and she could tell that Grisha was getting uncomfortable too. She watched as he lowered his gun for a minute to give his arms a rest. He then licked his finger and put it up in the air.

"I don't think you're far enough away to worry about factoring the wind into your shot," she chided him.

"That's not what worries me. The wind is blowing toward that building."

"I don't get it," she said. "What's that have to do with anything?"

"Your perfume," he said. "What if they smell your perfume?"

"My perfume is very mild," she defended. "And I'm pretty sure that I'm not the only one in town who wears perfume. Besides, if they smell anything, wouldn't it be better to smell something pretty and innocent than stinky and threatening?"

"I'm just saying," Grisha remarked, not wanting

to start a debate.

"You know I haven't had a shower in over two days," Lydia added. "Besides, they'd have no reason to suspect a woman was onto them."

Grisha shrugged it off. Either he didn't want to argue the point, or she had proven it sufficiently to satisfy him. In either case, he let it go.

Needing a stretch, he rested the gun and stood up for a few seconds. As he was doing this, the door to the building opened. He quickly crouched back down and grabbed his gun.

The man stepped out with a woman, and Lydia whispered, "Can you tell if it's him?"

Grisha whispered back, "No, that girl is in the way."

Lydia also kept her binoculars fixed on the two. They were standing side by side, the man's arm around the girl and hers around him. They walked a few paces then stopped. The girl looked at the man and said something that Lydia couldn't hear. The couple then stepped sideways and faced Lydia.

Lydia could not believe what she was seeing. It had to be a mistake, but she ducked behind the wall and pulled Grisha back with her. Grisha lost his balance and fell backward, but not before firing one round from the rifle, missing the mark.

"What the—?" he said, followed by some explicative language in Russian. "It was him, I could have had him. Why you do this?"

"I thought I recognized him," Lydia said as she labored to get a hold of herself.

"Who you think it was?" Grisha growled, knowing it was too late to catch them now.

"I know it sounds crazy," she said, "but he looked just like my husband, Flint."

Epilogue

Flint didn't start shaking until after they'd cleared the gate of the compound. The familiar smell of perfume reminded him of the jet he'd stolen back in Egypt. It was that same perfume that his wife had once favored. Flint also had no doubt that the man who'd shot at him was the Russian he'd fought back in Egypt.

Questions flooded his mind. He'd reconciled with Troy, so why would the Russian have attacked him? Also, who was the woman with him? The last time he saw a woman that reminded him of Lydia, he nearly lost his life and that of his friends.

Up ahead, Flint saw a small bakeshop and ushered Dusty over. The dull thud of his feet on the packed earth was muted by the louder thud of his own heart as it raced for answers. Once Dusty was sitting out of sight, Flint left her to spy on the GRIP agents. Carefully he edged his way around the bake-shop and peered at the gates of the compound.

Everything was still. If he was being pursued, they were being cautious about it.

Flint waited, not wanting to risk exposing him-self. He remembered how dangerous these people had been in Egypt. If only Troy was still here. This had to be a miscommunication. Flint was about to return to Dusty when the two characters emerged from the compound.

After they passed, Flint wished he hadn't spent so much time looking at the raging face of the Rus-sian. He totally missing his opportunity to study the female companion.

Like the time he first saw Dusty, he was now left with only a vague familiarity to his missing wife. *No,* Flint told himself. *I'm finished with these Martian off-spring. They're nothing but trouble.*

Flint never suspected that his little Egyptian va-cation would place him in the heart of a plot that could have destroyed the world. He was the hero that nobody would ever know and he got the girl. He should be happy. Maybe he was. His life might have returned to normal if all he did was save the world, but Dusty wasn't in any hurry to let him leave her life. *Maybe it's time to move on. Perhaps Dusty is just who I've been needing to meet to start a new chapter in my life.*

This could end happily ever after. He had a gor-geous woman that was head over heels for him and plenty of time to enjoy the remainder of his trip with her. Despite having told himself this, that empty pit, where his heart longed to place Dusty, was now a hungry chasm again. *Just be happy,* he scolded himself. As much as he didn't want to give in to the painful yearning, the last couple years of contemplating Lydia's fate were all too consuming. Of course it was stupid. By now Flint knew this better than anyone. But as he returned to Dusty, he feared that she could never fill that void as long as there was any remnant of Lydia in there.

Flint watched the taxi drive away. He didn't dare give those two a chance to see him. Of course, that meant that he couldn't get a better look at them either.

He turned to Dusty, then back at the taxi as it disappeared. He let out a slow deep breath. It may not make sense to anyone else, but he made his mind up. Now he just had to break the news to Dusty.

Don't miss
The Nephilim Effect
Book 2 in the Nephilim series

Words from the Author

Hi, and thanks for giving my debut book a try. After pouring countless hours into writing, re-writing, and re-writing... It's nice to have somebody other than me and my editor get to this part of the book. Of course the real test would be if you go on to read more of what I publish. Yes, I do plan on publishing more.

For me, the Nephilim series started out as a single book, but as I got more into the book, I realized that it was taking on new dimensions. I soon came to the conclusion that this would be one fat book, or three smaller ones. I opted for three smaller ones, with the hope that a smaller book size might not scare you, the reader, away. Unfortunately this means that they all have to be read in order to make much sense. If you're anything like me, then you might get a little annoyed with these type of serial books. This is why my next few books are going to be stand-a-lone novels, even if they are a little longer.

A little about me. I'm not a full time author, but I aspire to be a great storyteller and devoted family man. I currently am a general contractor. Yes I build houses, and I'm good at it, but telling stories fascinates me. Nobody will ever accuse me of being an elegant speaker, even if I can drone on for hours. But that's the magic of literature. I can spin a dream into reality, and fill you full of imagination. If I can't, at least I'm trying.

I live in Utah, and yes I'm a Mormon. I'm very proud of my heritage and my faith. One of the reasons I wanted to start writing books, was because I was getting fed up with the smut that many authors decide to publish. Admittedly, I have read many books by many authors, and books that wouldn't seem so, often have a few pages of pornographic literature. I don't want my kids reading stuff like that and you never know if the author is going to drop something like that in.

Many people I talk to get so fed up with this, that they exclusively read young adult fiction in an attempt to avoid such content. I've often thought that a rating might be nice on books. On my Goodreads account, I try to give a rating of the books I get through. It's not perfect, but it's my own little way of contributing. My goal is to always keep my books at a PG-13 rating or lower. You'll never find too harsh of language or sexual content in my books. Yeah, maybe a little violence from time to time. I haven't quite gotten away from that, but for the most part, I'm trying to be a morally conscious writer.

Since I'm not a full time author, I'm stuck writing only about an hour each day. At that rate, I can only produce about one novel every 12-18 months. So if you enjoy reading my books, please have patience with me. I will publish again, and hopefully soon after you read this.

Good luck in all you do, and if you don't mind, wish a little luck my way too.

-B.C. Crow